Midnight Lily

A Sign of Love Novel

Mia Sheridan

To my girlfriends, my soul sisters,
the ones who have saved me time and again.

Virgo

Persephone, Queen of the Underworld, destined to live half her life in the darkness, and half in the light.

PROLOGUE

I saw her everywhere. Walking down sidewalks, in crowded restaurants, once in the brief flash of dark hair and white lace right before an elevator door closed. Without thinking, my heart thundering in my chest, I'd run up four flights of stairs only to find that it was someone else. Someone holding a little boy's hand. She'd pulled him closer to her side as she'd exited the elevator, looking at me warily as if I might grab him and run.

Those were the times I still doubted my own sanity, still questioned whether she had ever existed at all. But then I'd remember the feel of her fingertips on my skin, the slippery silk of her hair, the sound of her laughter, and the way I loved her still, and I'd know, *I'd know*, deep down to my soul that she was real.

I dreamed of her, and in the darkness, she held me in her arms. In the darkness, she whispered that I was strong enough to hold on, that I was worthy of the love she'd given, and she reminded me who I was before I was anyone at all.

My Lily of the Night. Only of the moon.

Because now, just as then, when daylight came, she was no longer there.

CHAPTER ONE

Holden

The powerful whir of the helicopter propellers grew faint as they slowed and finally came to a stop. I opened my eyes blearily and stared out the window at the vast forest surrounding the grassy field where we'd landed. My muscles twitched and I fisted my hands on my thighs, but I felt a little better than when we'd taken off from San Francisco. At least I'd slept. Maybe for a couple hours? It was something, and more than I'd had the night before. Possibly more than I'd had in the last three days.

"You coming, man?" Brandon called as he threw the door open. "Sorry to wake you, but there's a bed inside that will be a lot more comfortable than that seat."

"I wasn't sleeping," I muttered, grabbing my duffle bag and moving slowly toward the door. A painful drumbeat pounded in my head, and nausea swept through me. Goddamn, I still felt like death warmed over. I grimaced as I hopped out of the open door. "I was praying."

Brandon chuckled. "Oh ye of little faith. Did you actually doubt I'd get you here in one piece? Mad pilot skills, bro." He turned and began walking, not bothering to close the doors to the helicopter, meaning, I supposed, that he wouldn't be staying long. I followed along behind him.

"You can't even hold on to a damn football half the time. And they pay you millions to do that. Why should I trust my very life in your

4

hands?" Brandon shot me a scathing look over his shoulder but then laughed.

"Still can't believe you bought a helicopter," I said, catching up to him as we stepped through tall, dewy grass.

Brandon shrugged. "I always wanted to learn to fly. Why not? Life's short. If you have the opportunity to cross a few things off your bucket list, I say do it. Plus, it takes three hours to drive here from the closest commercial airport. This was a whole lot quicker."

"Jesus, how far to any civilization at all?"

"About seventy miles to Telluride. When I said privacy, I meant *privacy*."

We walked through a sparse grove of trees and came out on the side of a massive, two-story luxury cabin, featuring floor-to-ceiling windows on both levels. As we walked closer, I could see the trees and sky reflected in the glass, as if the huge structure was part shimmering illusion. At night it must look like a shining beacon. I whistled, looking at the forest directly in front of it—what would be the view from inside. "Damn, when you build a remote lodge in the wilderness, you don't mess around. This is like the fucking Shining, dude. Does it come with a set of spooky twins?"

Brandon chuckled as I followed him up a large set of stone stairs. "Careful what you joke about. Last time I was here with a group, a couple of the girls swore they saw a ghost in the woods. Came in screaming and hollering from the hot tub." He shot me what I assumed was supposed to be an expression of mortal fear, and formed one hand into the shape of a claw.

I made a scoffing sound and rolled my eyes as he pulled out a set of keys and unlocked the door. "Sounds like a bad combo of alcohol and heat stroke." *And limited brain cells. That was always a factor when it came to the girls Brandon partied with. I should know. They were the same ones I partied with, too.*

"Either way, they required lots of protection from the heebie-jeebies just outside—*naked* protection. In my bed. Win-win. You know what's really creepy, though? Apparently there's an old, abandoned mental institution five miles or so from here. Isn't that fucking awesome?" There was no sarcasm in his voice. He meant it was awesome.

"Awesome," I repeated half-heartedly. *And creepy.* But I had a few problems bigger than an abandoned building miles away. Brandon threw the keys on a side table as we entered the massive room. The whole space was decorated in sturdy, masculine furniture, befitting a luxury ski lodge, arranged in small groupings to make it feel more intimate.

"I had a feng shui decorating expert out here to make sure the flow of energy was balanced and shit." I stared at him blankly before glancing around briefly.

"Is that what I've been missing? Balanced energy?"

Brandon shrugged. "Could be, dude."

I managed a soft laugh, dropping my bag and walking toward the window where I could stare at the view. From up here it was an entirely different experience. The beautiful vastness of deep woods all around, the cloud-capped mountains far beyond, the way dew sparkled on leaves under slants of late-afternoon sunlight. I silently stared for several minutes.

"So you're really going to leave me here, huh?" I asked without turning, my voice sounding more desolate than I'd intended. Nothing except air, forest, stone, and sky. Oh, and an abandoned mental institution. Couldn't forget about that. Well, and myself—the one thing I could never escape, although I was damned good at trying. Out here though . . .

Brandon paused. "Yeah, I really am. And you're going to be good—better than ever. You know it's—"

"Yeah, I know." My mind supplied what Brandon hadn't. A second chance, a *final* chance, the opportunity to forge a comeback . . . high time to get my shit together. I continued to stare out the window. The beautiful simplicity of the landscape felt like a mockery of the dirty, roiling complexity inside me. Or maybe it wasn't complex at all. Maybe it was the simplest thing in the world: I was a goddamned fuck-up. I'd gone so far up my own ass that I couldn't find my way out again.

Shaking my head to clear my thoughts, I turned back to Brandon who was looking at me with concern.

I ran a hand through my hair. I needed a shower. Cringing, I asked, "Will you tell me what happened last night?"

Brandon paused. "You don't remember any of it?"

"Bits and pieces." I sagged down onto the nearest chair, massaging my temples. I still felt the remnants of the massive headache I'd woken up with thanks to the copious amount of alcohol I'd consumed the night before. And the fact that I needed a fix. "I remember Paul tossing me out." *My agent, his face filled with red-hot rage as he very literally kicked me out of his house. Sprawled in the dirt, groaning, gritty saliva dripping down my chin as Brandon dragged me up.*

"You fucked Sabrina in the downstairs bathroom, man. The whole party heard it."

Sabrina. Paul's beautiful, blonde trophy wife.

Nausea rolled through me. *Oh shit. Fuck.* I fell back on the chair, trying to grab on to the pieces of memory that flitted through my brain. Sabrina had followed me to the bathroom and propositioned me and I'd . . . *Jesus, I'd taken her up on it?* I had no recollection of agreeing, just the vague vision of pounding into someone against the sink as she scratched at my back and made loud mewling sounds. Before I even realized what I was doing, I reached around to my back and when I pressed lightly, I could feel the sting of the wounds she must have inflicted with her long fingernails—the proof of my disgusting actions. Vomit threatened and I swallowed it down, running my sweaty palms over my thighs. "Fuck," I murmured. "Fuck, fuck."

"Yeah, well I guess that about sums it up," Brandon agreed. "On several levels." His expression was filled with pity and I looked away. There were a few beats of silence. "You can't keep going like this, bro. This isn't *you.* You can't keep living this way. You have to be the one to make the choice, though. Your life can be good again, man."

I nodded, even though I had no idea how it possibly could be. "Yeah, I know," I lied. "This is good. Man, I appreciate it." And I did. If it wasn't this, it would be celebrity rehab somewhere where paparazzi were hiding in the trees trying to get a picture of me sobbing in group therapy or some such shit. Instead, Brandon had picked me up off the ground—quite literally—and taken me home. Then in the morning, he'd shown up with coffee and Tylenol and offered me this place. As long as I promised to use it to get myself back on track. And I wanted to, I really did. I was so fucking *weary* of my life, of the endless parties and drinking, the desperate suck-ups, the meaningless sex, and the overly bright mornings that always arrived with shame, sickness, and depression. And so I'd packed a bag and taken him up on his offer. I knew I should look at it solely as a gift, but in reality, hiding seemed a lot more appealing than facing my numerous fuck-ups. So here I was.

Brandon came closer and grabbed my shoulder, giving me a supportive squeeze. "Before I go, I need to check your bag."

I glanced at him, narrowing my eyes slightly. But all I saw in his expression was concern and possibly some regret. He wasn't relishing playing warden. I considered telling him to go fuck himself, but the truth was I couldn't really afford to lose any more friends. I let out a breath. "Yeah, sure. Okay." I stood and grabbed my duffle bag, dropping it on the couch and stepping away as he did a search of the contents, looking for pills, I knew. He cared, but I guessed he also didn't want me overdosing in his remote lodge in the wilderness of Colorado. The media would have a field day with that. I tried to feel some sort of fear that that's exactly what would happen, but all that came over me was a distant feeling of curiosity. I wondered how long it'd take someone to find my body.

After a minute, he zipped my bag closed and pushed it away. "Take any of the bedrooms upstairs. A housekeeper was out this week. The pantry and the fridges in the kitchen and garage are stocked with about a month's worth of food. There's a full gym downstairs—*use* it, man. The altitude up here makes it a better workout than you'll get anywhere else. There's a Jeep in the garage, keys on the peg next to the door."

"I thought the deal was I stay holed up here for the next four weeks." Plus, he knew I wasn't supposed to drive.

"It is. You're still allowed to know where you are in the case of an emergency. You're not in jail." His gaze held mine for a moment. *Yet,* was implied in his expression. "If you have any questions, call me. Cell reception out here is decent. I've rarely had a problem." I just nodded. "Just lay low, man. Rest. Recuperate. Get your head clear." His eyes lingered on my face for a beat too long. He looked as if he wanted to say something else, but changed his mind. *Right. I knew what he meant anyway. Stay hidden. Banish yourself so you can't fuck up any more than you already have. Think long and hard about why you hate your life so damn much, you stupid, ungrateful bastard.* "Okay. I better go while flying conditions are still optimal." He clapped me on the shoulder and walked toward the door. A quiet click behind him and I was alone. Nausea hit me again and I sat down on the couch, pulling in deep breaths of air as I put my head between my knees. *All this quiet.* After a few minutes, the silence was broken momentarily by the distant sound of a bird screeching. It sounded vaguely human and caused a shiver to race down my spine.

A moment later, I heard the noise of the helicopter rotors and then it slowly faded. Brandon was gone.

I raked my hands through my short, dark hair and then sat up and reached for my duffel bag, zipping it open and feeling for the hidden pocket near the bottom that was sewn shut. I tore the thread and pulled out the plastic bag wrapped with duct tape. My hands were shaking as I ripped it open, swearing softly as two pills fell soundlessly onto the carpet at my feet, one rolling under the coffee table. I got down on my hands and knees and searched for it. My utter pitifulness in that moment was blatantly clear, even to me. I let out a relieved breath as my fingers found the small tablet.

I brought the taped-up bag into the kitchen, glancing around at the dark cabinets, industrial-sized stainless steel appliances, and dark gray granite countertops. I hid the bag behind some cereal boxes in the large pantry—I wasn't sure who I was hiding it from, but it was habit at this point—then popped the two pills that had fallen on the floor into my mouth, leaning over the sink to drink straight from the tap.

I was going to stop taking the pills. A couple days and I'd do it. I had a month before I needed to get serious about training. A couple more days wouldn't matter. I'd gather my strength, and I'd do it then. When I was ready. But not today. Today I needed the pills. I needed the blessed numbness the pills brought.

Again standing in front of the window looking out over the forest, I wondered what sort of wildlife lived in it. Bears? Did I need to worry about bears? Wolves? No matter. I'd stay inside. Bears or wolves were far less frightening than paparazzi trying to get a photograph of the former quarterback slash currently jobless, hot fucking mess.

I'd call Ryan—

I jolted and flinched at my own thought. Even after almost three months, I still went to call him sometimes when I needed my best friend, a person who knew *me*, before I belonged to everyone. Before I was Holden Scott, public property. And then I'd remember he was gone and it still *shocked* me. How long would that last? That now-and-again portion of a second when my unconscious mind believed he was still alive—just a phone call away? And did I really want it to go away? The very last portion of my brain that refused to believe he was really gone forever. My head throbbed again.

Turning away, filled with ugly self-pity, I flipped on the television and lay down on the leather sofa, hoping to the god of feng shui that good vibes were already flowing my way. I'd try to get some sleep. I needed sleep so fucking badly. I was just so damn tired. Maybe everything would look better after some rest.

****

Sleep didn't come. Sometime after midnight, I stumbled from the house to get some fresh air. The canned laughter of some late-night show grated in the background, the manufactured sound of happiness causing my jaw to clench and my skin to ache. Everything felt *wrong.* My legs wouldn't quit their restless, incessant movement, as if ants crawled through my veins. I couldn't fucking breathe. Even my thoughts were off. It felt like something or someone was knocking incessantly at my brain, as if trying to get my attention, and it *hurt*. I had stripped down to my boxers earlier and although the late summer night breeze was only mildly chilly, it felt good against my bare skin. I stood at the railing of the massive wrap-around deck, staring into the dark woods, inhaling the cool, crisp air as if it might somehow cleanse me of all my failings.

I startled slightly when I caught movement between two trees, the vague outline of a human form wearing white. Straining my eyes, I stared at the spot where I swore I saw . . . *something*. But after a moment, I looked away, rubbing at my tired eyes. Jesus, I was seeing things. It'd happened before when I'd gone days with no sleep. And now it was happening again.

Or maybe it *had* been a wolf, an animal, some trick of the moonlight that made it appear human. I raised my arms, laughing into the quiet void of night. "Hey, bears! Wolves! Listen up, motherfuckers. Do you know who I am?" My words echoed in the wide-open darkness. "I'm Holden Scott, the most lusted-after man in the NFL." I dropped my arms. "Formerly of the NFL. Disgraced, but still lusted after. Look at me. I'm a fucking GOD! Women everywhere want me. They want to have my babies. They sneak into my hotel rooms and hide under the bed. It's the craziest shit." I laughed, but it held no humor and sounded more like a strange bark. "They—" I let out a shaky breath. "They—" I sucked in sharp, cool night air, feeling waves of misery as if they were tangible, knocking me down, dragging me under, scraping me along the bottom, filling my mouth with the gritty taste of despair.

"See, here's the thing—I've got a back-up plan. I could start pimping myself out. No more freebies. I'd make a damn fortune. I'm a god among men," I called out again. And then my legs gave out as I fell to my knees under the silent judgment of the moon. And I hung my head. It felt like my soul was sleeping, and I had no earthly idea what would wake it up again.

CHAPTER TWO

Holden

The next morning dawned clear and fresh, the faint glimmer of yellow sunshine on the horizon. I'd managed several hours of sleep and felt a certain newness, standing at the railing of the deck with a mug of coffee, watching the pale light of morning chase the night shadows away. If only I could hold on to this feeling long enough to grasp my own new beginning. If not here, then where? Not on the field, a football clasped in my hands, thousands of fans cheering my name; not between the thighs of some vacant-eyed beauty; not even among so-called friends in my own home—always having to wonder what they really wanted from me, inevitably finding out it was something other than friendship. If not here, maybe nowhere. Maybe nowhere at all.

By mid-afternoon, the craving set in again, the beast hungering for a fix. I paced the deck, trying to convince myself to resist, knowing that in the end I wouldn't. Knowing I couldn't come up with a good enough reason. I was pathetic, I knew. How many people would switch places with me in a heartbeat? How many people would roll their eyes and play the world's smallest violin on their fingers as they wiped fake tears out of their eyes for the poor, rich sport's star who had everything and threw it all away out of stupidity? Or entitlement. Or both. Even I couldn't figure out exactly why. When I tried, my head started pounding, and I couldn't form a clear thought. If I *could* figure it out, maybe I'd have a fighting chance to change it. Or maybe I'd still be a weak fuck who knew what I needed to do but wasn't strong enough to try.

Because, frankly, it took a whole lot of available life comforts—not having to spend one second worrying about the basics—to sustain this level of self-pity. And I was lacking for nothing in that regard.

Not to mention that my fame insulated me from consequences others might face. "Yes-men" surrounded me—people who would rather make me happy than risk being ejected from my life and lose the status my friendship or business relationship provided. Once upon a time I thought it'd made me lucky. Now . . .

I stood in the kitchen for a while fingering the bag of pills like the plastic was a beloved's skin. Finally, with a sound of disgust, I tossed it down on the counter and went to look for some liquor. Maybe a couple shots would take the edge off. I'd never had a problem with alcohol—or rather, I'd never felt like I couldn't stop drinking if I really wanted to. Although I'd definitely done some stupid shit while under the influence, namely driving down Sunset Boulevard with two swimsuit models squealing out my sunroof and ultimately earning myself a well-deserved DUI.

Brandon had probably requested the place be free of liquor, but after rooting around in the very back corner of the pantry, I found a bottle of Johnnie Walker, still in the box, a bow affixed to the front—obviously a gift Brandon had forgotten about. Whoever cleared the place hadn't found it. It wasn't lost on me that the victory I felt at the find was probably at least a little bit tragic. I tossed back a shot anyway, grimacing as the liquid burned down my throat, resisting the urge to retch. I took a deep breath and did another, closing my eyes as warmth spread through my veins. But by six that night it wasn't enough and I gave in to my lover's call, downing several painkillers with a sip of Scotch and soda, the welcome numbness of the drugs and liquor cocktail flowing through my system.

I stumbled out onto the deck and fired up the grill, holding my glass up to the sky in cheers to the magnificence of the sunset, the sky awash in vivid swirls of pink and gold. "Impressive show. Good work."

As the steak began to sizzle, I stared out at the trees beyond, lost in my own scattered, half-formed thoughts. Movement. Something white. I froze, squinting into the dwindling light, a streak of excited fear shooting down my spine, somewhat muted by the chemicals but still there. For several beats all was still, the only sound the sizzling meat and a few distant bird cries. The hairs on the back of my neck prickled. *Something's about to happen,* my mind whispered. Strange thought, but the feeling accompanying it was familiar and the memory came back to me now.

It had been my senior year in college, and the final game of the season was about to start. There were scouts in the bleachers, at least two or three. I'd forgotten something in the locker room and had run back to grab it. Or had I been in the stands? Why would I have been in the stands? No, no, that wasn't right. Damn my memory. I really shouldn't have mixed alcohol and pills. Anyway, senior year . . . on my way out of the locker room—yes, it had been the locker room, yes, that was right—I had paused at the door, a feeling washing through me: *something's about to happen.* The same feeling I'd just had now. I'd been a warrior on the field that day, and three months later, I'd been drafted by San Francisco in the first round and signed one of the most lucrative contracts in the NFL.

My heart picked up in speed and adrenaline surged through my veins, now, just as it had then. *Something's about to happen.* Swallowing, I turned around and walked as casually as possible to the other railing and leaned against it, the forest where I'd seen movement now at my back. I took my phone out of my pocket and held it up to take a selfie. My muscles tensed. I waited. Movement again, this time in the screen of my phone. I clicked the button and took a photo. Turning around to the grill, I flipped the steak and opened the picture. A portion of my face blocked part of the background, but I'd taken a good shot of the trees behind me. And there it was—the movement I'd spotted. "Yes," I mumbled feeling a surge of success, widening my fingers on the screen to zoom in. I brought the phone closer to my face.

"Holy shit," I breathed. Whatever it was, I'd barely caught it with my camera—but it was *something.* I zoomed in more, but couldn't make out exactly what it was as it was too blurry. Perhaps a piece of white material? Dark hair? But I wasn't crazy, and I wasn't seeing things. And whatever had been there, it had waited until I'd turned my back to dart between trees. Were animals that intelligent? "What the hell?" I murmured, raising my head and looking around again, a chill moving through me. "What the hell?" I repeated.

I debated calling Brandon. Or maybe calling the police? But to report what? That I'd possibly seen a ghost? I laughed out loud. That'd go over well, especially considering I was clearly under the influence. Somehow it would get leaked. I'd be even more of a laughing stock than I already was, and sooner rather than later, there would be paparazzi hanging in the trees. Of course I *did* have the picture, but the photo was too unclear to be called any kind of proof. It would be explained away somehow, and I'd end up looking like a fool. Maybe I shouldn't trust myself too much anyway in the condition I was in.

I ate my dinner, sitting outside on the deck, my eyes trained on the woods, but I didn't catch sight of anything again that night. Finally, I stumbled inside, my phone clutched to my chest while I dozed on the couch as if the picture might cease to exist once I closed my eyes.

****

Stripping off my clothes, I climbed into the hot, bubbling water of the outside Jacuzzi, sighing as my muscles relaxed. It'd been four days since I'd arrived here and I was bored as hell. The bottle of Scotch was gone and I only had enough pills to last another week or so. I would be forced to go cold turkey. What the fuck had I been thinking agreeing to this? I'd have to take Brandon's Jeep and drive to the airport he'd mentioned and catch a flight. Brandon would be disappointed, but he'd get over it.

The warm water surrounded me, making my limbs feel like heavy jelly, the steam swirling, clouding my senses as my eyes fluttered closed.

"Do you believe in God, Holden?" Ryan's voice choked out.

Did I? I wasn't sure. My parents did. I was raised to believe. My mom was always going on about being a good Christian, but I'd never truly given a lot of thought to God. But what did I say to Ryan? His life was shit. His dad was a sadistic bastard. Of course he wanted to believe there was a purpose to all the pain he constantly experienced, all the fucking scars. Misery overtook me and I swallowed. My throat felt thick. "Yeah, man. Of course."

He nodded, his eyes closed, the bruise on his jaw a sickly, blackish purple, blood still caked on his lip. His dad had done that to him. I fisted my hands on my thighs, angry, helpless.

He gave me the barest glimmer of a smile, more fleeting than a single raindrop falling. "Okay, good because some days I don't think I can do this alone, Holden."

"You're not doing this alone. I'm here," I said. Something burned in my chest.

He smiled again. "I know. You've always been here. You, your parents." The smile slipped and he grimaced slightly.

"Maybe God sent me, you know?" I gave a short chuckle. "Jesus Christ Almighty, that sounds really stupid and self-important, doesn't it?"

He gave me the first small laugh he'd given in a while. "Yeah, it really does, you arrogant asshole." But his smile increased and he held up his hand, his fingers making a V, the gesture he always did from the stands at the end of a game, letting me know he saw me. I held up my own hand and grinned back at him.

Water filled my mouth and I choked, jerking upward and taking in a lungful of air. My body thrashed in the bubbling water of the hot tub and I looked around wildly, trying to remember where I was. Oh fuck, I must have drifted off. I had been dreaming about Ryan when we were kids, but to fall asleep in a hot tub? Jesus, if the alcohol and drugs didn't kill me, I'd manage it some other way—in a car or drowned in a damn Jacuzzi. My heart was beating a mile a minute.

I sat up and ran my hand through my wet hair, looking out to the trees beyond. There was a girl standing at the edge of the forest. I startled, letting out a small yelp. She startled, too, and turned around. Standing abruptly, I called out, "Wait!"

She hesitated and turned her head back toward me. I grabbed a towel and scrabbled out of the hot tub, almost slipping and head-planting onto the deck. She turned back to the forest and ran. "Wait!" I called again.

I ran down the stairs and across the grassy area in front of the lodge, wrapping the towel around my waist as I ran and holding it in place so it didn't fall.

I entered the woods where she had been and stopped, the light dimmer here, shafts of sunlight filtering through the dense trees. "Hello?" I called, but there was no answer and I could detect no sound.

I looked down at my bare feet and back from where I'd come, spotting the footprints of my own path. I walked back to where I'd entered the trees behind her and looked more closely, but there was only one set of tracks: my own. Frowning, I walked back toward the lodge, looking over my shoulder as I moved away from the woods, a chill moving down my spine. *First Ryan, now this.* Was I seeing ghosts? Is this what happened when you were so deep into addiction that chemical holes formed in your brain? Or was it the lack of sleep causing me to have visions? Was I cracking up? But no, Ryan had been a memory, just a dream.

"No," I repeated aloud, reassuring myself, "I saw her." Dark hair and a white lace dress. But who the hell wore a white lace dress in the woods? I knew she wasn't part of the paparazzi who normally stalked me. If she was, her purpose would have been to get a photo and the girl's hands had been empty. There'd been no camera. So where had she come from? There was nothing for miles around. And what did I do now? Clearly she didn't want to communicate with me. But if not, why did she keep coming back? It *must* have been her before. She was watching me. But *why?* What did she want?

****

I woke bright and early, showered, put on jeans, a T-shirt, and some sneakers. It was the first day I'd actually gotten dressed since I'd arrived at Brandon's cabin. The unfamiliar feeling coursing through my veins was . . . *excitement.*

I packed some food and water and made my way into the woods, a backpack on my back, entering at the same spot where the girl had entered the day before.

I didn't want to go too far and lose my sense of direction. There was no path to follow in this forest, nothing that spoke of anyone having been here before me. And it was just exactly what I needed—to get lost in the wooded darkness when there might not be a soul around and no one would know I was missing for another three weeks. I'd die alone, quietly, unceremoniously, and maybe someday they'd find my bones, or maybe not.

I walked for an hour or so, enjoying the fresh air in my lungs, the whisper of the foliage moving in the breeze, and the sound of bird cries in the trees above. I called out here and there just for the hell of it, but there was no answer in return. My legs began to cramp and I started to wonder if I really was crazy. What was I doing wandering through the woods looking for a vision that may or may not really exist? Suddenly I felt like a complete idiot. The excitement I'd woken with turned into sour foolishness. And I felt like shit physically, too. My body was achy and twitchy and I needed a couple pills. In my hopefulness that morning, I hadn't even thought to bring a few with me. I sat down on a rock and took out my water bottle, taking a long drink. I was cold and my T-shirt hardly provided enough warmth in the cool air of the forest, too dense where I was to allow for any sunshine. "For fuck's sake," I muttered.

I sat there quietly for a couple more minutes, gathering the strength to get up and turn back around. I'd been moving uphill, and I knew all I had to do was go back downhill to find my way out. Taking another drink, my eyes moved around the forest in front of me, my gaze caught by what looked like a small animal lying at the base of a tree. Frowning, I stood up and moved closer. A rabbit, it looked like. I knelt down and looked more closely. Its eyes were open and glassy and ants covered its bloody, matted fur. I whipped my head up, suddenly feeling . . . watched. It felt as if a clutter of spiders had scurried down my spine. I jerked to a standing position, turning around in a circle. The woods suddenly seemed oddly silent, the quiet oppressive, *wrong*. Walking backward, I moved slowly away from the dead rabbit, going back the way I'd come.

My shoulders relaxed slightly when I entered an area I'd walked through only ten minutes before—a grassy glade filled with warm sunshine, only a few trees dotting the mostly open area. But I immediately tensed again when I heard a high-pitched squealing, calling to mind some kind of wailing banshee. Drawing in a sharp breath, I ducked behind the nearest tree, pinning my back to it, my heart drumming in my ears. *Shit, shit, shit.*

Peeking out, I spotted the animal that was making the terrible shriek—it was a wild boar. And it appeared to be caught somehow, or possibly injured. Taking a moment to catch my breath, I leaned back against the tree and took in a big lungful of air. I almost laughed at myself. *Get your shit together, Holden. It's a fucking pig.*

Still, I'd be wise to move on. I didn't have a weapon and wild animals of any size could be dangerous. Hadn't the king on Game of Thrones been speared by a wild boar while hunting? Come to think of it, it wasn't the worst way to go: something very manly about it actually. Much better than being found in your own vomit on some bathroom floor, which would more likely be my end the way I was going.

Suddenly, the pig let out another high-pitched squeal, turning toward where I stood as if it had somehow sensed me. It doubled its efforts at struggling and wailing. I could see now that its leg was trapped somehow. It squealed and grunted fiercely, trying in vain to free itself. I was hit by a sudden head rush and leaned back against the tree, panting for air. Suddenly a bird came swooping out of the sky, barely missing my face. I felt the feathery brush of its wings as I yelped and fell forward, my heart rate spiking sharply when I saw that the pig was free and charging straight toward me. I scrabbled backward in the dirt and pine needles, letting out a deep yell, finally pulling myself to my feet.

Holy shit, holy shit, holy shit, my manic mind chanted. Fear arced through me as I pulled myself to my feet, turned and ran, tripping and sliding back down the hill, my thoughts pooling together in disjointed alarm, my stomach at risk of spewing its contents at any minute. My whole body was shaking. I'd never been so fucking terrified.

By the time I reached the lodge an hour later, I was breathing normally, and feeling like a complete and utter pussy. What kind of coward was I? Is that what a big, strong quarterback did? *Weak, weak, weak. Not strong enough . . .* Some far back corner of my mind screamed before I shut it down. I groaned. Sudden, intense nausea caused me to stop and draw in long breaths of air so I wouldn't lose the contents of my stomach. The headache was coming back again.

Weak, weak, weak.

No, it was okay. I just needed to get my thoughts in order, and the pills would help me do that. *Maybe just one to take the edge off.*

I imagined what I must have looked like running from that wild pig through the woods, and almost felt sorry for the paparazzi for missing that shot. Hysterical laughter bubbled up my chest. I was seized by it so violently I lay on the grass and literally rolled with hilarity. I stopped almost as quickly as I'd started, the laughter dying a quick death on my lips. Jesus . . . *Jesus. Somebody save me.*

CHAPTER THREE

Lily

I dragged the brush through my damp hair, angling my head toward the fireplace to help it dry more quickly.

I ran my hand up the bare skin of my leg, thinking about the girls I'd seen at the lodge at the edge of the woods—the ones who wore the tiny swimsuits and danced to loud music on the deck. I wondered what it'd feel like to be that comfortable in my own skin. I'd been too curious and leaned out too far. One of them had spotted me and they had all started shrieking and screaming and slipping on the deck as they clamored out of the hot tub and ran inside.

I'd wanted to laugh out loud, but I hadn't.

Then several men had come to the edge of the woods with flashlights. I'd just watched them from behind a spruce tree. I hadn't even had to work to hide.

Staring unseeing into the leaping flames of the fire, I wondered again about the man. He'd almost gotten himself speared by a pig today. If that low-flying bird hadn't caught his attention, he wouldn't have even known the pig was running right at him. I pressed my lips together, untangling a knot at the end of my hair.

Who in his or her right mind would leave someone obviously incapable of taking care of himself out here? Alone.

The man had spotted me a few times and I wondered if he would tell anyone about me? Would they believe him if he did? It seemed to me a case could be made that he was off his rocker. I'd watched him stumble around the lodge—I could see him outside on the deck and inside through the tall, uncovered windows, too. And he did a lot of yelling and ranting at no one in particular. And then the day before yesterday he'd stumbled halfway down the outside stairs before he'd caught himself and fallen on the ground half-moaning/half-laughing. I'd waited to make sure he could actually stand up before leaving. Yes, most likely, he was insane. I supposed there was some kind of irony in me pointing out his insanity, being that I was locked away in a mental institution and all.

But anyway, he *was* handsome; I'd give him that. More than handsome, beautiful even. Could men be beautiful? Well, he was. Evidently he knew it, too. He'd ranted about that a whole lot out on the deck by himself. I myself might have found him appealing if he wasn't so obviously crazy and useless. I shook my head, my brush running through the partially dry locks of my long hair, the rhythm and the fire putting me into some sort of mild trance as I thought about *him*.

What was it about him that made me so curious despite his obvious lunacy? I laughed quietly to myself. Okay, so, maybe he wasn't a lunatic, but there was definitely something wrong. The thing was, he wasn't *only* crazy, he was sad, too. He seemed very . . . *alone*, and not because he was actually living a solitary existence, at least for the moment. For some other reason I couldn't understand. But I could relate and perhaps *that* was why I was drawn to him. Yes, maybe that was it.

"Why is he so sad?" I whispered to the fire. It was late August, and the night was only mildly cool, but it was so drafty in here. So big, so cold. The warmth felt nice. The fire snapped as if in answer to the question I'd asked, a log rolling over suddenly and breaking apart, a small spark jumping out and landing on the rug at my feet. I used my brush to smash it out and then went back to brushing my hair, wondering where the man was right now—inside or outside? Howling up at the moon perhaps? I smiled to myself.

How long would he stay? I assumed the lodge in the valley was more a vacation home than anything, used primarily in winter when the ski slopes were open. Although why he wanted to vacation all alone during *any* season, I wasn't sure. I wondered again what the man who'd called out his own name—Holden Scott—was doing right that very second.

CHAPTER FOUR

Holden

I was vomiting. Again. Kneeling on the floor and gripping the porcelain bowl, I emptied the contents of my stomach and then groaned in misery as I fell over onto the floor, resting my cheek on the cool tile. "Fuck me," I moaned hoarsely.

I closed my eyes, but the room started spinning and so I opened them immediately, staring at the baseboard in front of me. *You can't keep going like this. You can't keep living this way.* Brandon's words came back to me and I groaned again, pulling myself up. "Jesus, I know, okay? I know."

I made my way into the living room and flopped down on the couch, keeping my eyes fixed on the enormous, bronze chandelier hanging from the beamed ceiling above. I was just so tired, always so tired, but I could never sleep for very long. Outside the window, the first light of dawn was shading the sky a thousand hues of gray. If only I could sleep . . .

I didn't see the kid sitting on the ground on the side of the bleachers, his head in a book, until I practically tripped over him. "Darn, sorry," I said, hopping quickly to the side, righting myself and switching my football helmet to my other hand. The kid looked up at me, revealing a large black and blue mark on his right cheekbone, the eye on that side of his face red and partially swollen shut. "Whoa, what happened to you?" I asked. "Are you okay?"

He frowned and then reached his fingers up to touch the bruise lightly as if I'd just reminded him it was there. "Yeah, I'm fine," he muttered, shaking his shaggy, dark blond hair so it fell over his forehead into his eyes, hoping I'd go away.

"You sure? 'Cause that looks like a real shiner. How'd you get it?" I knelt on the grass next to him. His expression was confused as if he didn't know how to react to someone talking to him.

"Uh, I walked into a door by accident," he said.

I tilted my head, considering him. He was lying. He'd probably gotten into a fight. I raised my eyebrows. "Nah, you can come up with a better story than that. That one's been used a million times." He looked surprised for a second and then he made his expression go blank again.

"Story?" he asked.

"Yeah, like, you know, you gotta be more imaginative." I tilted my head and looked up at the sky, thinking until it came to me. I looked back at the kid. "That creepy janitor who always just happens," I set my helmet down and used my fingers to make air quotes, "to be walking through the locker room when we're changing tried to abduct you, but you fought him off with the Ninja skills you learned from the old Chinese guy who manages your apartment building when he's not growing bonsai trees."

The kid looked at me silently for a couple seconds and then said, "I don't live in an apartment building, I think you mean Japanese, and that story is not imaginative at all—it's a clear Karate Kid rip-off. And also, it could get an innocent janitor in a whole lot of trouble—maybe even fired from the job he might need to feed his three foster kids."

"That guy has three foster kids?" I did a fake shudder.

He shrugged. "He could."

"See, that's what's wrong with social services. They give foster kids to guys like him. I hear, like, the whole system is a joke."

The kid narrowed his eyes—well his one good eye at least—and stared at me for a few moments. Then his lip tipped up slightly and he laughed a short laugh. When he stopped, he looked . . . bewildered. Yeah, bewildered. That was the word. And it'd just been on a vocab test the week before. I took a moment to pat myself on the back for using it.

"I'm Holden," I said. "Holden Scott."

He paused for a second before reaching out and gripping the hand I held out to him. "Ryan Ellis."

Two guys from my team walked by and I heard them snicker under their breath. "Hey, Holden, dude," Vince Milne said, "is it adopt-a-loser day and no one told me?" He ribbed Jeremy Pratt who was walking next to him and Jeremy laughed.

"Yeah it is, Vince," I called. "Are you already taken?"

"Eh, fuck off," he muttered under his breath before walking away. I hated that asshole. And he was a suck-ass football player, too.

I turned back to Ryan who was trying to look like he was busy organizing his backpack and hadn't heard anything Vince and I were saying. I could tell he had though because his face was hot and bright red.

"Anyway, what way do you walk? I'm headed home if you are, too."

"Uh, I walk toward Bridgetown Road," he muttered.

"Me, too. Come on." I stood up, gathering my helmet, and he stood slowly as well. We were about the same height, although Ryan was real skinny. He zipped his backpack and hefted it onto his shoulder.

"Your backpack looks like it weighs two hundred pounds."

Ryan smirked. "It does. It's how I got all these muscles."

"Ha. So what grade are you in?"

"Seventh, same as you," he said.

I nodded, feeling bad that he obviously knew who I was, but I'd never noticed him before. I cleared my throat. "So, hey, do you want to stop at Skyline and get a couple Coneys? Are you hungry? I'm starving. I go there after practice a lot. Some of the other guys might be there, too. The cool ones."

He shook his head. "No, I can't. I have to be home."

"Oh, okay. Another time then."

As we started walking, Ryan said, "So you, uh, obviously play football."

"Yeah, I love it. Man, it's my life. I'm number twenty-two. I'm gonna go pro someday," I said excitedly. "I'm gonna live in a big mansion and date celebrities, and have my own personal chef, and drive the coolest cars." It was all I ever dreamed about. "Do you play at all? Even just for fun?"

Ryan shook his head, sticking his hands into his pockets. "Nah. I like watching, though. I like the Cowboys."

I turned to him. "That's my favorite team. Holy shit, they're awesome!"

Ryan smiled and nodded.

"If you like football so much, why don't you play?"

He pressed his lips together and stared down at his shoes as we walked. "My dad . . . the gear and stuff, you know. It's just . . . not in our budget." His face turned kinda red. I nodded so he would know I understood.

"My parents are on a budget, too. I know what you mean. My dad had to pick up extra hours so we could afford for me to play."

Ryan nodded, looking like I'd made him feel better. "I go to all the school games. I think I've seen your parents at them, too—holding up number twenty-two signs."

I nodded. "Yeah, that's them, all right." I rolled my eyes. "The one's dressed entirely in our school colors, waving pom-poms, foam number-one fingers, and holding up signs with my number. It's so embarrassing." I kept talking. I always talked so damn much. Like my brain had no off switch. All my thoughts just flowed right out of my mouth. "My parents thought they couldn't have kids. They tried for years and nothing, then, boom! When my mom was forty-nine, she found out she was pregnant with me. You should see her, when she tells the story, she looks all dreamy like God himself came down and knocked her up, you know? So they kinda go overboard with the whole parenting thing. Like I'm their miracle child."

Ryan smiled a small smile. "I guess you kinda are."

"Yeah, I guess," I said. "So what about your parents?"

Ryan stiffened and stared down at his shoes again. "It's just me and my dad." I waited, but he didn't go on. I glanced at him out of the corner of my eye as we walked in silence for a few blocks, getting up the nerve to ask the question I really wanted to know.

"Did your dad do that to you?" I asked as casually as possible, nodding to his eye when he turned his head to me. His expression was surprised for a second, then he looked kinda mad, then he closed his eyes and looked ahead, deciding to answer honestly.

"Yeah."

I was quiet for a minute, wondering what it was like to have a dad who hit you in your face. What did a kid do to deserve something like that? "Your dad sounds like a real asshole."

"Oh, so you know him," Ryan said sarcastically.

I breathed out a small laugh. "Hey, you know, so, why don't you come over sometime? We could watch a game. And it would give my parents someone else to fall all over."

Ryan looked like he might be just a little bit mad about the offer, but then he shrugged. "Maybe. Hey, this is my street. I gotta go."

"Okay," I called after him as he walked away. "See you tomorrow then."

He didn't turn, but I heard him mutter, "See you tomorrow."

I woke up with Ryan's name on my lips. I sat up abruptly and groaned at the pain that throbbed in my head. I was sprawled on the couch in the living room, the morning sun streaming through the floor-to-ceiling windows. I'd fallen asleep at dawn so I couldn't have been asleep for long. But I'd dreamed. For the first time in a really long time. I lay back down. Something about the dream niggled at my brain, but I couldn't figure it out. Something felt *off.* But it'd left a lingering feeling of . . . happiness. *That* was it—I'd had the first *happy* memory of Ryan. I laughed softly to myself. Maybe there was something to this feng shui after all. And maybe, just maybe I'd venture out into the woods again to look for my ghost. Something in me was having a hard time believing she didn't exist—I'd *seen* her. Besides, what the fuck else did I have to do? Wild boars be damned.

CHAPTER FIVE

Holden

Late that afternoon as I sat outside in the fresh mountain air, drinking a steaming mug of coffee, I felt a little more alive. I'd taken a pill—just one. Just to take the edge off. I'd woken from my dream . . . *hopeful* I guess, and I'd tried to go without today, but the nausea was just too severe. I'd wean myself off . . . I'd take fewer and fewer until . . . I let out a long sigh. I'd tried that before and it hadn't worked. But maybe up here it'd be different. *You have to be the one to make the choice . . .*

The girl . . . if she *was* out there, what was she doing right now? Was she in those woods? Alone? She must be well equipped to take care of herself, which made me feel even more lame for having let a pig put the fear of the devil into me. Hadn't I been fearless once upon a time? Hadn't I? Why had I run? I couldn't remember now. But then again, I couldn't remember a lot these days.

Sitting there on the deck, staring into the forest, the vague hint of hope coursing through me, I made a decision. I was going back in those woods *today*, I was going to find her, and I was going to solve the mystery of who she was.

An hour later, feeling that same excited resolve I'd felt when I'd first set out to find her, I entered the woods.

The day was mild and the forest floor was cool and misty under the thick canopy of trees. I walked what I thought was the same path I'd walked the last time. Determined to shake off the strangeness and the fear of my last trip into these woods, I made a concerted effort to appreciate the wild beauty around me, bending to look at hollowed-out logs and clusters of wild mushrooms.

For a Midwestern boy like me, these woods were all new and different and for the first several hours, I was again caught in that lost place of boyhood adventure. As a kid I would have loved this forest—building forts out of rocks and sticks, pretending to be an explorer. I'd been filled with life and hope and excitement once, hadn't I? I must have—I couldn't grasp the feeling now, but I knew I had been a happy kid, a boy who'd dreamed anything was possible and found joy in simple things. Maybe even a boy who should be mourned, because *he* was gone now, replaced by the wastrel of a man I'd become.

I called out for the girl but with a little less enthusiasm. It'd been hours and I was starting to doubt myself again.

I walked for a while longer, before I finally decided to give up and go back. I was getting cold despite the mild weather outside this thick forest, and I hadn't brought the proper layers, underestimating the temperature drop as the day wore into evening. And I was feeling sick again. I needed a fix. My ears were ringing slightly, and my skin felt strange like it did when I hadn't taken a pill for a while: pulsing and electric. I hated it. And I was disappointed, depressed even. I hadn't even seen a whisper of the girl.

I started back the way I'd come but suddenly realized I'd been walking over flat ground for a while—not uphill like I'd done the other day. Then it had been easy enough to get a feel for direction, because I'd simply returned downhill. But now, looking around, worry began fluttering through my gut. A crack of thunder cut through the trees. "Fuck," I muttered. Surely I wasn't lost. I started walking back the way I thought I'd come, but I felt turned around, unsure, my heart now pounding out a staccato beat in my chest. Branches swayed in the mounting wind and a sudden bolt of lightning streaked across the sky, for a brief instant lighting the forest an eerie, glimmering white.

And then the rain came.

The muted light shining through the trees dimmed even more as dark clouds moved across the twilight sky, casting the forest in silvery shades of gray.

I pulled out my cell phone, trying to get a signal, but it was useless. Of course there wouldn't be service up here in the midst of this thick forest. "You're in the middle of fucking nowhere, idiot," I mumbled to myself. Walking again, I moved more quickly, fighting brambles that seemed to reach out and grab me, twisting away from branches that snagged my clothes, tripping over things I could no longer see at my feet, falling once and feeling sharp pine needles and pieces of fallen bark dig into the flesh of my hands.

"Motherfucker!" I yelled, standing up and stopping, turning in a full circle. What in the hell had I been thinking? I'd tried this before and been beaten then, too. Why had I imagined it was a good idea to give this another go?

Because of her.

I was such a stupid fuck sometimes. So now I had to face the facts: I was alone in the woods, no shelter in sight, in a hostile environment that had already gotten the best of me in more ways than one, in a fucking rainstorm.

Out here it didn't matter that I had millions of dollars in the bank. It didn't matter that I was a superstar in some people's minds, or a tragic fuck-up in other's. It didn't matter that I had a Super Bowl ring or a fleet of cars.

It didn't matter because the forest didn't care.

And truthfully, it didn't matter in general. None of it had brought me happiness, not one single bit. And what were you supposed to do when you had everything in the world and not a goddamned *bit* of it brought you joy? Where did you go from there? What was left to offer any hope?

I'd tried it all . . . I'd tried it all. Goddamn, I'd tried it all. I sat down heavily on a large boulder, looking around bleakly, hardly able to see anything through the heavy sheets of rain. I was going to die here, either of exposure or by being skewered by a wild boar. Or maybe worse.

Probably worse. And I cared about the dying, but I wasn't sure if I cared about being dead. There was peace in death. Quiet.

I was lost, my hands bloody and abraded, out of breath, nauseated, and so damn . . . sad. *I was so fucking sad.* I felt stripped bare, and all that was left was fear and such terrible sadness. I tilted my head up to the rain and felt it mixing with the hot tears running down my face. Christ, now I was crying? This forest had unmanned me in ways I didn't even want to think about, especially now when I was directionless and alone.

"You've lost your way," came her voice. I lowered my startled gaze and found her standing next to a tree, watching me. Her hair and clothes were drenched by the rain, although she didn't seem to notice. It was as if she had been formed from a magical combination of my own desires and the night itself.

I hesitated for a long time, just looking at her, wondering if she *was* a dream, letting her words sink in through my skin, right into my heart, my soul. "Yes," I whispered. "Yes, I know."

She nodded slowly as if in complete understanding. "Come," she said. "I'll help you find your way again."

Relief flooded my system so fiercely it made me dizzy, as I stood and walked toward her, my eyes taking in her details as I drew closer. Her hair was very dark, maybe even black, though it was difficult to tell since it was soaking wet. She had it braided, and it was hanging over one shoulder. Loose tendrils had escaped and were stuck to her cheeks. And her face, God, her face.

She was . . . *beautiful.*

For a moment, I simply stared. *Was* she real? Her white lace dress was plastered to her body, showing delicate curves beneath. She had on a pair of brown boots with thick socks sticking out of the top, but no jacket.

"Aren't you cold?" I asked dumbly, a shiver wracking my body, my teeth visibly chattering.

She smiled, her face moving from stunning to breathtaking, her beauty almost otherworldly. "No."

I blinked at her, wondering at how she'd appeared out of the mist.

"Are you a dream?" I mused aloud. "Or maybe a . . . ghost?"

She tilted her head, her gaze intent. "I can't imagine being anyone's dream. But a ghost?" She looked thoughtful for a moment, something entering her expression that I didn't know how to read. "Maybe," she whispered. "Yes, I think I might be." And with that she turned and moved in the opposite direction I'd been walking.

I wanted to speak to her, to ask her what she'd meant, but my teeth were chattering so violently I could barely form words, and the headache that had begun earlier was now a hammer pounding at my skull. So instead, I focused on her back and the sweet curve of her ass under her wet dress as she moved surely and swiftly through the forest, leading me out of the darkness, into the luminous glow of the moon. The rain dwindled and then stopped altogether, the night birds seeming to come alive all around us as we walked.

"What's your name?" I finally managed as we walked through the glen I recognized from the other day—the one where I'd seen the pig— and started downhill.

She glanced back at me, biting at her lip, seeming to be considering whether she'd answer or not. But finally she said, "Lily. My name is Lily."

"Lily what?"

"Just Lily."

I caught up to her and walked beside her now that the trees were sparse and there was room for two. Her breath clouded in the air just like mine. If she was really a ghost, she was unlike any ghost I'd ever imagined. Okay, so she didn't want to tell me her full name, but I had to find out something about her. "Where do you live? I was told the nearest town is a couple hours away."

She nodded, looking at me warily from under her lashes. "I live close by."

"But—"

"You shouldn't come into the woods if you don't know where you're going," she said, looking ahead again, back to where we were walking.

I stopped moving and she stopped next to me, gazing up at me questioningly. I hadn't been prepared for *her*. But I definitely hadn't been prepared for her eyes in the light of the moon: wide and almond shaped, true violet, framed by lush, dark lashes. For a moment my breath hitched. I'd never *seen* eyes like hers. "I know. I . . . well, I was looking for you," I said distractedly, before I could consider a different answer.

She studied me, her expression suddenly perplexed. "Me? Why?"

I ran my hand through my wet hair, feeling more off balance than I ever had in my life. Why did I suddenly feel like an eighth grade boy at the middle school dance, trying to make conversation with a girl? "I . . . well I saw you, um, the other day . . ."

"At the edge of the forest? Yes, I know. I thought you were going to drown in that hot tub." She cocked her head to the side.

"Oh, uh . . . yeah, it probably looked that way. I just fell asleep. Thank you, though."

"For what?"

I shrugged and rubbed at the back of my neck. "For caring about me." I cleared my throat. "The thing is, Lily, I thought I saw you a few times, and I was curious about you. I wanted to . . . introduce myself." *Introduce myself? Really? What the fuck is wrong with you, Holden?*

Lily swiped her tongue along her bottom lip, her brow creased, staring at somewhere just behind me. Finally her eyes met mine again. "Well, it's nice to meet you, Holden Scott, God Among Men."

I stared at her blankly for a moment, memory finally dawning. "Oh, shit," I muttered under my breath. "Uh, about that . . . I uh—"

She laughed suddenly, her white teeth flashing at me in the light of the moon, and then she turned. "I should apologize for spying on you." But she didn't sound sorry. "Goodbye, Holden Scott."

I stepped after her. "Wait! Please don't go. I live right over there . . . temporarily, I mean. For now. I live there. Do you want to come in for a drink? A beverage or . . . or a meal or something?" *A meal? Like she was homeless?* "Not that you look hungry. Just that I'd like—" *Jesus.* I grimaced.

Lily laughed softly again and I couldn't help but join her, feeling

35

embarrassed, glancing at my feet before looking back into her eyes. "That god among men thing was obviously a gross overstatement."

She raised one brow. "Obviously." But the smile turned her full, berry-pink lips up again, and there wasn't anything mean in her expression.

"Do you know who I am?" I asked.

Lily looked at me in confusion. "I just told you I know your name. Holden Scott."

"No, I mean, not my name, but do you know who I am?"

The look on her face was utterly confused and I let out a long exhale. "Never mind."

"You should go warm up and get some sleep." When she began to turn again, I stepped after her once more.

"Will you come back tomorrow?" Even I could hear the desperate note in my voice.

Lily paused and regarded me for so long, my heart began to thrum faster with nervous hope. "Yes. Meet me right here tomorrow at sunset." She looked up at the moon and then back at me. Victory coursed through my veins. She was going to meet me again tomorrow. "I have to go."

"Okay, Lily of the Night. Thank you."

She turned around, walking backward as she went. "Okay, Holden, God Among Men. You're welcome." And then with a small laugh she turned and ran into the woods, disappearing into the darkness.

I looked down, smiling at my own feet, noting the mud caking my shoes and the deep footprints of where I'd stepped in the soggy ground. My eyes kept roaming, looking for Lily's footprints next to mine, but once again, it was as if she'd never been there at all. Not a trace of her was left.

CHAPTER SIX

Holden

I stood over the toilet, holding the bag of pills in my clammy, shaking hands. I hadn't taken any when I'd returned home the night before, though my body had been demanding them, and it was now daybreak. Letting out a deep groan, I threw the bag on the counter and slammed the lid of the toilet. I wasn't ready. I opened the bag hungrily and threw back two pills, cupping my hand under the faucet and swallowing big gulps of water.

For a moment, I stood looking at myself disgustedly in the mirror. *God among men.* It made me laugh at myself.

Lily. Her name is Lily. And she's beautiful.

I needed the pills if I was going to spend any time with Lily. If I went cold turkey today, I'd need at least three or four days to detox and recover. *At least.* There was no way I could meet her tonight if I was in the midst of withdrawal. And I wanted so badly to meet with her again. It was the first thing I'd actually wanted in a very long time. God, I had a million questions about her. Who was she? Where did she come from? Where did she live? Why had she watched me?

After taking a long shower and drinking half a pot of coffee, I went down and checked out Brandon's home gym. Switching on the light, I glanced around and let out a low whistle. Mirrors covered the entirety of the far wall. Top-of-the-line workout machines and weight benches were spread throughout the impressive room. There was a large-screen TV mounted in the opposite corner with a sound system set up beneath, its speakers fastened to the walls.

I spent half an hour on the treadmill, winded after fifteen minutes, but pushing myself to finish the full thirty. Then I spent a few minutes lifting, breaking a sweat after two reps. *Fuck, I was out of shape.* I'd been out for a season and a half and I'd done nothing but party and pollute my body. And now I knew I was not only emotionally depressed, but my body was broken down, too. Feeling defeated, I flipped the lights off and left the gym.

I was antsy for the rest of the day, checking the time over and over. I'd looked it up online and the sun was supposed to set at seven twenty-one. At six thirty, I was walking toward the woods, telling myself I didn't want her to wait for me in case she got there early. My heart was thumping steadily and anticipation filled my chest.

It was a beautiful evening, the air crisp, but not overly cool, the sun warm on my back. I took my heavy sweatshirt off and tied it around my waist so I was just wearing a long-sleeved T-shirt. Pushing my sleeves up my arms, I entered the woods and leaned as casually as possible against a tree to wait.

When was the last time I'd waited for a girl? I honestly couldn't recall. High school, maybe? There was something deeply satisfying about it, with an edge of nervous excitement. What if she didn't come? What if she *did?*

When seven twenty-one came and went, the sky changing from soft blue to bright shades of orange, I rubbed my palms on my jeans. *Would* she stand me up? Disappointment filled me as I considered that I might be walking back to the lodge alone in half an hour, Lily having never shown. Maybe she had forgotten. Maybe our "date" just didn't mean much to her. Maybe something had come up. Maybe I was an idiot for expecting her to want to come at all.

I looked up and she was standing a little ways away, watching me. Relief and happiness brought an immediate smile to my face. "You made it," I said, stepping toward her.

She tilted her head to the side, her black braid swinging over her shoulder. "Did you think I wouldn't?"

"I wasn't sure."

She tilted her head backward. "Come on, I want to show you something I think you'll like."

I followed. Again, she was wearing a dress—blue with buttons up the front. It looked as if it was from an era when women wore short, white gloves and small hats on a regular basis. Despite the old-fashioned look, the dress fit her well and I couldn't help that my eyes lingered on the feminine lines of her body. She was wearing black canvas sneakers on her feet and again, no coat. I felt my lips curve up and wondered who this girl was. *A girl. A flesh and blood girl.*

We trudged through the woods, as the light around us grew dim. I couldn't see the horizon above the trees anymore and the sky was a pale shade of orange overhead. The air was fragrant with the tangy scent of pine, just covering the musky smell of the damp, rotting leaves underfoot.

"Watch your step," Lily said, pointing to her right. "There's a snake in the grass by that dead log."

I swiveled my head left as Lily giggled. I looked at the log and at the ground around it but didn't see a thing. "Were you kidding?" I asked.

Lily glanced at me. "No. It won't hurt you, though. Not unless you get in its way."

I cleared my throat doing my best not to shudder. I hadn't even thought about snakes being in these woods. I fucking hated snakes.

I chuckled, feeling like an idiot. But when I looked over at her, she was smiling at me in a way that made me smile back.

I watched her walk away for a moment and then jogged to catch up. "Lily, do you . . . what I mean is . . ." The area directly ahead of us was bare of trees or bushes and so I walked more quickly to move in front and turned around so I was walking backward and she was looking at me.

"Be careful you don't step on a snake walking backward like that. It isn't smart to turn your back on what you can't trust."

I laughed softly and turned so I was walking next to her and she smiled in obvious amusement. "Ha ha. What I was trying to ask is, do you *live* in these woods?" *Was that even possible?*

She shot me a strange look. "No, Holden, I don't *live* in these woods. I'm just familiar with them. Come on." She turned abruptly, pulling my arm so I'd follow her.

"Well, where do you live? I don't mean to pry, it's just I was told there was no one close by."

"I live a little ways from here."

I looked around, wondering what she meant by a little ways from here. It was the same answer she'd given me before. From what I could see from the deck of the lodge, there was nothing but woods for hundreds of square miles. "Oh, okay, so like in the middle of nowhere then?"

Lily laughed. "Yes, I guess you could say that. But then again, so do you."

I smiled. "True, but just temporarily."

"Maybe I'm only here temporarily, too."

"Oh, so what do you—"

"Why so many questions?"

"I just want—"

"Follow me," she said as she made a sudden turn between two trees. The terrain grew slightly rockier, the forest less dense. I followed behind Lily because the trees were spaced in a way that didn't leave room for two to walk side by side. After ten minutes or so, the trees opened up even more, and I caught up to Lily. A few minutes after that, we came to the edge of a cliff, and I cautiously looked over. It wasn't very far to the ground and I released a huff of air, turning away anyway. I'd never minded heights particularly, but after Ryan . . .

"Over here," Lily said, giving me a hand gesture to follow her. I did. She looked down. "It starts here." I joined her and saw a crude set of stairs carved right into the rock.

"Whoa," I said, looking down. The steps went all the way to the ground below. "Who made these?"

"I don't know," she said, taking a step down.

"Wait, Lily, let me go first," I said.

She looked back at me. "I've been down them before."

"I know . . . I just . . ." *They could be crumbly, you could fall. I can't let you fall.* "Just humor me." I smiled. "Please."

She hesitated, but then moved aside as I passed her. "Thanks," I said, smiling at her again.

The color of the sky dimmed, and the moon appeared, lighting the small canyon with a muted glow. When I'd almost reached the bottom, the last two stairs fell away. I hopped down and then reached my hands up to Lily. "Here," I said, placing my hands around her waist, "let me lift you down." Something about my hands around her waist felt more intimate than I'd intended and warmth filled me as I lifted her down to the ground and she stood in front of me, looking up into my face. "Okay?" I asked. My voice sounded strange in my ears, hoarse, gravelly.

"Yes, I'm good. But you're still . . ." She looked down to where my hands still rested. I pulled them away quickly.

"Sorry," I breathed, shaking my head. I looked up and around. "What is this place?"

"I'm not sure," Lily said, stepping away from me. "But here, look." She moved to a large rock at the edge of where the rocks met vegetation and pushed some leaves aside. Carved into the rock was a kind of very small room with a window, perfectly square and obviously man-made. And at the top of the window was a carving of some sort. I looked more closely.

"Are those hands?" I asked.

"Yes. They look like they're reaching for each other, the fingertips just barely touching."

"Huh," I said in wonder.

"There's a place several hours from here where ancient people built whole houses under cliffs—right into the rock. It's almost like they just barely started one here and then decided to go somewhere else instead."

"Hmm," I hummed. "I wonder why." I ran my hand along the sill of the window before moving aside and leaning into the small opening, barely big enough for two people to lie down. When I leaned back out, Lily was tracing the carved hands with her finger.

"It's just so strange to think about someone standing here once upon a time carving these hands, thinking whatever he was thinking, maybe worrying about something, maybe annoyed about someone." She smiled softly as she watched her own finger moving around the carving of the hands. There was something sensual about watching her finger move that way, and I almost felt as if I could feel it on my own skin, tracing, exploring . . . I couldn't help the warm shiver that moved through my body.

"Maybe thinking about a girl," I supplied.

She looked at me and her smile grew. "Maybe." She looked back to the window and put her hand on the sill, tilting her head. "Seems so funny that a person, all his thoughts, all his ideas, all his feelings, can be here one minute and just . . . gone the next."

I studied her profile as she continued to stare through the window. And I knew just what she meant. I'd thought the same thing when I'd lost my best friend. How could he be so alive, so vibrant, so filled with all those things that were only *him*, and then just . . . gone. Where did he go? "I know what you mean, Lily," I said. "I've thought the same thing."

Lily's lips tilted up ever so slightly though she continued to stare ahead. "But you know what's even worse?" She looked over at me, her smile fading, her expression becoming sad. "Leaving nothing behind. No proof that you ever existed, not something like this," she moved her hand on the sill, "and no one to remind the world that you were here, even for a small moment in time. No one who might brush their fingertips against your own and know the feel of you, even in the dark."

I blinked at her, opening my mouth to speak and then closing it again. What she'd said hit me as so very *profound*. For some reason I felt filled with emotion. That was my job now. My job was to keep my best friend's memory alive, the him that only I knew, the him he didn't show anyone else. His parents were gone; he didn't have any brothers or sisters. I was the only one here on earth who had known the *real* him. Something about that thought, the responsibility it suggested, both filled me with a sudden surge of joy, and a strange aching sadness, maybe even fear. "I . . . yes," I said, my voice cracking slightly. Lily seemed to come back to the moment, shaking her head slightly.

"I guess this place just makes me sort of introspective." She gave me an embarrassed tilt of her lips "And something about it makes me feel as if I've been here before. A sort of . . . déjà vu maybe. Isn't that strange?"

I looked at the small rock space, thinking that maybe I felt the same way, too. There was something about the width of the sill beneath my hand that had felt familiar somehow, as if my skin knew every bump and groove before I'd really even felt it. No, not entirely strange. "Maybe we *have* been here before," I teased. "Maybe you were an Indian princess and I was a . . . chief. Maybe we met in another lifetime." I grinned at her, leaning my hip against the rock.

She laughed, the sound of it echoing into the cavernous space in which we were standing. "How come when people imagine their past lives, they always cast themselves as someone famous or important?" She tilted her head. "Everyone is Elvis or Cleopatra or Einstein. Why wasn't anyone ever Joe Green, a mechanic from Long Beach in a past life?"

I chuckled. "When it comes to other lives, I say dream big or go home."

She laughed as she shook her head, raising her delicate eyebrows. "I'd rather be someone simple, with a simple life, simple problems." She looked around. "Not a princess. Maybe just a gatherer. I'd walk the forest all day looking for roots, flowers, and herbs, and I'd be happy. It would be enough." She shot me a smile. And I had to agree with her, because I'd had all the fancy things, the best that money could buy, and yet, in this quiet place, there was . . . happiness? Peacefulness? The very antithesis of everything else in my life: simplicity. Surrounded by nothing but trees and sky, in the middle of the forest, with this girl felt . . . *right*. We were looking at each other seriously now, a current of some kind flowing between us. Something I wasn't entirely sure I understood, because it seemed like so *much*, so soon. Lily looked away first, just as I caught the first tinge of blush in her cheeks.

"Here, there's one more thing I wanted to show you." She turned and I followed her. "Look," she said, bending to something lying on the ground beneath a nearby tree. I went to her and bent down, too, the light from the moon casting just enough light for me to see what she was pointing at. I picked up one small, shiny, black piece of rock, holding it up and marveling.

"Arrowheads," I murmured.

"Yes. What's strange is that there are so many of them, all in one place," she whispered.

"Huh," I said, feeling something like wonder, putting the black one down and picking up a different reddish one, realizing who would have loved these even more than me. "Ryan loved history. He would have loved these. Damn." I picked up another one from the ground and held it up. It was a soft pink color, the tip still pointed and sharp.

"Who's Ryan?" Lily asked.

I snapped my head up, not even realizing I'd mentioned his name out loud. I studied her for a moment. "Where do you live?" I asked, raising a brow.

Lily laughed softly. "Ah, tit for tat?" She was quiet, but she didn't appear to be angry. I waited, watching her. "I live with my mother not far from here. A couple miles or so."

I nodded, clearing my throat. "Ryan, he was my best friend. He . . . he passed away recently."

Lily studied my face, her violet eyes seeming to look right into me. "Oh, I'm sorry," she whispered.

Uncomfortable, I looked away, back to the arrowheads. "It is strange that they'd all be together like this, as if someone collected them from all over the forest."

"That's kind of what I thought, too," she said.

"Hmm," I said, frowning. "Weird."

She shrugged. "I know. It's interesting to look at all the different kinds together, though. This one's my favorite." She picked up a white pearlescent one, so thin you could see through it in spots. "It looks so delicate," she said softly, "and yet it could take down a large animal, or even a man." She smiled a little and then looked at me. I realized I was staring, my eyes soaking in the beautiful lines of her face, the sweep of her long lashes against her cheeks, the way inky tendrils of hair had escaped from her braid and were curling around her jaw. I wanted to keep staring, but I forced myself to look away.

"You said you wanted to show me something you thought I'd like. How'd you know? That I'd like these?"

For the first time since I'd met her, an unsure look passed over her face and she pulled her bottom lip between her teeth.

She let out a soft laugh and shook her head, beginning to stand. "Well, I just figured all men like weapons."

"I do like them," I quickly reassured her, reaching for her arm so she remained kneeling. "I like them. They're amazing. This *place* is amazing." *I think you might be amazing.*

She had offered me one of the only things she probably had to offer. I didn't know a lot about this girl . . . yet. But she must live a simple life. The things she had to give were . . . here. And she'd given one to me.

For an instant, our eyes met in the dim, golden-hued light of the night. Lily stood and I followed her up, feeling confused and lost for some reason I couldn't comprehend. Lily reached out and took my wrist and put the white arrowhead she'd said was her favorite into my hand and closed my fingers around it. Her skin was warm and I could feel very light calluses on her palms. I wondered what they'd feel like against my lips.

"I suppose it's not actually mine to give, but I don't think anyone will mind if you keep it."

"Thank you." I slipped it into the pocket of my jeans, feeling as if I'd received something precious. "Here," I said, picking up a small, sharp rock and returning to a portion of the cliff wall a few steps away from the strange little windowed-cave. I used it to draw two stick figures, one with a triangle skirt. "Long after we're gone, this will still be here. And maybe someday someone will come upon it and wonder who these figures were.

We'll live on forever."

"Except you probably just defaced an historic archeological find."

I blinked at her and her lip quirked up. "You're teasing me," I said.

She laughed. "Mostly. Come on." I looked back once at the carving of the hands and then followed her, laughing softly.

We ascended the crude steps and started walking through the open, rocky area toward the more dense forest. I walked close to Lily, brushing against her arm on purpose. Each time I did it, it felt as if a thousand nerve endings came alive on the patch of skin that touched hers. She didn't speak and I wondered if she felt it, too. I felt fifteen again. I felt like I'd just discovered there was still something innocent about me, something pure and untouched, despite my past. I hadn't known that a girl could still make my heart race and my mouth go dry. Especially one I'd just met. More so, one who wasn't scantily dressed and trying to get into my pants. No false platitudes, no rambling, self-centered prattle. Just . . . calm. Still. It was as if my soul yearned to meet with hers, to understand all of her, to know every detail of her life.

She glanced over at me, perhaps thinking something similar because she asked, "So, Holden, what are you doing out here?" Referring to the lodge in the middle of nowhere, I assumed.

I sighed. I hardly wanted to get into that. "I'd tell you all about it, Lily, but I'm afraid you wouldn't respect me anymore."

"What gave you the idea I respected you?"

My own surprised laughter rang through the trees. "Everyone respects me. I'm a superhero. A god among men."

"Hmm," she hummed, sounding unimpressed. "So what's your superpower?"

I scratched at my neck as I stepped over a tree root, taking a moment to think about it. What *was* my superpower? Everyone else would say being a football player. But that wasn't really a superpower. That was something I'd worked my ass off at practically my whole life. I was naturally gifted, sure, but I'd still had to put the hours in. Plus, I didn't necessarily want to tell Lily about that right now. "I can fly," I said, grinning at her.

She looked over at me. "Oh really? What a coincidence. So can I."
I laughed softly and we walked for a moment. I was having trouble concentrating because her arm kept brushing mine and every now and again, I caught her scent, something fresh with the very faint undertone of wildflowers.

"Where do you fly, Lily?"

She stopped walking and turned toward me. "Anywhere I want. Sometimes I go to a crowded city, and other times, a deserted island. Once I went to Jupiter."

"Jupiter? I've never been. What was it like?"

She hugged her arms around her body. "Cold."

I laughed, and then regarded her, feeling suddenly serious, my smile faltering. "Do you think we could figure out a way to fly together?" I gave her a teasing smile, but she didn't smile back.

She tilted her head, her expression becoming thoughtful, almost tender, "I suppose anything's possible."

"Where do you land?" I whispered. She regarded me quizzically. "I just mean, flying is only good if you have a place to land where someone else is waiting for you." *Where had that come from? I didn't know, and yet the truth of my own statement hit me in my gut. Who was waiting for me?*

She was silent for several heartbeats, something moving behind her eyes that I couldn't read. Her mouth opened and then closed again, her brow creasing slightly, as if the answer had skated through her mind, and then moved just out of reach. "Do you always think so much, Holden Scott?" she finally asked, giving a barely perceptible shake of her head as she started walking. I shook my head slightly, too, shaking off the strange moment. *Did I always think so much? Yes, I supposed I did. Always had.* I jogged a few steps to catch up to her.

"I think I do. Yes." We walked out of the trees, into a more open area.

Lily laughed softly, looking up at the sky. I followed her gaze. "I've never seen so many stars," I said. "They're so clear."

"I'll show you the best place to see them. And then I'll walk you back. It's getting late."

"It's not that late," I said, not ready for my time with her to end. "You could come back with me and hang out for a little while," I suggested, but Lily shook her head.

"No, not tonight."

Not tonight. But that meant maybe another night. I'd hold on to that. *I barely know you, Lily, but I already like you. And somehow, I feel like I need you.*

The forest felt alive all around us: movement in the brush, soft scampering on the ground close by, wings flapping softly in the trees. Maybe I had tuned it all out when I'd been here alone not wanting to consider what was making those noises. But suddenly, with Lily at my side, I felt no anxiety. She obviously knew this place well. If she wasn't nervous, neither was I.

We came to a rock formation, and I followed her as she began climbing it. At the top there was a large, flat rock and she dropped down and lay back, gazing up at the stars. I lay down next to her and looked up. The sky was glittering and sparkling above and it took my breath for a moment. It didn't feel like I was looking *up* at it, but like I was *part* of it, like I was floating amongst it. It was as if we had stepped off some magical cliff and tumbled straight into the sky.

"I feel like this whole night is a dream," I said. "I feel like I'll wake up in San Francisco after having fallen asleep for a minute and realize I dreamed this entire thing. Dreamed *you.*" I turned my head and found that Lily was already looking at me, watching me as I watched the sky.

She smiled and propped herself up on one elbow. "San Francisco? Is that where you live?"

I came up on one elbow, too, and faced her. "Yeah." I almost told her that I played football for the 49ers, but it was as if here, in this forest, *that* life didn't exist. I wanted to leave *that* Holden behind, just for now and continue as we'd started, sharing things we chose to share, but not everything, not now. Here, I didn't want to be . . . *him.* I just wanted to be *me.*

I suddenly realized I didn't want to explain my life to her. I looked away, embarrassment at my own situation assaulting me. I'd never had to explain it to anyone. The vast majority of the world already knew. Saying it out loud, choosing the words, would mean taking ownership of it somehow, and that's what made me hesitate. If I told my story out loud, and if I told it truthfully, I would be forced to claim it. Until now, there had never been reason to do that.

Maybe that was it, this strange removal from my own life. Ever since I'd been drafted and become part of the tabloid fodder, I'd begun feeling like I belonged to the world. I'd started looking to the opinions and judgments of the general public as the narrative of my own existence. It was dissatisfying and arduous, and because of it, I'd spent the last three years never feeling truly *known* by anyone, maybe even myself. Of course, I hadn't helped my situation with my choices— everything I did these days practically guaranteed judgment and condemnation and was talked about in big, bold headlines. It was . . . lonely.

But I didn't want to think about all that now. I didn't want to see an expression of disappointment and disdain on Lily's beautiful face. I didn't want this girl to know what a mess I was. I wanted to leave that behind and enjoy the one simple moment of peace I'd had in years.

Lily's eyes had been moving over my face as if trying to read my thoughts through my expression. I turned, looking momentarily back up at the clear starlit sky. "How old are you, Lily? Have you lived here all your life?"

She paused for a moment and then said, "Nineteen, almost twenty, and yes, I've lived in Colorado all my life. I grew up near Telluride."

Nineteen. That was young, and she seemed very innocent . . . yet somehow very wise, too. I was six years older than her. But in that moment it didn't seem to make any difference at all.

I smiled, my eyes moving over her beautiful features again and lingering on her full lips for a moment. I wondered if they'd be as warm as the rest of her, or if they'd feel cool against my own. "Tell me something about *your* past," she murmured. *Tit for tat.* I searched my mind for something to give her about my own childhood.

"I was a Boy Scout. I earned all kinds of awards, actually. I was the pride of troop one sixty-one." Confusion made my head throb for a moment. Yes, yes I *had* been a Boy Scout. I'd forgotten that.

Lily laughed, falling back, and bringing me back to the moment. "I'll build a rock shrine in your honor once you leave these woods."

I laughed. "*If* I leave these woods. I've obviously required some assistance in the recent past."

"Your secret is safe with me. Troop one sixty-one will never be the wiser." She leaned up again and grinned over at me, and my heart picked up speed.

"Did you like it? Being a Boy Scout?"

I tried to remember, but my memory was so foggy these days. I had such a hard time grasping specific events. But I could . . . feel it. Being a Boy Scout. I closed my eyes for a moment. Yes, yes I'd liked it very much. "Yes," I answered finally.

"What else? What else do you like?"

A lock of hair fell over my eye, and Lily brought her hand up and brushed it away and then froze as if she'd caught herself doing something she hadn't meant to do. She blinked as her eyes met mine. "I'm sorry," she said, pulling her hand back.

I reached out and took her hand in mine, swallowing. "No, please, that felt nice. I don't mind if you touch my hair." Truthfully, I wanted her to touch me anywhere and everywhere. I wanted to feel the warm touch of her fingers on my skin, I wanted her to move closer and lie beside me so I could feel the length of her body next to my own. This moment suddenly seemed more intimate than any I'd ever experienced before, and we hadn't even removed one item of clothing. We hadn't even kissed.

Lily brought her hand tentatively back to my hair and wove her fingers into it. I moaned and lay back, closing my eyes. God, it felt good. It'd been so long since someone just . . . touched me. *Forever* . . . She continued to thread her fingers through it with obvious curiosity as if she'd never touched a man's hair before. Was it possible she hadn't?

Feeling relaxed and half in a trance, I said, "I like sports, especially football, Star Wars, and jazz music. Not together, necessarily."

I quirked my lip up and raised one brow before closing my eyes again. "And I like the old jazz, you know, like Miles Davis or Coltrane." Lily's hands kept moving in my hair, causing me to sigh.

"What else?" she whispered.

"I like, uh, comic books . . . I like museums, fireworks . . . travel. I like breakfast for dinner, and . . . movie theaters. I like movie theaters. And I especially like going when there's no one else in the theater but me." I felt like I could fall asleep. "I like Tuesdays."

"Why Tuesdays?"

"Because no one else likes Tuesdays. I get it all to myself. Tuesday is all mine."

I somehow heard Lily's lips move into a smile, but didn't open my eyes.

"And snowstorms. I love winter and snowstorms." I paused. "Why do I feel like I'm writing a personal ad?"

Lily laughed softly, her fingernails raking lightly across my scalp. I was half asleep and half turned on, and it felt so damned good. "What about you? What do you like, Lily?" I felt like my voice might be slurring a little.

"Hmm," she said, pausing for a moment. "I like to read. And I like history."

"What else?"

She paused again. "I don't know." She sounded sad.

I opened my eyes half-mast and gazed at her sleepily. "What kind of music do you like?"

She tilted her head, watching her hand in my hair. "My mom used to play these love songs from the forties. I haven't heard them in a long time, but I used to love them."

"What did you mean yesterday when you said you thought you might be a ghost?" I asked, my eyes falling closed once again as I enjoyed the delicious feeling of her warm hand running through my hair and across my scalp. I resisted the urge to moan out loud, thinking any sound like that might scare her away and stop her from touching me.

She was quiet for a long moment, and I got lost in the comfort of being touched gently. Nothing in my recent past had felt gentle. And that's what Lily was: gentle and pure. Being with her made me starkly aware of how harsh and dirty my own life felt. "I just mean that sometimes I don't feel like I'm part of the world. I don't feel like my life is . . . real," she finally answered softly.

I opened my eyes, gazing at her lovely face. *Yes.* "I know what you mean," I said. "I feel the same way. I feel the exact same way. But this, this feels real. Does it feel real to you, too?"

She nodded down at me, her expression very serious. "Yes," she whispered. I closed my eyes again.

I could feel the familiar clawing inside me needing a fix, and I knew I should probably leave, though I didn't want to. But I was so tired. I hadn't slept more than a few hours in the last couple days, and Lily's hand in my hair was heavenly. If I just closed my eyes for a few minutes . . .

I woke up dazed and alone, the first light of dawn appearing in the eastern sky. I sat up abruptly, the sweatshirt Lily must have laid over me falling aside. A sharp pain sliced through my head and I groaned.

But I'd slept. I laughed softly to myself. I felt grateful to Lily as if somehow it'd been her who had given me that small gift. And although I needed a pill or several, I could feel the healing effects of more than a few hours of sleep. "Lily?" I called, but there was no answer. I stood slowly, being careful not to jar my aching brain any more than I had to. My skin was clammy and prickly, and I needed to get home, but I smiled anyway, recalling the magic of the night before. It had felt both like an escape, and the first real moments of peace I'd experienced in so very long.

Standing up on the rock, I noticed several small pebbles laid down in the shape of an arrow and looked in that direction. Over the tops of the trees, I could see the very tip of the roof of Brandon's lodge. I wasn't too far, and I knew which direction to go. For once.

Lily had again shown me the way.

CHAPTER SEVEN

Lily

I heard his voice through the woods. I hesitated before standing slowly, trying to control the sudden wild beating of my heart.

I refused to appear too eager to see him. But I did. Oh, I did want to see him.

Where do you fly, Lily?

I wished so badly I could ask my mom about the protocol on how to act with a man, but I knew that would not go over well, and so I didn't dare. Besides, it had been years since she'd been anywhere near a man, so she probably wouldn't be the best source of advice anyway. So instead, thus far, I'd followed Holden's cues and did what felt comfortable to me. There had to be *some* instinct to this whole getting-to-know-you dance between a man and a woman. I sighed. Who really knew if any of what I was doing was right?

I *liked* him. And I'd liked spending time with him. Already. So much. Too much. And it scared me.

It's only because even before you came here, you were so sheltered, Lily. Of *course* I was bound to be captivated by the first man who caught my attention.

But at least I'd learned that he wasn't as crazy as I'd originally thought. He *was* sad, though. I'd been right about that. I figured all the strange behavior was due to drinking too much. A gardener we'd had when I was a little girl had liked to drink, too, and I saw him stumbling around sometimes when he was off duty. But that'd been a long time ago . . . I hadn't seen anyone drink alcohol since then. But I was pretty sure my memory of the effects was correct.

I should stay away. This friendship or whatever it was between us was bound to lead nowhere, but try as I might, I just couldn't. I wanted so many things it wasn't smart for me to want. I *wanted* to know about Holden, I wanted to talk to him. I wanted to see that sweet, lopsided smile of his, and I wanted to feel the wild thrill of delight I felt when his eyes lingered on my lips for too long. And I wanted to be kissed. Even just once, I wanted to be kissed. And I could be wrong, but I thought Holden might want to kiss me, too.

I didn't dare ask him too much about himself, though. That would just cause him to ask about me. Questions invited questions, and I couldn't give him many answers. But I figured if we just stuck to topics that made little difference, it would be okay. And very soon, he'd go back to San Francisco, his vacation or whatever would be over, and none of this would have mattered. I would know little about him, and he would know little about me. I tamped down the disappointment the thought brought—it was the way it had to be. I adjusted the backpack I was carrying and walked more quickly to his voice calling through the trees. So we still had now, and even if we didn't come to know each other's secrets, we could still enjoy some time together. And for now, *just for now*, I didn't have to be so lonely.

When I stepped up behind him and tapped him on his shoulder, he let out a small yell and whirled around, shock and fear in his expression. I couldn't help laughing just a bit. "Jesus, how do you walk so quietly?" he asked, his hand over his heart.

At the sight of his face, butterflies took flight in my belly, and I did my best to ignore them. I smiled. "Habit, I guess. It's best not to make a big racket in the forest. I thought a highly decorated Boy Scout would know that better than anyone," I teased. He was so very handsome up close like this. His hair was the color of rich honey and his eyes were as blue as the summer sky, fringed by dark lashes, tipped in the same deep golden color of his hair. He was tall and slim, but I could see that he had well-honed muscles through his clothes when he moved. There was something very graceful about him—something almost *quiet* about the way he moved—well, when he wasn't stumbling around drunk anyway.

"So, there must be a better way to contact you than yelling your name in the woods," Holden said.

I shook my head. "No."

His face sobered. "Okay." He looked as if he wanted to say something, but changed his mind and settled on, "How are you?" His eyes moved over my features in a way that made me feel good. He seemed to like what he saw. I brought my hand up to my cheek and wondered exactly what that was.

"I'm well. And you?"

Holden laughed, showing me his beautiful, wide smile again. He clasped his hands behind his back and rocked on his heels. "I'm very well, too. Thank you for asking."

I grinned, turning and glancing back to make sure he was following me. He walked quickly to catch up.

"So what are we doing today?"

"You're the one who was calling for *me*. Didn't you have a plan?"

"*My* plan is to be amazing and awesome so you want to spend more time with me." He tilted his head and gave me a hopeful smile and, God, he was so cute. It wasn't right to be that cute. I couldn't help smiling back, and I was pretty sure my cheeks were red. "And I never got to say I'm sorry I fell asleep on you last night."

I shook my head, glancing at him. He suddenly looked unsure, slightly embarrassed. "It seemed like you needed it," I said. "I didn't mind."

Holden stopped and I did, too, looking at him and wondering why he had halted. He ran his hand through his hair, making me want to touch it again. I knew now it was soft and thick and it would tickle my fingers as it fell between them. "I did. I did need the sleep. The truth is, Lily, I haven't felt real well lately—for too long, actually—and I wanted to spend time with you today, and to thank you for last night, but I also wanted to tell you that I'm going to need to take a week or so to try to feel better. I," he ran his hand through his hair again, "I think I'm ready. I hope . . . well, I hope you'll wait for me, wait for me to explain it to you. I hope you'll trust me." His expression was filled with something that looked like regret or maybe fear. Maybe both.

"It's okay, Holden. You don't owe me anything," I said hesitantly. I was confused about what exactly he was telling me. But the dark circles beneath his eyes, the way he'd tremble sometimes for no apparent reason, told me something wasn't right. Was he an alcoholic? Was it that bad? Or did he have some other sort of illness?

He looked at me for a second, and again, I could see how tired he was, how sad. "Maybe not," he muttered, looking away. "No. No, I do. Even though we barely know each other, you've made me feel peaceful in a way I haven't felt in a very long time. Truthfully, Lily, you've made me want to feel better than I do. And so yes, I do owe you. And I owe you an explanation about why I won't be back for a little bit."

Disappointment filled my chest, but he looked so troubled and confused, and so I grabbed his hand and held it in mine. "It's okay. I understand," I said, even though I didn't entirely. What I did know was that he was struggling and whatever he was considering, it was taking all his strength to do it. And he'd said he'd be back. *And* he'd said he wasn't leaving for good—not yet anyway. He had decided he needed to do something difficult, and I wouldn't make it harder on him.

"Yes," I said.

"Yes what?" He tilted his head.

"You asked me if I could trust you and the answer is yes. I trust you." And I did. Inexplicably, perhaps, but I did.

Holden let out a breath. "Thank you. That means a lot." He smiled at me and squeezed my hand. "So how are we going to spend this day? I was hoping you'd have some ideas."

I laughed a small laugh. "Actually, I was going fishing before I heard you calling me." I shrugged my shoulder, indicating the backpack I was carrying.

"There's somewhere to fish around here?"

I nodded, stepping over a fallen branch. "About a mile from here there's a stream."

"What type of fish?"

"Trout."

"Where's your fishing pole?"

"I leave it there if I know I'll be back in a day or two. There are only a handful of days left to fish."

As we stepped into a clearing, the sight of something moving caught my eye and I looked across the open space to see a male elk—a bull—mounted on a female. I'd seen animals mating plenty of times before, but for some reason standing there watching it with Holden felt . . . strange. It made my skin tingle and my nipples harden and it made me intensely aware of him beside me. It made me intensely aware of *his* maleness.

Suddenly the day seemed overly bright, the sun very warm upon my skin. I looked up into Holden's face and saw him looking in the same direction . . . and his cheekbones were flushed. He caught my eye and then raised his eyebrows and laughed in that self-conscious way he sometimes did. I found it incredibly appealing. He had called himself a god among men, and yet his expressions spoke of a man who was self-conscious, almost shy. I wasn't sure who the real Holden was just yet. I wondered if he even knew himself.

"I think we might be intruding."

I let out a breath. "I think you're right. Here, let's go this way." He followed me as I took an alternate route, and we walked in silence for a while, both of us lost in our own thoughts, me trying to regain the relaxed feeling I'd had only moments ago.

I remembered back to him yelling on his deck about how lusted after he was, how he could start pimping himself out. I suddenly wondered exactly what that meant. I hadn't caught every word of what he'd been saying as there'd been a lot of slurring, but I thought I understood the gist of it: women wanted him, and he rarely said no. Women. *Plural.* Whatever life Holden Scott came from, there were lots of women waiting for him. I stopped suddenly, causing Holden to come up short, and I turned toward him. He had been right on my heels and now we were face to face. I cleared my throat. "I . . ."

"What is it?" he asked, concern in his expression.

I pressed my lips together, not knowing how to ask him the questions I wanted to ask, not knowing how to get the reassurance I needed. *What exactly did I need to be reassured of?* I wanted to know if he thought about kissing me as much as I thought about kissing him. I wanted to tell him that I'd never kissed a man before. "I heard what you said, on your deck, most of it anyway, about the women . . . you . . . well—"

"Christ," he interrupted me, putting his hands in his pockets. "I really made an ass of myself that night, didn't I?"

"Um, I—"

"You don't have to answer that. It was rhetorical." He paused, a frown creasing the skin between his brows as he glanced around the forest. "I did. I made an utter ass out of myself. The truth is I've been making an ass out of myself for a really long time. But I want to stop doing that." He looked back at me. "What I meant earlier, and the reasons I'll have to stay away from you for a little while, is that I'm going to stop doing things that lead me to acting like the ass I was that night. I'm sorry you had to be a witness to any of it. I'm ashamed of that because that's not who I want to be."

I shook my head and put my hand on his arm. "No, you don't need to apologize about that night. You thought you were alone. I'm the one who should be apologizing for spying on you. I just . . . I did hear that," I licked my lips and Holden's gaze moved to my mouth, his eyes seeming to darken to a deeper blue, as if a summer storm was coming, "about the women, I mean, and so I'm just wondering if . . ." I stopped again.

Why had I brought this up? I needed time to consider what I was even trying to ask him. I needed time to get my thoughts in order before bringing any of this up with Holden. Or maybe it shouldn't be brought up at all. We barely knew each other. I resisted the urge to turn and simply run away from this terribly awkward moment.

When I looked back up into Holden's face, he had the glimmer of a smile on his lips. "Lily, are you wondering if I have a whole horde of women waiting for me back in San Francisco? A girlfriend? Maybe even a wife . . . or two?" His smile grew bigger and I blinked. He was teasing me, but yes, I had been wondering those things. I'd been wondering those exact things. "Are you wondering if I want to kiss you? Are you wondering if I think you're the most beautiful girl I've ever seen? Are those the things you're wondering, Lily of the Night?" He used his index finger to run down the curve of my cheekbone.

I blinked. My cheeks felt hot and I was slightly stunned. And Holden looked so very pleased with himself. *Infinitely* pleased with himself. "I . . . no, I was actually just wondering how they all work out the sharing of you? Do they each get different days? Or is it just a virtual free-for-all? Just . . . curious because it sounds very complicated. No wonder you're so tired."

Holden's face went blank for a brief moment and then he leaned his head back and laughed. After a minute, he looked back at me. "I deserved that." I laughed, too, and turned, glancing back at him once to make sure he was following me. He ran to catch up.

"What exactly constitutes a horde anyway?" I asked, looking at him sideways, trying not to smile, biting my lip so it didn't turn upward of its own accord.

"A horde? Oh, um, three. A horde is made up of three."

I laughed. "Liar." Holden laughed, too, and then grabbed my hand, swinging it between us as we walked. His skin was cool and smooth and my hand felt small in his. We both continued to smile at each other in this goofy way that made my heart expand. Finally, I looked away, a small smile remaining on my lips. Yes, I trusted him. I *did*. I didn't have any experience to gauge whether I was trusting blindly or not. I only knew I liked him, and that I felt *safe* with him.

"By the way," he said after a minute, taking me from my reverie, "even though you *weren't* wondering, the answer to the question about me having hordes of women—all three that is, waiting for me back home—the answer is no. And as far as wanting to kiss you, the answer is yes. A definite yes. And as to whether or not I find you stunningly beautiful, that answer is yes, too. I know you don't care, I know you're *not* wondering, but just so I get it off my chest. It's been a tough burden to bear alone." He grinned a crooked grin but stuffed his free hand in his pocket and a slight flush colored his cheekbones. I couldn't help grinning back. I felt giddy again and warm and vibrantly *alive* for the first time in so very long.

When I looked back at Holden a few minutes later, though, he looked deep in thought. I could hear the soft rush of water nearby. We'd almost arrived at the stream. "I want to tell you all about my life, Lily, the things that brought me here, but I want to tell you when I've cleaned some of it up. I know it probably seems like I'm talking in code, and I'm sorry about that."

The look on his face was so troubled, so somber. I nodded. "It's okay. I already said I trust you." Holden smiled and yanked my hand so I was walking right next to him, his body touching mine and the mood seemed to lighten immediately. We walked through the trees and came out on the bank of the stream. He let go of my hand.

"So where is your fishing pole?"

"Over here." I had left my fishing pole leaning against a rock formation on the other side of the stream. To get there I jumped across the water from one rock to the next—about six—landing on the mossy shore on the opposite side of the stream. Turning around, I saw that Holden was still standing on the other side, looking dubiously at the rocks I'd just used for steppingstones. "Come on. It's easy," I called.

Holden took a deep breath and then stepped tentatively on the first rock, balancing both feet there as he judged the distance to the next one. "You have to do it quickly," I said. "If you don't you'll—"

I sucked in a breath and brought my empty hand up to my mouth, trying not to howl with laughter as Holden fell face first into the water. He came up sputtering and flapping his arms and I couldn't help it. I doubled over, holding my stomach. "Okay, so you're no athlete," I said through my laughter. Holden pulled himself up slowly, coming to his full height, his shirt and jeans molded to his body in a way that made the hilarity die in my throat. I swallowed, letting out a few last coughs of laughter.

"You set me up." He narrowed his eyes, but there was amusement in his expression. He wasn't really mad.

I shook my head. "No, I swear, I didn't. I thought you would make it. I'll just grab . . . this," I said, picking up my fishing pole, "and come to your side." Holden took the few steps in the thigh-high water and pulled himself onto the bank. He shook his head like a dog and then looked up at me and grinned.

"Get over here," he called. I hopped easily from rock to rock and landed on the shore next to him. "Show off," he muttered. "You know usually *I'm* the one who excels at everything. Being with you has been a very humbling experience, let me tell you."

"Maybe you needed one, Holden Scott, God Among Men," I said, laughing a bit more.

He chuckled. "You're probably right." He started slowly peeling his shirt off and I stepped back. "This was your master plan, wasn't it? To set me up to fall in the stream so I'd have to strip off my wet clothes?"

I shook my head, my mouth suddenly going dry. "No, no. Really, that's not—" He pulled the wet piece of material over his head and my eyes slid down his bare chest to his ridged stomach and then back up as his shirt came off completely. He was too skinny, but his muscles were defined and his shape very masculine. Broad shoulders tapered into a narrow waist and his jeans looked as if they were barely holding on to his slim hips.

Feeling off balance in a way I wasn't used to at all—and not knowing how to act next to a beautifully half-naked man—I turned and walked on unsure legs to a fallen tree trunk on the bank of the stream where I usually sat when I fished. It was in a bright patch of sunlight and at the perfect spot right in front of a fishing hole. I bent forward and dug in the soft mud at the edge of the stream for a worm, spearing it quickly on the hook once I found one. I cast my line into the water just as Holden sat down next to me.

I kept my eyes focused on the water for a few minutes, finally braving a glance at him. He had his face tilted up to the sun and his eyes were closed. I allowed myself a moment to admire him, the light bringing out the gold in his hair and in the very slight scruff on his face. He must not have shaved today. I let my eyes drink in the strong, masculine lines of his jaw and cheekbone, my gaze resting on his well-shaped lips, slightly parted, his expression one of peaceful contentment. My eyes wandered down to his naked torso and I stared at his smooth, tanned chest, resisting the instinct that urged me to reach out and run my hand down his stomach and back up to the male contours of his shoulders and arms.

A slight breeze rustled the trees and the rushing sound of the stream lent a soothing background song, as a whippoorwill called to his mate incessantly in a nearby tree. When Holden's eyes suddenly opened, I startled slightly and looked back to the water. "Repetitive sucker, isn't he?" Holden asked, nodding to the bird sound coming from right behind us.

I smiled. "They go on for hours sometimes. The males are very persistent when they want a female."

"Is that what that is? His mating call?"

I nodded, setting the fishing pole in a small hole in the trunk we were sitting on, propping it up.

"Want me to hold that?" Holden asked.

I shook my head. "There's no need to hold it. I usually just put it here next to me. I'll grab it if there's a tug." I glanced at him, and he was looking at me with a small smile on his lips.

"As for the whippoorwill, yes, that's his mating call."

"Will she answer him?"

"Eventually, I suppose. Or maybe she's not interested in that particular whip-poor-will. Perhaps she doesn't want to be part of his *horde*. All three that is."

The corner of Holden's lip quirked up and there was a twinkle in his eye as he tilted his head and said, "A persistent fellow like him? Nah, I thought all women liked persistent."

I made a small snorting sound. "Perhaps you don't know as much about women as you believe." I gave him a teasing look. *Or maybe you know way too much.*

Holden laughed. "I'm beginning to think you might be right." He tilted his head back up to the sun. "This is nice, peaceful."

Yes it was. Even sitting here with him for the first time felt very right, natural. "I know. I come here as often as possible in the summer."

"Alone?"

"Yes, yes, alone."

"Doesn't your mother ever come with you?"

I looked at him sharply, but when he didn't withdraw his question, I sighed, already weary of the tit for tat. It was too much work. "No, my mother doesn't come outside very often. She . . . well, she was injured years ago, and she stays in."

"Injured—"

"What about you? Do your parents live in San Francisco, too?"

Holden paused, his blue eyes lingering on my face for a few moments before he looked out to the water. "No, I'm originally from Ohio, but both my parents have passed."

I watched his profile again as he stared forward, that sad look of loss on his face that he'd had when he told me about his friend, Ryan.

I reached out and put my hand on his thigh, and his gaze jerked down to where my hand touched him. "I'm sorry, Holden. I know what it's like to feel lonely." I felt the heat rise in my cheeks. I shouldn't have said that.

His eyes met mine and though there were questions in his, he simply grasped my hand. "Thank you."

Something electric filled the air, sizzling through the ozone the way lightning does right before it flashes across the sky in a sudden, thrilling arc of intense light. I pulled my hand away and stood up quickly. "Want to see a quicker way of fishing than waiting for a fish to bite the worm?"

Holden laughed. "Yes. Show me."

I removed my boots and my socks and hiked my dress up, tying it in a knot at the side of my thighs. I began wading into the shallow water and when I looked laughingly back at Holden, his gaze on me was intent and filled with something I couldn't define. Something that looked *hungry.* He looked down to my bare legs and back to my eyes. I swallowed, but brought my finger up to my lips, instructing him to stay very quiet. Then I stood very still in the water, which was just brushing the bottom of my tied-up dress. I didn't move a muscle as I tracked the movement of the fish that swam by my legs, two large trout. In a lightning-swift move, I plunged both hands in the water and made a sound of dismay as I came up empty-handed. Focusing again, I stood still for a long, quiet minute, my eyes again tracking the slippery, silvery bodies of the fish moving past me. Again, I plunged my hands into the water, reaching just slightly in front of where the fish I was tracking swam, laughing out loud when the fish slipped right past my grasp. I jumped to the side as another one swam next to me, again coming up empty-handed. Holden was laughing on the shore. "Have you ever actually caught one like that?" he called.

"Not yet, but I will before this summer is over," I said, laughing back. He grinned at me and my heart skipped at least three beats in a row. This was the first time I'd seen him looking genuinely carefree and happy, the small lines between his eyes completely smoothed out. When I realized I was simply standing there staring at him, I turned back, looking down to the water again. Out of my peripheral vision, I saw Holden walk to the edge of the water. I looked over to see him rolling up his still-wet jeans. He waded in next to me.

For the next fifteen minutes, we tried in vain to grab a trout, both doing ridiculous-looking little hops as fish darted by. Once I almost face-planted in the water, and Holden grabbed me as we both laughed, his arms staying around me for a beat too long as my breath caught and our eyes met.

"Last try," he said. I nodded. We stood still and silent. Suddenly Holden's hands plunged into the water and when he brought them out, a fat trout was wiggling in his hands. I gasped, my mouth falling open. Holden rose slowly to his full height, letting out a small shout.

"Oh my God!" I exclaimed, grinning wildly at Holden, the flailing fish finally stilling in his hands. "I can't believe you just did that."

"I can honestly say I can't either," he said, shaking his head, a look of awed disbelief on his face.

"Beginner's luck," I mumbled, trying to sound displeased. But it came out breathy and impressed. I *was* impressed. "Or maybe you have experience and didn't tell me."

He laughed. "How long did you say *you'd* been doing this?" There was boasting amusement in his tone and I rolled my eyes.

Placing the fish in the plastic bag I'd laid down next to my fishing pole earlier, he chuckled and then returned to the stream to rinse his hands. I bent down next to him and washed my own, a wave of insecurity suddenly coming over me. We had just gone fishing with our bare hands on what was a sort of date. He'd participated, but he must have thought I was some sort of heathen or cave girl—or foolish little kid. That's it, this was him re-living his childhood with me. Ugh. I was sure those girls I'd seen dancing on the deck would never do something like this. They'd probably think it was gross. When I came back to the log he had already returned to, I shrugged self-consciously. "Too long. Obviously I have far too much time on my hands." I attempted a self-deprecating laugh, but it sounded sort of strange and choked.

"Hey, don't be mad because I'm naturally better at it than you."

I whipped my head toward him and saw that he was teasing me. He winked, looking so happy that I couldn't help but to laugh again, the self-consciousness that had come over me, melting away. I shook my head. Holden leaned forward and scratched his ankle and I noticed his back. I bent forward and touched his skin gingerly and he sat up quickly, his eyes meeting mine.

"You have so many scars," I said.

He smiled a tight smile. "My job isn't easy on my body. I've been injured more times than I can count."

"Your job . . . " I sat back down next to him, frowning slightly, wondering what in the world that could be. He nodded his head to the ground at my feet.

"What are you reading?" he asked, obviously changing the subject.

Glancing in the direction he was looking, I saw the edge of the book of poems peeking out of my backpack. I shrugged. "Oh, nothing," I said, using my foot to push my bag closed.

"Nothing? That looked like a book to me. What? Is it a tawdry romance novel or something?"

I laughed. "No. Just . . . a book of poems."

"You like poetry?"

I could feel the heat of his gaze on the side of my face and felt the color moving up my neck to my cheeks. Something about him knowing about my love of poetry felt very personal. "Yes," I said softly. "I do."

"Can I see?"

I hesitated briefly, but couldn't think of a good reason to tell him no. Plucking the book from my backpack, I held it in his direction without looking at him. He took it from my hand and was silent for a moment. "Romantic poetry." I heard him flip through it and then stop as he read to himself. My curiosity too great, I couldn't help but look over and see which poem he'd stopped on.

"She walks in beauty, like the night," he read, "of cloudless climes and starry skies, and all that's best of dark and bright." He looked up and caught my eye. "Lord Byron." He paused. "I never knew that this one's about you," he said softly. I felt my blush deepen and looked down at my own hands.

"It's written about Mrs. John Wilmot, Byron's cousin by marriage. She was in mourning when he met her."

He hummed. "Maybe for Byron it was about her, but for me, it's about you." I brought my gaze to his and for some reason I wanted to weep. How often had I sat alone reading that poem and dreaming of someday being admired that way? "Lily of the Night," he said gently. "I knew it was the perfect way to describe you." My heart bursting with joy, I could only smile. He handed the book back, and I replaced it in my backpack.

"You knew it was Byron," I said. "Do you like poetry, too?

"I like literature," he said, a confused look crossing his face, his brow furrowing. He brought his hand up to his head and massaged his temples as if he was grasping on to a memory and it hurt. "Yes . . ." he said, bringing his hand down and smiling at me. "I haven't talked to anyone about that in a long time."

I nodded, feeling pleased that he'd shared something personal with me.

We spent the next hour or so talking about the things around us, the birds in the trees, the types of plants that grew next to the water. I knew the names for some of them, but not all. I'd received a book on Colorado flora and fauna years back and had attempted to learn as much as I could, but as I soon learned, it'd take a lifetime to know it all. And who knew—maybe that's what I had. I'd frowned with the thought, something desperate and yearning that I didn't know how to define filling my chest and making my heart squeeze. *I wanted more than what my life was now. More than the small, dark, lonely world I lived in.*

I wanted someone to save me. But I didn't know what to do about that.

As the hour wore on, I noticed Holden's hands begin to shake, and although the sun was shining on us, he began to perspire in a way I thought was excessive for the weather. I'd seen signs before that he was sick, but I didn't know how—or if that was part of what he was going to address in some manner while he stayed away.

"You should get back," I finally said, my eyes landing on his trembling fingers. He rubbed his hands on his thighs, looking nervous and sad.

"Yes, I should. This has been one of the best days I've spent in years. Thank you for giving this to me. Thank you for spending your time with me."

I shook my head. "It was really . . . I enjoyed it, too." That felt like such an understatement, but I didn't know how else to express to him how much I'd enjoyed our time together, how he'd made me forget that I was so lonely, how I never wanted this day to end.

I collected my things, rolling the fish up in plastic—the one Holden had caught with his hands and two others I'd caught with the pole—and placed them in my backpack. I left my fishing pole behind as I usually did.

We walked in silence most of the way back, Holden looking increasingly nervous. My heart was pounding, too. I didn't know when I'd see him next, and I already missed him. And that terrified me. I wanted more time. *Don't go,* I wanted to say. *Please don't go. Not yet.* But I couldn't, and I wouldn't, and he'd asked me to give him time. Lost in my own thoughts, I hardly noticed when we arrived at the edge of the woods where he would leave me for his lodge. Holden leaned back against a tree and crossed his arms over his chest. He'd put his T-shirt back on, and it was mostly dry, but his jeans were still damp. He closed his eyes, his expression pained.

Forcing a smile and suddenly feeling very awkward and shy, I took a deep breath and stepped closer to him. "The look on your face . . . you look as if you're going off to war," I teased, trying to lighten the mood.

Holden released a gush of air. "Not exactly . . . but it kind of feels like it. Will you be waiting for me, Lily?"

I wasn't even sure exactly what I was waiting *for.* Holden Scott confused me, and I felt completely out of my depth. But, for me, there was only one answer. I smiled. "Yes." His eyes roamed over my face.

"Why do you look at me that way?" I asked softly.

"What way?"

"Like you're trying to memorize me. Like you think I might disappear."

"I didn't realize I was," he said, moving a piece of hair away from my face. "Please don't disappear."

I shook my head. "I won't." I stepped even closer, and he suddenly seemed to become very aware of me, standing taller, his eyes intently focused. I took one final step into his space and went up on my tiptoes and pressed my lips to the side of his mouth, just intending to give him one simple kiss.

For a second he seemed frozen, and then a strange guttural sound came from his throat and he turned his head so that my lips slid on top of his and our mouths were pressed together. I jolted slightly and his arms were suddenly around me, making it impossible to move away as I'd almost done. I opened my eyes and saw his were closed and there were lines creased between his brows as if he were in pain. I wasn't sure what that meant, so I let my lashes flutter closed again and waited to see what he would do next. I startled when I felt the tip of his tongue come out and run along the opening of my lips. Instinctively, my own tongue came out to lick my lips where he had so that I could taste him on my mouth. He made another one of those growling sounds I thought meant he liked what was happening and used his tongue to open my mouth wider so he could slip inside. I let out a quick panting breath and opened for him as intense pleasure shivered through me. Holden's hand came to the back of my head and he tilted it, which brought his tongue deeper into my mouth. His kiss sent sensation from the tip of my tongue all the way to my knees, and I let my weight fall against him as I met his probing tongue with my own. I wanted to be closer, to absorb all of him, to experience the shimmery feeling flowing through my veins for as long as possible.

I ran my hands up his back. The feel of his shifting muscles under my hands enhanced the pleasure of the kiss, and I couldn't help moaning into his mouth. He pulled me closer, answering my moan with one of his own.

Our kiss deepened as I followed his lead, letting my tongue dance with his, tasting his masculine essence. He tasted salty and sweet and more wonderful than I ever could have imagined.

I didn't know how long we kissed, but after a little while he pulled back, sprinkling smaller kisses all around my mouth and down my jaw. I gave another little shiver when his lips brushed against the sensitive skin of my neck. "Lily," Holden said and his voice sounded breathless and hoarse, "the things you're doing to me right now. I'm trying to control myself, but—"

"Don't control yourself. Please just kiss me one more time," I whispered against his mouth. "I want to taste your tongue again."

Holden groaned and put his hands on the sides of my face and kissed me again, our tongues stroking and tangling for long delicious minutes. When he finally ended the kiss, he was panting again and I could feel the slight shivering of his body, as if he was barely controlling something.

"I have to stop, Lily. I don't want to, but I have to. I'm going to catch on fire if I don't." I nodded. He sounded so desperate as if he was in some sort of agony. I had a vague idea of what he was feeling. *My body felt hot and achy and unfulfilled despite having just experienced something so incredible.* If more kissing led to more hot achiness, I might catch fire, too. I raised my eyes to his and he looked at me tenderly, using his knuckles to run along my cheek. I leaned in to his touch and smiled. I felt dreamy and giddy and so very, very happy. He leaned forward and kissed my eyelids and I laughed softly at the ticklish feel of his lips. He rubbed his rough jaw against my cheek and I giggled again, feeling the smile on his lips. "Lily," he whispered. "Lily of the Night. How do I say goodbye to you now?"

"With happiness," I whispered, "because we'll see each other soon. And when we do, you'll kiss me again."

"Yes," he choked out, "yes, I will." I kissed him one final time, softly and sweetly on the corner of his lips, the way I'd first intended. And then I backed away from him, our arms extended, our fingers joined, until they slipped apart. And then I turned and walked away, looking back only once to find Holden still leaning against the tree at the edge of the forest, watching me as I left him where he was.

CHAPTER EIGHT

Holden

Watching her walk away was the hardest thing I'd ever done. But I knew what I needed to do. Lily had shown me. She didn't know it, but she had, by giving me a taste of peace, of happiness and comfort. I wanted those things. Craved them with an ache deep in my soul. I'd forgotten, and she'd reminded me what joy felt like, reminded me that I was still capable of holding happiness in my heart. *It wasn't too late. Not if I didn't let it be.*

The way she'd tasted . . . like *hope*, both familiar and unknown. I wanted to beg her to hold my hand as I did what I knew I needed to do, to soothe me as my body withdrew from the numbing chemicals I'd been using to escape my pain and unhappiness for far too long. But I knew this was something I had to do alone if I wanted any chance of offering her all of me—not this fragmented man I was now. And if Lily saw who I really was, saw what I'd done to my body, I knew it would only scare her and probably drive her away. Brandon had been right—*I* needed to be the one to make the choice. And ultimately, I was the only one who could do the work. And though I wanted Lily in my life like nothing I'd wanted in a very long time, I also had to do this for *me*. I had to want to get better for myself, most of all.

Closing the door of the lodge behind me, I went straight to the kitchen where I'd left the plastic bag with the handful of pills I still had left. Not allowing myself to think, I walked straight to the bathroom and opened the bag over the toilet and flushed, watching the water swirl and drain, the pills disappearing. Just for good measure, I flushed again. And then dread filled me. And so I closed my eyes and pictured Lily. Beautiful, mysterious Lily. I would go back to her better than I'd been and I'd ask her to share all her secrets. And maybe I'd be brave enough to share mine.

****

"**F**uuuuuuck," I groaned miserably. By the next afternoon, every muscle in my body had seized up and my stomach was wracked with agonizing cramps. I writhed in pain on the couch, my legs pulled up to my stomach. Sweat dripped down my forehead. I was going to die. There was no way I could survive this misery. Why had I tossed out the pills? God, *why?* Not able to sit still for more than a few minutes, I got up and staggered into the kitchen and poured myself a glass of water, shaking so badly, I'd spilled most of it by the time I got the glass to my mouth.

I wanted to escape my own body—get out, get free. The feeling of claustrophobia compounded the fear and anxiety I was already feeling. I was trapped now. Trapped in my own skin. There was no way I could drive and it would take someone else at least a day to get to me. And then longer to get me anywhere I could convince someone to write me a prescription for the pain pills I needed so badly.

Sometime later that evening, I heard the sound of someone's feet coming up the stairs. I was sitting on the floor of the shower, my arms wrapped around my legs, lukewarm water raining down on me. It had started out hot and had worked for a while to soothe my screaming muscles, but now it was barely tepid. I'd thought about getting in the hot tub, but decided the shower was wiser given the state I was in. If I fell asleep, I'd be safer here. My body was in so much agony, the footsteps barely stirred any emotion in me. I supposed I should be concerned, alarmed, curious at least, but I couldn't figure it out, much less drum up an appropriate response.

"Well, this is not how I expected to find you," came the female voice. *Oh no. No. Fuck no.* I was dead. I was dead and I was in hell. And one of Satan's servants had just shown up to torture me. I turned my head and looked blearily through the glass of the shower door. *Taylor.* The 49ers' manager's daughter and my ex-girlfriend.

"What are you doing here?" I managed.

Taylor opened the shower door, causing me to fall out onto the floor in a groaning heap. "Holy fuck. What the hell is happening with you?" She actually sounded a little concerned.

I crawled over to the toilet and threw up. "Oh God! Jesus," Taylor yelled, the noise making me feel ten times worse than I already did. I hadn't thought that was possible. I heard her heels clicking on the bathroom tile. A minute later she came back with a washcloth, ran cold water over it, and leaned over me to wipe my forehead and around my mouth.

"What are you doing here, Taylor?" I mumbled bleakly.

"I came to see you, to spend some alone time with you." There was a note of disgust in her voice. Clearly me vomiting upon her arrival had not been part of the plan.

"Why?" I closed my eyes, feeling a cold sweat break out on my skin again. "We broke up over four months ago." The cool washcloth was back on my forehead and it felt good. My brain was so hazy.

Taylor was silent for a minute. "It was four *weeks* ago. Do you have no concept of time? And we did *not* break up. You just started acting all weird and distant and I needed a breather. Anyway, none of that matters. I've been thinking about you. And when I figured out where you must be, I knew I needed to come to you. This is the perfect place to get reacquainted, don't you think?"

Think? What? No. "Will you help me get to the couch?" I didn't have the strength to listen to her, much less argue or care about anything she was saying.

Taylor helped me stand up and I grabbed a towel with my shaking hands, wrapped it around my waist, and limped downstairs to the couch where I fell onto it.

"What's wrong with you, anyway?"

"I'm withdrawing, Taylor. Just leave me here to die, please," I mumbled into the leather.

"Oh, shit. Listen, I applaud your efforts to get clean, but going cold turkey is just stupid. I've seen this before. I brought you some pills—you left a couple bottles at my apartment and I threw them in my suitcase. You need to wean yourself—"

I brought myself to a sitting position, grimacing and clenching my jaw as my muscles locked up. "You have some pills?" I asked desperately. Oh sweet fucking relief. I'd do anything to feel better, even just for an hour. *Anything. Anything.*

"Yeah, a couple bottles." She came over me on the couch and straddled my lap. She used her index finger to trace my lips and leaned in slowly and kissed me, her long, dark hair creating a curtain around us. "Say please," she said silkily.

"Jesus fucking Christ, just give me the damn pills," I almost shouted.

Taylor stood up, giving me a sulky frown. "Okay, okay, testy. Relax." She moved toward some luggage sitting next to the front door and rooted around for what seemed like forever. I wanted to scream. I got up and walked over to her, letting the towel fall to the floor. I didn't give a damn. "Ah, here we go." She held up a bottle of Percocet and I greedily grabbed for it, trying twice to open it with my shaking hands before finally prying the top off and downing two pills without any water. I made my way to the kitchen and drank from the faucet, then stumbled back into the living room and sagged down on the sofa, breathing rapidly, already feeling the drug coursing through my veins bringing relief. Sweet. Blessed. Relief.

"There, that's better, right?" Taylor asked, again straddling my lap. I put my hands on her hips to move her, but then found I didn't have the strength. "Why are you doing this anyway? Why like this?"

"Because I need to get back to my life. Back to the team."

"There's no rush, though, is there? They can manage without you while you take your time getting better."

I didn't bother explaining anything to her. Either way, *she* wasn't part of my future. "Get off me, Taylor."

She wiggled. "Aw, come on. Now that you're feeling better and I'm here, let's have a little fun. You do remember fun, don't you?"

"I don't want fun. I want to sleep. And I need you to leave."

She trailed her finger down my chest, looking thoughtful. "Hey, I know you're still messed up about what happened. We all are. But wallowing won't bring him back. He'd want—"

"Goddammit! Get *off* me!" *You wouldn't know a fucking thing about what he'd want. You didn't even really know him.*

She sat up straight, but didn't move away. "Well, isn't that a real nice thanks I get for coming all the way out here to Bumfuck Egypt, bringing you what you obviously needed at just the moment you needed it, and even," she trailed a nail down my naked chest, "intending on showing you the fun you've obviously been missing. I even brought some toys. You missed me, didn't you, baby? Come on, we had a good thing, and we only barely got started." She leaned in and sucked on my earlobe.

I again thought about pushing her off, but the intense relief of finally getting a fix—of the agony in my muscles releasing—was so wonderful, I suddenly couldn't even bring myself to be overly annoyed by her unwanted attention. "Didn't you?" she purred. "I know I missed you." She reached her hand down and squeezed my dick. "I missed *this*."

"Enough," I slurred, pushing her hands away. "Get off me."

She sighed loudly but removed her body from mine. "Fine. I get it. You need to freshen up. Let's go to bed and in the morning, you'll feel better."

"Who brought you here?" I asked, my eyes still closed.

"Kelly. She was here for one of Brandon's parties and kept the directions. She'll be back to pick me up in a few days." *Jesus, presumptuous much?*

"How'd you know I was here?"

"Brandon told someone who told someone . . . you know how it goes." No, that didn't sound like Brandon. More likely she used some more devious method to find out. What Taylor wanted, Taylor got. *Conniving bitch.*

I sighed. "You need to call Kelly and tell her to turn around."

"Excuse me?"

"Call Kell—"

"I'm going to make myself a drink," she said. "You want something?"

"No. And there's no alcohol here."

"Not to worry," she sing-songed, her voice fading as she moved toward the kitchen. "I brought my own."

Jesus, what a clueless idiot she was. And so was I. I'd slurped down her pills without a second's thought. And now the past day and a half was all for nothing. *Nothing.*

I gripped my hair, self-hatred assaulting me. I sat up slightly and turned my head toward the window.

Lily was standing just a couple feet from the deck staring upward.

I bolted to my feet, clutching my scalp and yelling an obscenity as the blood rushed straight to my brain, causing the throbbing in my head to sharpen. I picked up my towel, covered myself, and ran to the door, calling Lily's name as I threw it open. She'd turned and started to head back toward the woods, but when she heard me calling her name, she halted, but then picked up her pace again, now running.

The look on her face . . . pure devastation.

Oh God. Oh God. She'd seen Taylor sitting on my lap fondling me, seen my hands on her hips, but not pushing her away. "Lily," I called again, clutching the towel around my waist. I wanted to shout out a stream of expletives. "Lily, please," I begged.

When she reached the shadows at the edge of the woods, she finally slowed and turned toward me. "I'm sorry. I shouldn't have come. I was just worried about you. I just . . . wanted to make sure you got home okay. That you saw . . ." She bit her lip. "I just wanted to check on you. It was . . ." She shook her head as if she didn't know how to continue. I wanted to grab her and haul her body into mine. I wanted to tell her how to me she was an oasis in the middle of the desert I'd been crawling through for the last day and a half.

"What are you *doing* out there?" Taylor yelled from the deck.

"Jesus Christ! Go inside, Taylor. Now," I yelled over my shoulder. Taylor crossed her arms and even from the distance, I could see she was glaring daggers at me.

"God, Brandon said you were acting nuts!" Taylor shouted and stomped inside. "But you're really just a fucking dick!"

When I turned back to Lily, she had moved more deeply into the woods. "Wait," I called, running after her, holding the towel around myself, my body only barely strong enough to run at all. Lily started moving more swiftly.

"Lily, Lily, please, just listen to me," I called after her. "Wait, please, Lily. I want . . . I want . . ." She whirled around, her cheeks flushed, her eyes wells of hurt.

"What?" she demanded. "What *do* you want, Holden? What do you want with *me*? It certainly doesn't look like you're lonely."

I shook my head. "Please, what you saw back there is not what you think it was. Taylor is not my girlfriend. Or at least . . . I didn't consider her my girlfriend. She . . . the point is, I haven't thought about or seen her in months. Please, it's not what you think," I repeated.

She shrugged, letting out a small brittle laugh. "I don't think anything. I have no idea what to think. God, what do you want with *me*? What do you want?" She turned without waiting for an answer and for a moment I stood frozen. What did I say?

A wave of insecurity washed over me. What *did* I want? *To get better. For you. So I can kiss you, so I can plant my nose in the soft, fragrant spot between your shoulder and your neck and feel like I'm worthy enough to be there, to date you, romance you . . . however that might work. To know about your life. To tell you about mine. What? What did I want?* "To spend time with you," I finally managed. "Just . . . to be with you, Lily. God. I want to be with you."

She stopped and turned toward me slowly. Shrugging, she said, "It just won't ever work. We just don't make any sense together."

I shook my head and leaned against a tree. God, I was still so weak and sick. "You're the only thing that's made sense to me in a very long time. If you only knew." Sweat had broken out on my forehead, and I swiped at it, gripping the tree so I stayed upright. Lily looked at me warily.

"You should get back, Holden. You're not even dressed." I wanted to resist. I wanted to fight for her, but I couldn't and I hated myself.

"Please," I whispered, "please . . ."

Lily walked back to where I stood and brought her hand up to my forehead. "You're so warm," she said. "You should go back inside."

Behind me, Taylor was shouting on the deck again about what a dick I was. I ignored her and Lily did, too, pretending she wasn't there at all. "I want to come with you," I sighed. Her hand slipped down to my cheek. Behind me, Taylor's voice rose and the door slammed again, causing me to curse her name under my breath.

"Didn't I tell you that you should learn to recognize a snake? Or you're likely to step right on one."

I sighed again. "I know," I said wearily. *And they're everywhere. My life is so full of them I'm scared to make a move.*

My eyes slipped closed, and I pressed my back against the rough bark of the tree. When I started to slip down the trunk, I caught myself, jerking back to reality.

Lily was gone.

****

I made my way dazedly back to the lodge, my bare feet scratched and wet. When I got inside, I sagged down onto the couch. Taylor was glaring at me from the other side of the room, her arms crossed under her large breasts. "What in the hell were you doing out there in a towel?" she asked.

I shot her an impatient look. I barely had the energy to deal with her. "I was talking to Lily," I said.

"Who's Lily?" She looked at me blankly.

"The girl. Didn't you see her?"

Taylor narrowed her eyes. "I didn't see anyone. It looked like you were shouting into the woods. What's going *on* with you? I'm seriously worried."

I let out a long breath. What had I been thinking, spending any time with her at all? Oh right, I *hadn't* been thinking. I'd been drunk or high or both. Suddenly I not only felt exhausted, but I felt depressed. A soul-shaking depression that made me want to fall into a black hole. I'd tried so hard to get off the pills and the second, the very second, they were put in front of me again, I'd given in. Of course, it had been in the midst of intense physical agony, but even so . . . I'd hoped I was stronger than that. And now I had confirmation I wasn't. So was I going to give it another try? I shuddered with the memory of how completely awful I'd felt. Was I willingly going to go back there so soon? Somewhere in the background I heard Taylor's phone ring and she answered it, walking into the other room. I didn't attempt to overhear her conversation. When she came stomping back into the room, she said, "Kelly will be back in the morning. She's staying at a hotel in Telluride tonight."

"Good," I murmured, leaning my head back on the couch and throwing my arm over my eyes to block out the light above me.

After a minute, Taylor came over and sat down on the couch next to me. "Can I at least sleep in the same bed as you tonight? I miss you. I miss your arms around me," she said sweetly, trying another tact.

My head felt so woozy, and all I wanted was for Lily to come back. But she wouldn't, and I couldn't go after her in the condition I was in. I had *promised* myself. And I'd promised her. She didn't know it, but I'd promised her, too. Not in those words—but it was what I'd meant all the same. And I *refused* to break a promise to Lily. I just had to make things right with her first, though. "Taylor," I started, "why did you date me anyway? What did you see in me? What did you like about me?"

Taylor looked confused for a moment. "You know what I like about you. Was I so hard to read?" She ran one finger down my arm.

"Other than the . . . physical, though."

Taylor sighed. "Does there have to be more than that? Isn't that enough?"

I thought about that for a second. I guessed, for a while, that was all I went after. But had it ever brought me more than momentary satisfaction? "No, it actually isn't. And Taylor, you can do better than that, too, whether you realize it or not," I said, pulling myself up into a standing position, one hand on the couch for leverage. "Good night. If Kelly gets here before I get up, I'll say goodbye right now. And for the record, we are broken up."

I heard her gasp of surprise, but she didn't come after me. I locked the door behind me once I'd climbed the stairs to my bedroom. And with that, I collapsed on the bed and fell fast asleep, Lily's sorrowful face following me into my scattered dreams.

CHAPTER NINE

Lily

"The garden is bursting with flowers," my mom said, picking up a stem and clipping the bottom before placing it in the vase with the others. "Smell those roses? That's what real garden roses smell like, not those store-bought ones that barely have any fragrance at all." She made a clicking sound as if the idea of store-bought roses offended her greatly.

I looked up from my book. I'd been reading the same paragraph again and again and still didn't know what it said. "They're beautiful," I murmured. "I like the white ones with the yellow in the middle."

"Narcissus," she said softly before I tuned her out again.

A woman. There'd been a woman with Holden. A beautiful, half-dressed woman. My gut clenched and I felt tears threatening. *You're so stupid, Lily.* Of *course* I was stupid. Holden probably thought I sounded like someone who'd never left her house, rarely interacted with anyone at all. Because that was the truth of the matter. The women he dated were probably sophisticated and worldly. They probably talked about . . . talked about . . . I huffed out a breath. Well of course I had no idea what they talked about. Which was actually the whole point. Despair overwhelmed me.

" . . . glad you agree!" I shook my head as I realized my mother was speaking again.

"I'm sorry, Mom, were you saying something?"

My mom rolled her eyes. "Yes, but it really wasn't anything important. I answered for you. Recently I've been having the most interesting conversations with myself—very stimulating actually."

I offered a small smile. "Sorry, I got lost in my own head."

"What have you been thinking about so intently lately?" She gave me a speculative look. Half speculative, anyway. The other half of her face, the deeply scarred half, mostly failed to move at all.

Shaking my head, I said, "Nothing in particular." I pretended to read the book again. In my peripheral vision, I could see that she watched me for a moment and then sighed before going back to her arranging.

"Purple crocus, royal blue iris," she said, placing flowers in the vase. She brought one to her nose and inhaled. "Mmm. Hyacinth," she said. "Doesn't it smell wonderful?" She clipped the stem and placed that one in the vase as well. "There are so many vegetables in the garden here, too—lettuce and cucumbers, beets, potatoes, squash."

I nodded absently. My mind wandered again. Had Holden lied when he'd said there was something he needed to do? Was that just something he'd said so I didn't bother him while the woman was there? So he could walk around naked with her to his heart's content? Because that's what he'd been doing. I'd gotten an eyeful, and it was not disappointing. I kind of wished it had been. And yet, despite what I'd seen, he'd run outside to *me*, leaving her there. I didn't know what to feel . . . confusion, sadness, hope?

I shook my head, trying to shake off all the questions, all the doubt. I shouldn't care so much. So he had kissed me. So what? It wasn't like this could go anywhere. It was worthless to mourn the loss of something that could never be. I'd just . . . I'd thought he liked me the way I liked him. Despite not knowing him very well, I'd *trusted* him. My stomach cramped with remnants of the terrible, painful jealousy I'd felt when I'd seen them through the window. Her on top of him, his hands on her hips. *Naked* him. *Beautiful* her. And watching from the distance . . . *idiotic* me.

Maybe the other woman didn't even matter. Even if he really did want to spend time with me here, maybe it was better that he'd have someone to go home to. It wasn't like he was going to stay in Colorado permanently.

I glanced over at my mom and saw her grimacing and moving her face as if flexing it, as she placed the last flowers in the vase. Sympathy overcame over me. Lost in my own world, I'd been ignoring her lately. "When was the last time you applied any of the cream the doctor gave you?"

She shook her head. "Not in a couple days."

"Mom, you need to use that consistently. It works best that way and you know it. Your skin is all tight now because it's dry. No wonder it's uncomfortable. Here, let me put some on for you."

She nodded and went into the other room to wash her hands and then came back and sat down in the chair next to the fireplace, leaning her head on the back, her shoulder-length blonde hair cascading over it. I could see strands of gray woven through it now and they sparkled in the firelight as if they were glittering pieces of tinsel like she used to toss onto our Christmas tree. We didn't use tinsel anymore. I wondered why not. I supposed it had gone out of style, but I'd loved it. Shaking my head free of the memory, I grabbed the small tube of cream and stood behind her, using a small bit of it on my fingertips to massage it into the thick, crisscrossed scars on the left side of her face, and down her neck. She sighed. "Thank you, darling, that's better. What would I do without you?"

I smiled, but my heart squeezed painfully to think of her without me. All alone. Sometimes I dreamed of going somewhere where there were lots of people, where I could sit and watch them without hiding, where maybe they'd even talk to me, too. I dreamed of things I didn't dare share with my own mother. I dreamed of things I knew could never be real.

"I like that dress, by the way," my mother said.

I smiled. It was my favorite, too. The white lace.

"You probably shouldn't wear dresses into the woods, though. You're bound to ruin them."

I shrugged. "If I don't wear them, they'll eventually just rot away.

They deserve to live a little, don't you think?" I asked, smiling. "What will be done with them otherwise? Donated to some vintage clothing store eventually?"

My mom smiled back, the right side of her mouth tipping upward more than the left. "I suppose they do deserve to live a little, being that they've been packed away in a dark basement for so long," she said and cracked one eye at me, smiling bigger. Why did I feel like that was a good description of *me*? Kept in the dark. *Forgotten.*

"Well good, because I'm giving them plenty of new memories." I continued rubbing the cream into her skin. *I'd even received my very first kiss in one of them.*

After a minute, she asked. "Where do you go, Lily? When you go into the woods—where do you go? You're away for so long, all day sometimes."

"Not far," I answered. It was a lie, I knew. "I like it there." *It was where I felt alive.* "Sometimes I just wander and . . . lose track of time, I guess."

"I worry about you. It can't be one hundred percent safe."

"Nothing is, Mom." I sighed. "There's no need to worry, though. I promise."

"You don't go far? You won't get lost or anything?"

"No, I won't get lost."

"And you don't ever *see* anyone, do you?"

"Who would I see? It's the middle of nowhere, in the woods."

"I don't know, hikers or—"

"There are no trails in these woods, Mom."

My mother's eyes, clear and green, were opened now and she studied me closely, her expression a mixture of confusion and sadness. She seemed to look at me like that a lot lately. All the time, actually. But she didn't ask any more questions, and I was relieved.

"You could come walking with me, you know."

She pressed her lips together. "I walk in the garden. That's enough for me."

I sighed. She'd never change, never venture out. So where did that leave me?

"We have to think about leaving, you know. We only planned to be here for the summer. It's already the end of August. It's going to be your birthday soon. What do you think about leaving right before?"

I frowned. Despite what had happened with Holden, I wasn't sure I was ready to leave yet. Here I had freedom. "Can we think about it? It's still so beautiful in the forest. And you love the garden, right? You're happy here, Mom?"

She nodded, and I smiled down into her beloved face, my eyes moving over the familiar lines of her features, my heart suddenly filled with a terrible, aching sadness. "I love you," I said, swallowing the strange emotion.

That whole business with Holden had crushed me more than it should have. I had trusted Holden, been swept away, and now I was left empty and confused. My emotions were all jumbled up. My mother gave me a tender smile.

"I love you, too, my darling Lily. I always, always will."

As I continued to smooth the cream over the half of her ravaged face, my mind insisted on returning to Holden. *Will you be waiting for me, Lily? Yes.* I'd been foolish to promise something so recklessly. So, how far *would* I go back into the woods? I wouldn't go near his lodge. I wouldn't. I'd stay away. I would not subject myself to the pain he was sure to bring. I'd received my first kiss, and I'd have to hold on to that. It didn't have to mean any more.

CHAPTER TEN

Holden

I went into the woods every day for the next three days, wandering aimlessly, calling for Lily. A couple times I even tried purposefully to lose my way, but I must have started noticing things about this forest that I hadn't meant to keep track of. "How the fuck can a person fail to get lost in a remote forest when he's actually trying?" I muttered. "That proves it, Holden, you are hopeless. Completely hopeless."

Returning to the lodge, I paced relentlessly. There was so much good pacing area out here. I could pace for days and only occasionally cover the same ground. It was a pacer's heaven. *Fuck.* Lily. I ran my hand through my hair. I was going to pace a track onto the deck and go prematurely bald from all the hair raking.

How in the world had things gone downhill so fast? Fucking Taylor, the snake. What *had* I ever seen in her?

She's good in bed.

I'm sure she is. She gets plenty of practice.

The words flitted through my mind, causing my head to ache. I brought one hand up and massaged the back of my neck. *Ryan*, I'd had that conversation with Ryan. I'd had that conversation with Ryan *that* day. I shook my head. No, no, I refused to think about that day. I pushed it out of my mind forcefully. *No.*

I had to explain things to Lily. I had to let her know that what happened wasn't my fault. I had to know if she'd give me another chance. Never mind that I'd need to start all over with the detoxing. I couldn't do it until I knew things were settled with Lily. And now, thanks to Taylor, or maybe *no* thanks to Taylor, I had a fresh supply. But, no, that was good because I had to make sure Lily and I were okay. I had to know she'd be waiting for me on the other side, so to speak. Knowing that would help get me through the darkness. *Her.* So if she wasn't in the forest, where was she? She'd said she lived nearby, but where?

Going back inside, I pulled my laptop out and sat on the couch with it on my lap. I used Google Earth to look up the lodge. The only building for miles and miles was the abandoned mental hospital Brandon had mentioned. Whittington, Hospital for the Mentally Insane. I did a Google search and scrolled through a couple pages of information.

The Whittington Hospital for the Mentally Insane, later renamed simply Whittington, was first constructed in 1901 on a forty-acre spread of land. The sixty-thousand-square-foot building was designed by Chester R. Pendelton who believed the mentally ill should be cared for and treated with kindness and compassion, away from the many stressors of the outside world. That translated into luxurious interiors including chapels, auditoriums, libraries, private rooms for the patients, all with vaulted ceilings, and large and plentiful windows to allow for maximum sunlight and ventilation. The expansive grounds and gardens featured beautifully ornate statues, fountains, and benches, and excellent walking paths.

I scrolled through the few black and white pictures online, not noting the exact year they'd been taken. Despite the fact that the interior was indeed, very appealing—light and airy—the outside of the building looked like something out of a horror movie. Enormous and gothic with tall, ornate towers, grandiose arches, and sweeping windows. There were even screaming gargoyles flanking the upper windows. I was sure nothing put the mentally ill at ease quite like monsters outside their rooms. I couldn't help shivering.

Whittington was built over twenty miles away from the nearest community to ensure that should a patient escape, there was no risk to outside inhabitants. Whittington was a privately owned hospital whose patients were comprised mainly of members of wealthy families who wished to keep their relative's condition private. In later years, though still privately owned, Whittington began accepting donations, grants, and some state funding for the less fortunate.

Despite the good intentions of its design and beginnings, Whittington, originally intended to treat three hundred patients, had a population of almost fifteen hundred by the twenties. The staff numbers, however, remained stable. This meant the patients were often severely neglected, becoming sick and filth-ridden from lack of care, and the staff was unequipped to offer them more. It wasn't uncommon for a patient to die and not be discovered for days, even weeks sometimes.

In 1915, Dr. Jeremiah Braun became the director of Whittington and instituted treatments that have been associated with the horrors of psychiatric facilities of the past: padded cells used for solitary confinement, mechanical restraints including straightjackets, the over-medicating of those difficult to control, insulin shock therapy, psychosurgery, and the lobotomy. The icepick lobotomy, which was essentially an icepick to the eggshell-thin bone above the eye, was a radically invasive brain surgery used to treat everything from delusions, to migraines, to melancholy, to deep depression, to "hysteria," a term used for women who exhibited sexual desire and strong emotions. In the unfortunate patient, the frontal lobes would be disconnected from the rest of the brain by a simple, quick side-to-side maneuver, leaving the individual with irreversible effects. In a 1941 interview, Braun described Whittington's mentally ill as docile and compliant under his direction, however, visitors to the facility told of patients wandering aimlessly in a daze, sometimes into walls, vacantly staring at their own feet, and hitting their heads repeatedly on tables with no intervention by staff.

Eventually, Braun's beliefs regarding mental illness became even more bizarre and dangerous. When he noted that very high fevers could cause hallucinations, he theorized that infection didn't just cause *diseases of the body, but of the mind as well. In 1923, he began extracting patients' teeth, and often their tonsils as well, though X-rays didn't always confirm infection. When this didn't cure his patients, he began removing other body parts such as the stomach, portions of the colon, gall bladder, spleen, ovaries, testicles, and uteruses, although he had no formal training as a surgeon. Moreover, these surgeries were often performed without consent from the patient or family, and sometimes, despite their vehement protests. Braun cited cure rates of over 90%, but in actuality, his surgeries very often resulted in death. This, however, did not deter him from his "pioneering work." What made the practices of Braun more disturbing, was that he regularly published his findings in highly read psychological papers and medical journals. And no one in the psychology community did a thing. Braun passed away in 1962.*

Sickened by what I'd just read, I skimmed down the article a little more and found that by 1988, all but one wing of Whittington was closed. The entire hospital had been shut down just five years ago.

I sat on the couch for a little while longer, staring at the screen. Swallowing down the lump in my throat, I closed the cover of my laptop. Jesus, it was a fucking house of horrors. Or it had been. Something about the fear and anguish of those who had been locked inside . . . I didn't want to dwell on it for very long, didn't want to consider the details.

But I suddenly had a deep curiosity to see it in person—to find out if the pictures online really did it justice. Mapping it out, I found that Brandon had been right. It was about five miles away and a straight walk through the woods.

It was only mid-morning. I gathered some supplies—food, water, a sweatshirt—and set off in the direction of Whittington. The terrain was deeply wooded for the most part, but there were no cliffs to scale or rivers to cross—thankfully—and it took me a little over three hours to make the walk through the misty forest. I called Lily's name intermittently, but received no answer.

I came out of the trees and was standing before what I recognized as Whittington, the gargantuan, gothic, stone building. My heart began to beat more quickly. It looked like a living, breathing thing and I shivered. Now that I was right in front of it, I couldn't help but imagine all the pain and unfathomable suffering that had gone on behind those walls. All because no one had been willing or brave enough to help. Those people had been invisible to society, deemed throwaways because of something they weren't responsible for. The weakest of the weak. And in that moment I felt the terror and hopelessness of that down to my bones, in my very marrow.

And *yet*, as I stood staring at it, tilting my head very slightly, it also exuded a strange sort of magnificent beauty, some hidden sorrow that lay just beneath the stone surface, as if the building itself wanted to say, *what happened here was not my fault.*

My gaze traveled upward until it settled on the highest window, something stirring deep inside, the grandeur of the structure stealing my breath for a moment.

I looked to my right and drew back slightly when I saw what must have been the asylum cemetery. I walked toward it, taking note of the crumbling gravestones, some topped with angels, reaching toward the heavens. This must be the oldest part of the cemetery. The farther I walked, the newer the stones looked, the dates carved into them corroborating my observation. Weeds thrived, almost completely covering some of the smaller markers. I wondered who was buried here—patients who had died with no family? Otherwise, wouldn't they be in family plots or closer to the homes of loved ones? Feeling totally creeped out, I turned around and walked back to where I'd started.

The massive, wrought-iron gate creaked loudly as I pushed it open and walked through. The walk from the gate to the front steps of the asylum was about a quarter of a mile. My feet crunched on the gravel, what had originally been a very long driveway, now overrun with weeds, grass and wildflowers growing in random patches. The sky overhead was a grayish-blue and filled with billowy clouds. Off in the distance, I could see a few approaching rain clouds, but nothing that looked like it would produce much of a storm. *Hopefully.* I still had to make it back.

When I finally arrived at the front steps, I climbed them slowly, glancing around. Everything seemed very still. I tried to turn the doorknob of the massive, double wooden front door, but it was locked. Looking around, I spotted a broken window on the first floor and it was easy enough to lift myself up to the windowsill and duck through. When I stood and had brushed off my jeans, I was standing in a dirty hallway. It was cluttered with debris, had paint peeling from the walls in large strips, and a rusted wheelchair lay overturned in front of me. I moved it aside with my foot and walked down the hall, craning my neck to see into rooms before I'd walked in front of the doorways. In one, there was an old gurney against the wall and in another there was a standing harp, most of the strings broken and curling wildly in every direction like the hair of some wild shrew. This place was creepy as shit. I expected Freddy Krueger to turn the corner toward me at any moment.

"Lily?" I yelled loudly, not truly believing she'd be inside this deserted place but finding a strange comfort in hearing her name echo through the empty halls. I walked through corridor after corridor calling Lily's name.

As I walked past one of the large windows, I caught movement. Far away, at the edge of the forest, Lily was on her knees doing something on the ground in front of her. *Lily!* My heart sped up and I turned and walked as quickly as possible through all the debris on the floor toward the front door. I was able to open it from the inside and I took the stairs two at a time, running back down the long driveway and out the front gate toward Lily.

"Lily," I said breathlessly as I finally came up behind her. She jerked slightly and turned, tears streaming down her cheeks. "Hey, what's wrong?" That's when I saw an owl on the ground in front of her and I went down on my knees beside her. "Oh shit, is he okay?"

Lily shook her head. "No, he's . . . dead." She heaved in a shuddery breath and used both hands to wipe at her tears. She shook her head. "I just found him out here, lying on the ground. He must have just . . . died of old age. There doesn't seem to be anything wrong with him." She sniffled.

"I'm so sorry."

She nodded and used a sweater that was tied around her waist to scoop him up. "I don't think owls have very long life spans. I have to bury him."

"I'll help. Do you have a shovel?"

She shook her head. "No, I'll have to use a stick or something. The ground is very soft in certain parts of the forest. It should be okay." I walked a little ways into the woods with her, and as she held the owl, I dug the small grave in the soft earth of the forest floor. We didn't speak, which made me aware of all the sounds around me: the birds twittering in the trees, foliage swishing in the breeze, and Lily's occasional sniffles. When I was done, she lowered him into the ground, the sweater wrapped around him, and stood as I covered him up, another tear rolling down her cheek.

"You must think I'm so silly crying over an owl," she said. "It's just that he used to come sit on the fence over there, every day, and I kind of got used to him." She shrugged. "Whenever I passed by and saw him, I came to think of him as good luck, a sort of wise sentry who might show you the way if you were lost and afraid." She tilted her head, looking sad but thoughtful.

"I don't think you're silly." *I think you're the most beautiful, tenderhearted girl I've ever known.*

She nodded, finally looking at me.

"Once when I was younger, I found a baby owl on the edge of our property. I was angry with my mother and I'd run outside and had lain on the ground under a fir tree. I was crying, and suddenly I heard this tiny sound like something very small hitting the ground next to me. I looked over and there was this helpless baby bird that had just fallen out of his nest, thankfully onto a bed of pine needles and leaves. He was so fuzzy and so tiny. I picked him up and tried to see the nest he'd fallen from, but it must have been so high up, and so hidden, I couldn't spot it. I didn't have a way to climb the fir tree, so I took him home with me."

"Home . . ." I murmured. "Is it close by?"

She smiled. "Not far." We began walking. "Anyway, I didn't think he'd live. But he did. He lived and he got strong, and eventually I released him back to the forest. I guess I kind of imagined this owl might be the same one."

I smiled. "Maybe it was. Maybe he recognized you. Why were you mad at your mother?"

"Hmm?"

"You said you ran outside because you were angry with your mother."

"Oh." She furrowed her brow. "I wanted to go to a party, and she wouldn't let me. Just a silly party . . ." She smiled, looking at me sideways, her smile fading. She looked down at her feet as she stepped over a fallen branch, biting her lip, obviously considering something. Finally, she asked, "What are you doing out here, Holden?"

I sighed. "I was trying to find you."

She stopped, looking straight at me. "Why?"

"Because I wanted to make sure you understood about the other night . . . that you were okay . . ."

"Oh," she said, biting her lip. "I see."

"Lily," I said, grabbing both her hands in mine. "I'm so sorry about that. I swear to you I had no idea Taylor was coming to visit. If I had, I would have told her not to come. I got rid of her. She's gone."

"Why? Not because of me. Because—"

"No, not because of you. Not entirely. I would have told her not to come because I'm not interested in spending time with her. But I do want to spend time with you. I meant what I said."

Lily licked her lips, her eyes on the ground as if she was thinking. "You were *naked*, and she was . . ."

I grimaced. "I know. God, I'm so sorry. It wasn't what it looked like. She surprised me and I wasn't at my best." *Jesus, the understatement of the century.* "I didn't know she was coming. Please trust me. Please give me a second chance. I've spent the last three days wandering through the woods looking for you. I'll make the three-hour walk out here every day if I have to. Or to your house if you'll let me. I'll come to you, so you don't have to walk all the way to me, especially now that I know how far it is. I'll do anything you ask me to do. Just please don't tell me you don't want to see me anymore."

She let out a big breath, pulling her hands from mine. "It's just not a good idea, Holden. I thought—"

"That can't be true. It can't be wrong to want to spend time together. I know there are things I'm . . . dealing with, and I know you don't trust me enough to share your life with me yet. And I know the whole Taylor thing hardly helped that." I rubbed the back of my neck. "But I'm hoping you will. I'm hoping you'll let me earn that. Please don't tell me to go." I put my hands in my pockets, swallowing, feeling intensely vulnerable in front of her. *Why would she want you? Why would she give you a second chance? Why?*

"Oh, Holden . . ." She looked away for a minute, and I held my breath. After a tense minute, she sighed and gave the smallest nod of her head, practically imperceptible. My heart soared.

"Was that a yes?"

Her lip quirked up. "A half yes."

"What should I do to earn a full yes?" I bent slightly to look up into her lowered eyes, her dark lashes fanning across her cheeks.

Her lip quirked a bit higher, and her eyes met mine. "I'll let you know when I think of something." I couldn't help smiling, couldn't help *marveling* that she had given me another chance. *A half chance.* And I'd take it. I'd take whatever she would give me.

"How'd you find me out here anyway?" she asked after a moment.

"Truthfully, I didn't know you'd be here. I just hoped. I came to check out Whittington."

Lily looked over her shoulder at the abandoned hospital. Turning back to me, she said, "Creepy, isn't it? Terrible things happened there."

"I know. I read about it online."

She nodded, her brow furrowing slightly. "It was open until somewhat recently, but in the last several decades lack of private donations and state funding turned it into what it is." She waved her hand toward it. "A crumbling mess. It's eerie." She looked thoughtful for a moment. "Something good should be done inside, don't you think?

Something to prove that humans care about one another." She glanced back quickly again. "If locations hold pain, maybe love and kindness set it free." She looked thoughtful as she bit at her lip.

My eyes washed over her troubled expression. *She's so compassionate.* "That's a nice thought. I think you might be right. What would you do with it?"

A ghost of a smile moved across her face. "I'd help those who can't help themselves."

"Like who?"

She shrugged. "There's always someone society chooses not to see. There's always someone who is invisible through no fault of their own."

I nodded. "Mental health care is a lot different now than it was back then. A lot more understood."

"Yes. For the most part, I think. Do you want to walk with me?"

As we began walking, she said, "There were two different patient escapes at Whittington. One happened during the coldest winter on record. A young girl, sixteen at the time, climbed out a window and somehow made it through the gate and into the woods. It was determined that she'd been highly medicated and simply wandered away. A search party was sent out, but she wasn't found. It was assumed she perished somewhere in this," she waved her arm around, "vast wilderness. Experts said there was no way she could have survived the temperatures."

"That's awful," I murmured. "Only sixteen? Jesus. I didn't realize teens had been there, too."

"Oh yes. Children and teens were there from the time it opened." We were both quiet for a moment, me pondering the terror a child must have felt in a place like that. "Sometimes I wonder if I might come upon her remains out here," she said, shooting me a glance. "Is that totally macabre?"

I managed a small smile. "Yes. But I guess it really is possible. Might be nice for her family anyway—to be able to bury her."

"That's what I thought, too."

I frowned. "What other escape was there?"

95

"Six years ago, on a July night, there was a summer storm that caused a power failure at Whittington. All the lights went out for several hours. During that time, many of the patients escaped to these woods. They wandered until morning when a search party was sent out, and all but one was rounded up."

"Who wasn't found?" I asked.

Lily was quiet for a moment. "A nineteen-year-old man, the son of a rich executive from Connecticut. The subsequent search parties didn't find him either. He survived out here," she waved her hand around again, "for over five months before he snuck back to Whittington probably intending to steal food. As it happened, it was a visiting day. While the families of the patients were inside, the escaped patient climbed into the trunk of a car. The family unknowingly transported him to their estate, where their teenage daughter discovered him later hiding in their stables."

"How do you know this?" I asked, intrigued.

"I found the stories in old newspaper clippings," she said, looking ahead.

"Where? Inside?"

She glanced over at me and nodded. She'd been curious, too. I wondered if I should tell her it wasn't safe to be wandering through abandoned buildings, but I didn't know how to word it so it didn't sound condescending. Especially since I'd just been inside myself.

"What happened when the girl discovered the escaped patient in her stables?"

"They fell in love," she said simply.

"The patient and the daughter fell in love? Wow. How'd that happen?"

Lily shrugged. "He was handsome and kind. Very, very troubled, but very, very kind. She harbored him. She fed him, and clothed him, kept him warm, and eventually, she gave him her heart."

I looked over at her. The expression on her face was wistful. She looked at me. "I imagine," she said and gave me a slight smile. "Maybe that's me romanticizing it, but that's how I picture it happening." She shrugged.

"What happened after that?" I asked.

"He ended up back at Whittington eventually." She shrugged again. "These things never end well, I suppose."

"Don't they?" I asked. "Maybe he got better. Maybe he found the right treatment, and found her again. Maybe they ended up together after all."

She tilted her head. "Why, Holden Scott, I do believe you're a romantic, too."

I chuckled. "Now that's something I've never been accused of before."

She smiled. "No?"

I shook my head, taking her hand in mine. She looked down at our joined hands and smiled softly. "I missed you," I said.

She glanced at me. "For three days?"

"Yes. Didn't you miss me?"

She paused before answering. "Yes."

"Do you think he's the one who collected the arrowheads?" I asked after a moment, suddenly remembering them.

"I wondered that, too," she said. "I like to think so. I like to think he found ways to keep his mind occupied. Maybe he even liked it out here." She smiled. "I do."

"I think he'd be lonely, though. Maybe that's the reason he went back. Maybe it wasn't for food. After all, the forest could provide for a man if he knew what he was doing. Maybe he decided he'd rather be locked up than be lonely."

"Would you?" she asked.

"Rather be locked up than be lonely? It's hard to say. I've never been locked up before. But based on what I read online, I'd probably choose loneliness. It sounded like being locked up was the least of the torments that patients experienced at Whittington, at least in the older days. And maybe he was even lonely *while* he was locked up. I guess out here at least he had freedom."

Lily was quiet for a moment. "Yes. Freedom." She paused. "I

suppose we'll never know *what* he was thinking exactly."

"No, I guess not."

Lily looked up at the sky. "It looks like it might rain. I hate to think of you walking all the way back in bad weather."

"I made it here. I think I can make it back."

She raised her eyebrows, looking dubious. "How about we wait it out for a little bit, Boy Scout?" She pulled my hand and we ducked beneath some low tree branches.

The rain was only sprinkling at the moment, and the thick canopy of branches provided complete shelter as we sat down on a dry patch of ground, me leaning against the tree trunk. The air was cool, but I was wearing my sweatshirt. I took it off and wrapped it around Lily's shoulders, putting one arm around her and pulling her close. She laid her head on my shoulder and we sat there for a few minutes, just listening to the rainfall on the leaves overhead.

I barely knew anything about this girl. I only knew that when I was with her, the entire world felt different. It was like this forest was our own secret land, and *here*, we could be anything we wanted to be. Anything at all.

"Feels like a different world here," I said, voicing my thought.

She hummed. "I know." She tilted her head and looked up at me. "Are *you* lonely out here, Holden? In that house all by yourself, I mean."

"I feel like I've been lonely for a very long time, Lily. It's not so much the location . . . it's just . . . me, I guess." I put my lips to her forehead. "I don't feel lonely when I'm with you, though," I murmured, brushing my lips over her cool skin, feathering kisses against her as lightly as if she were made of moonlight.

She raised her face so that her lips were almost touching mine. "I don't feel lonely when I'm with you either," she whispered, raising her mouth and pressing her lips against mine. Desire arced down the center of my chest, and I turned so I could bring my hands to her face and claim her mouth completely. Our tongues met and tangled and Lily moaned, climbing over me so she was straddling my lap as we kissed. "I've missed you so much," she said, between kisses. "So much it scared me."

The sweatshirt fell off her shoulders, exposing us both to the mist, but I didn't think it mattered. My own body was so overheated by her sitting on my lap, I thought I might suddenly self-combust.

"I'm sorry," I said. Because it was my fault we'd spent the last few days apart. My stupid life that had found me, even all the way out here, and had come between Lily and me. I felt ashamed. I had so much to feel ashamed about. Lily kissed the corner of my mouth, her lips sliding down my jaw and around to my ear. A muffled groan escaped my lips as her tongue traced the outer shell.

"Is this okay?" she whispered, her breath hot against my skin.

"God, yes," I panted, the entire forest disappearing around me. It was only her. Only her fresh scent, the feel of her weight on top of me, her hands, her skin, her lips. Only her.

The rain picked up, the sound of it beating more steadily on the leaves above, the air growing more humid around us, a cool drop of rain or two finding its way between the branches to splatter on our skin. My heart beat frantically, my excitement growing by the second. I wanted Lily so much it hurt.

"Show me what to do," she said. "Show me what you like."

"There's nothing you can do that I won't like. I promise you. Oh, God," I moaned as she bit lightly on my earlobe. My erection throbbed.

She kissed along my jaw again. "You make me want things I shouldn't want," she said.

"Why shouldn't you want them?"

"Because," she said, bringing her mouth to mine and kissing me again, "this is just temporary. It has to be, Holden. Eventually you'll go back to where you belong."

I could hardly remember *where* I belonged. Lately, it seemed like I didn't belong anywhere at all. "We can figure something out. We can be together. It's up to us. There's always a way . . ."

She smiled against my lips. "Just kiss me." I did, my mind emptying again as I focused on the sensations she was creating in my body. She leaned her head back as I kissed down the silken skin of her throat, darting my tongue out to taste her there. I wanted to taste her everywhere, learn the taste that was her and nobody else.

"Lily . . ." I reached for her dress. A few buttons and the top slid down her shoulders, the creamy swell of her breasts rising and falling above her white bra. I reached behind her and unhooked it, her breasts spilling free, the deep pink nipples already tight and hard. I took a shuddery breath and leaned forward, kissing the space between her breasts, breathing in her scent, hot and concentrated in that spot. All Lily. The effect she had on me was new and familiar all at once—as if we really had known each other in another lifetime—and my soul held the mere hint of a memory, even if my mind and flesh were just learning her now. I felt woozy with the mixture of deep emotion and powerful lust.

Lily gasped and brought her hands to my head as my mouth closed over one sweet nipple. I swirled my tongue around, pulling gently and then moved to the other one. Lily ground down on my erection, and I hissed in a breath, stopping momentarily to get hold of myself. "Oh, don't stop," she gasped, pushing her damp breast into my mouth. I smiled against her skin, taking the nipple into my mouth again and sucking lightly.

Quiet sounds of pleasure rose from her throat, and she slid lower, bringing her mouth back to mine. "I want you," she whispered.

"I want you, too. So much. But not out here. Not on the ground. I have to . . . I have to give you better than that."

"This is fine," she said, and I couldn't help smiling at the desperate note in her voice.

"No. It isn't fine. But I won't leave you unsatisfied. Can I touch you?"

Her eyes met mine and widened very slightly. They were a darker shade of violet, glazed with passion.

"Yes," she said. I brought my mouth back to hers, reaching beneath her dress and letting my hand trail up her thigh. She froze.

"Trust me," I said. Her body relaxed, and she began kissing me again.

I used my finger to trace the waistband of her underwear and she shivered above me. Reaching inside, I found the small swollen nub hidden at the top of her folds and circled my finger around it. She pushed herself into my hand and moaned. I thought I was probably going to come in my pants at the excitement of seeing her so aroused. I parted my own legs under her so I had room to bring my hand lower and slipped one finger into her wet entrance. "Oh, God," I murmured. "You're so wet, so sweet." She brought her face into the side of my neck and I felt her mouth open on a gasp as I went just a little deeper with my finger, using my thumb to circle and play with her sensitive peak. Her hot breaths against my neck made me lose my mind with desire. But this was about her. This was about bringing her pleasure.

Just as I thought it, Lily's body went taut, her small cry muffled against my neck as she shuddered and came on my hand. After a moment, I slipped my finger out of her and brought my hand to her neck so I could lift her mouth gently to mine. Before our lips met, I glimpsed her face, drunk with pleasure, a small smile on her lips. I kissed her slowly, trying desperately to rein in my own unfulfilled need.

Lily let out a small sigh, resting against me for several moments. We breathed together, the downpour shifting to a gentle smattering on the leaves above. "The rain is stopping," she murmured softly.

"Does that mean we have to go back?" I asked.

She smiled and put her lips back on mine, nodding her head.

"Come back with me. Stay with me tonight."

"I can't. My mother . . ."

"You're a grown woman, Lily. Surely she can't expect you not to live your life."

She sighed, pulling away from me and scooting off my lap. I was still half hard and I adjusted myself slightly. "That's exactly what she expects. For her, I'll never grow up. It's . . . complicated."

"Then explain it to me."

She stood up and I did, too. "I'll find a way to come to your lodge in the next few days, okay?" She smiled. "And in the meantime, we still have the forest."

"I'll take whatever I can get, Lily of the Night." I smiled and kissed her again. *We still have the forest.*

CHAPTER ELEVEN

Holden

The next few days were among the happiest I'd ever spent, despite feeling sick and chained to the pills I hadn't yet found the courage to stop taking. That chore weighed on me, a dark shadow in the back of my mind. I knew I needed to do it and do it soon—I wanted Lily to know all of me, not the shell of the man I'd become.

Plus, the headaches were getting worse. I was sick in a way the pills had never made me sick before. I needed to get off them and regain my health before I could begin to give anything at *all* to another person. But in the meantime, I reveled in the wonderful, seemingly dreamy world Lily created. We walked through the forest hand in hand as she pointed out all the things I'd have missed if it was only me: the wood thrushes and butterflies, the columbine bushes, now maroon in late summer. We drank the cold, sweet stream water that flowed from the mountains above and fed each other wild strawberries.

We kissed everywhere, against trees and rocks, in wide-open fields and at the edge of the stream, lying in the sunshine as the water gurgled and splashed next to us. She worked me into a frenzy of lust so powerful I could barely catch my breath some days. I wanted her with every cell in my body. And the way she moved her hips against mine, the way her eyes glazed over when we touched, I knew she wanted me, too. I had never known this type of physical *want*, even stronger than the craving I felt for the pills. It made me crazy, but it brought me hope. The numbing peace the pills brought was an illusion. Lily, Lily was real. And with her, I didn't need to be any of the titles I'd collected. I didn't need to be my mistakes or my pain. I was just . . . *me*, and I started to finally hope that that was okay.

But I also knew very well Lily was innocent—her tentative touches, her surprised reactions, the unabashed delight she showed each time I touched her in a way that brought pleasure, told me all I needed to know.

Maybe once I got off the pills, we could just stay in this forest until the end of time. A simple life suddenly seemed like a wistful, impossible dream. To spend days walking through the fresh air of the woods, talking about everything and nothing, and to enjoy evenings in front of a warm fire, reading, and then making love late into the night, celebrating life in the most ancient of ways. I wanted to *dive* into that kind of deeply beautiful simplicity, suddenly longed for it clear to my soul. It sounded like . . . *freedom*.

I walked to meet her at the edge of the forest a couple days after I'd first touched her under the boughs of a tree in the mist of the rain. It was a sunlit evening, and as I stepped into the dim light of the woods, she turned slowly toward the sound of my footsteps. She was wearing a pale purple dress and her brown boots. Her lips tipped up in a beautiful smile, and the whisper of a breeze picked up a lock of her hair.

Suddenly, a pale beam of sunlight shifted through the trees, casting a light across her body, seeming to make her *shimmer*, waver between this world and another. And my heart shimmered, too, at her awe-inspiring beauty. She was so gorgeous, I ached. *A dream. A vision.* No, no, *real*. So very real. The moment wasn't shimmering with dreaminess, but with a sudden, sharp reality. Because the emotion I felt couldn't be denied: I was in love with her. Deeply, madly, sweetly in love.

And I couldn't tell her. It wasn't fair—I was only half a man right now. So I'd keep it to myself, for now. And I knew: I had to get clean. I couldn't put it off anymore. Tonight would be our final night together until I could come to her as she deserved.

I walked to her, my body suddenly trembling at the realization, my head beginning to ache, as it seemed to have done all week.

"Hi," she breathed, wrapping her arms around me and immediately bringing her lips to mine.

I kissed her and then laughed softly when she pulled her head away.

"What?" she asked.

"I like that you can't keep your hands off me."

"How could I? Am I expected to resist a Boy Scout with high honors, one who kisses like you do? I'm only human, after all."

"True. You were a goner the minute I stepped into these woods."

"Hmm," she hummed as she wiped a bead of moisture off my bottom lip. "I know."

I cocked my head to the side. "Can you come to the lodge tonight? You haven't been inside it yet."

She bit her lip but then nodded her head. I took her hand and led her across the open grassy area to the stairs of the lodge. She looked a little nervous, but I squeezed her hand and pulled her along.

When we stepped through the door, she hesitated and looked around. When she finally moved farther inside, she placed her hand on the back of the couch, looking up at the high, beamed ceiling. I followed her gaze—remembering the speakers in the walls that I'd noticed the first week I'd arrived—and walked over to the shelf where I turned on the iPod docked there. A cover of Elvis's "Can't Help Falling in Love" filled the room and Lily turned to me smiling. I walked back to her, suddenly feeling shy. I wiped my palms on my jeans and took her in my arms, swaying to the music. "I'm not a very good dancer," I admitted.

"This feels nice," she said, pressing closer to me. "I've never danced before."

I drew back slightly. "Never?"

She shook her head. "See, you shouldn't have told me you aren't a good dancer. I'd never have known." She grinned and my heart stuttered.

"Until you danced with someone else."

For a moment, she simply gazed at me. "I don't want to dance with anyone else."

I swallowed. "Me neither, Lily." I pulled her closer as the song continued, thinking how the lyrics applied to me. Because I couldn't help it. I was in love with the girl in my arms and it seemed . . . meant to be, like fate. Beautifully designed. That we had, against all odds, somehow found each other out here in the middle of nowhere. Two people who needed each other so desperately. The song ended and we drew apart, Lily kissing me softly.

"Thank you," she said, "for giving me my first dance."

I smiled back and went to turn off the music. She wandered through the living room and I followed her, not saying a word as she went into the kitchen, trailing her hand along the granite countertops. "This is nice," she said. "It's so strange to be seeing it from the inside, instead of through the window." She gave me a small, embarrassed smile. "Said the stalker."

I laughed, leaning a hip on the doorframe and crossing my arms. I'd be happy just watching her forever. The way she looked, the way she moved . . .

She gave a slight shake of her head, walking to the refrigerator where she took a moment to look at the pictures affixed with magnets— so many. I hadn't even taken the time to look very closely at them. Mostly party pictures, it looked like, now that I was noticing, probably from the different get-togethers Brandon had had out here. She smiled, leaning in so she could look more closely here and there. "So many friends . . ." she murmured, a note of . . . jealousy? Was that jealousy in her voice? No, nothing that strong. Maybe wistfulness? As if she didn't have any friends.

"I—" I frowned, stopping myself from asking her to tell me every detail about her past. I wanted that, *needed* that, but I also wanted to give her the same and—I massaged my temples—I couldn't do that until I was clean. *Let it be your reward,* my mind whispered. Yes, Lily would be my reward.

"Where do you sleep?" she asked, her smile returning.

"Upstairs," I answered. *God, I wanted to lead her to my bed and spend the night worshipping every inch of her skin. I wanted to lose myself in the warm heaven of her body.* "Do you want a drink? A soda, or . . ." My voice sounded hoarse.

Lily nodded. I went to the cabinet and started making her drink as she walked to the window and looked outside for a moment. My breath faltered as I glanced at her profile. She was so beautiful. Would I ever get used to the effect she had on me? She wandered back into the living room. When I walked into the room a minute after her, holding her drink, she was standing by the window, a magazine in her hand. I supposed she'd found it in the basket next to the large, overstuffed leather recliner, the one filled with all sorts of reading material.

I froze as she turned toward me, her face pale, arrested. *Stricken.* She looked from the magazine to me. "Holden Scott," she said softly, blinking at me. "This is . . . this is . . . *you?*" she asked. From the small amount of cover I could see, it was a Sports Illustrated. I didn't know which specific edition it was, but I'd been on the cover several times, it could be one of many. I nodded. She looked from the magazine cover back to me again. Her body was stiff, and she looked as if she was in shock.

"I know, I didn't tell you I'm a football player, or that I'm, well, very well known," I said, setting her drink on the coffee table. I ran my hand through my hair, as she eyed me. She blinked, looking confused, wary. "I'm sorry," I mumbled, stuffing my hands into my pockets. "I just . . . I just didn't want to be *him*," I nodded my head to the magazine, "out here, with you. You helped me remember that that's not who I am. And, God, it's been so painful." I frowned, clenching my eyes closed for a moment. "I guess I'm not making sense, but you've helped me. You've helped me so much, and I don't even want to explain it all to you until I'm well again. Can you trust me?" I walked toward her. When I came to stand in front of her, her eyes moved slowly over my face as she chewed on her lip.

"Is that why you're here?" she asked. "To get well?" Her voice cracked on the last word, and she again, glanced at the magazine and back to me.

I nodded. "Yes. And I'm trying. I'm trying so hard to get well." She continued to stare at me, something working behind her eyes that I had no idea how to read. I stilled as I waited for her reaction. Finally, she reached out and tentatively took my hand in hers, looking down at the back of my hand as she ran a finger over each knuckle. I shivered at her touch. Her eyes met mine, that gorgeous violet gaze seeming so very grave.

"Yes, Boy Scout, I trust you. I want you to be well again."

My breath came out in a rush and relief flooded my chest. To have someone who had faith in me made my heart squeeze with gratitude. "This has to be our last night for a little bit. Just a week, hopefully. But I . . . I need to—"

She put her fingers to my lips. "I know. So let's make the most of the time we have, okay? I want to spend the night with you. Is that okay?"

"God, yes, of course. There's nothing I want more than that."

She took a deep, shuddery breath, seeming to compose herself. "Okay. Okay. So how about we go out on the deck?"

I smiled, feeling elated that she was going to stay. "I have s'mores," I said. "Up for roasting some marshmallows?"

She let out a breath and gave me the glimmer of a smile. "Definitely."

I walked back into the kitchen and grabbed the bag of marshmallows, a few bars of chocolate, and a box of graham crackers. We went out on the deck, and I pulled a couple chairs up to the fire pit. Lily was quiet as I lit the fire. When I looked over at her, she was gazing out to the forest where the sunset's shafts of gold were streaming into the trees. In the woods, everything must have looked as if it were gilded.

I ran back in and got a plate and laid out the ingredients for the s'mores. Lily seemed to be deep in thought and I didn't interrupt. I was sure she was thinking about me being famous. Surely she hadn't expected that. I wondered if she thought it would impact her own life. I wanted it to, once I was better. The thought itself startled me, but not in a way that brought fear. Instead, in a way that brought . . . peace. It felt *right.* I wanted to take her out of these woods, to bring her home to my apartment . . . No, I didn't live there anymore. I massaged my temple. Back to the mansion I'd recently bought and hadn't even enjoyed. I wanted to bring her there, to learn her secrets, to take care of her, to make her mine.

Above us, the sky was turning a deep shade of indigo. The small fire crackled and jumped. "Do you want a blanket?" I asked.

Lily shook her head.

I felt nervous around her again, like I had the first few times we'd hung out. "I suppose you're going to mock my Boy Scout skills," I said, pointing to the small fire pit, the one I'd used matches to light. "Flint is generally my preferred method of fire lighting, of course, but it's scarce out here. The first rule of Boy Scouting is you have to make do with what you have." She laughed softly and raised her brows.

"Boy Scouting?"

"That's right."

"I thought the first rule of *Boy Scouting* was always be prepared."

"Right, but if you're not, figure it out anyway. Make it work. It's in the fine print. Sort of an amendment to the first rule."

"Ah, I see. Well you would know the rules of Boy Scouting better than I." She dragged her chair closer to mine, and I relaxed. Things seemed less awkward, less strained, than they had a few minutes before.

"I like two marshmallows on my s'more. How about you?"

She smiled over at me and nodded. I relaxed even more, my shoulders lowering. She stood up and grabbed the skewers sitting on the edge of the fire pit and stuck one marshmallow on the end of each, handing one to me. We sat in silence as the marshmallows sizzled and turned golden, the sweet, sugary smell rising in the air around us, mixing with the smoke from the fire. "Will you tell me about Ryan?" she asked softly.

I startled, glancing over at her. "Ryan?" I asked, my voice cracking.

She nodded, her eyes filled with something I was having a hard time interpreting. Sorrow? I inhaled a deep breath of smoky, sugary air, pulling my stick out of the fire when I realized my marshmallow was quickly blackening. She had already pulled her marshmallow from the fire and was gingerly pulling a piece off with her fingers. She put it in her mouth, but didn't appear to derive any pleasure from it. "How did he die?" she whispered after a minute.

I put the skewer and the inedible marshmallow aside, leaning my elbows on my knees and staring into the flames. Something about the jumping fire calmed me, was almost hypnotizing. "He fell. He fell to his death." I paused, still not looking at Lily, but I could feel her calming presence right beside me. "We were partying. Or . . . he was at least. They all were . . ." I grimaced, the foggy memory I'd tried to push aside spreading its spindly fingers over my brain, pushing into my flesh, causing my head to throb.

"He had been so damned unhappy in those months leading up to it." Was that right? Why did that feel wrong? I had pushed the memory away so harshly, covering it with drugs and alcohol. I needed to remember.

Oh God, getting off the pills meant I'd have to remember every bit of it. There would be no distractions . . . no physical needs to cover the emotional pain. I sighed. Lily reached out her hand and placed it on my thigh, giving it a gentle squeeze. *You can do this.*

"He fell, and I'm not sure if he meant to or not," I finally said, the words bursting forth on one long exhale of breath. The ache in my chest increased. It felt like a giant weight was sitting on top of me, and I was at risk of being crushed beneath it. "But I . . . I couldn't save him. I couldn't save him. I tried. I tried, but I couldn't. I tried to hold on, but he, he slipped away. Just slipped away." I wanted to wail with the agony that truth brought me. I wanted to raise my head to the heavens and curse a god that would allow my best friend's hand to slip from mine. *I hadn't been strong enough.* My head throbbed and I gripped it, moaning.

"I grew up with him. He was my best friend, my—"

"He was your hero." Lily's voice came to me as a whisper. "And you never got to tell him."

I nodded my head, the pain easing slightly. "*Yes,*" I said. "Yes."

"Oh, Boy Scout," she said, and I heard the tears in her voice. I turned in to her and she was there, her arms open. I leaned forward and laid my head on her lap and she wrapped her arms around me and rested her head on top of mine as the tears fell for my best friend. Her clean, comforting scent enveloped me, and I felt safe. Finally. I finally felt safe. I felt loved. "I think he knew," she said softly. "I'm sure of it. And you never really lost him. He'll always be a part of you. Always."

After what seemed like hours, but in reality was probably more like ten minutes, I began to sit up, the embarrassment that I'd fallen apart in Lily's arms overwhelming. I hadn't put any more wood in the fire pit, and for a moment I stared at the low, dying fire, trying to get a grasp on my emotions. There was a certain feeling of relief at having shared some of that terrible night with Lily, but I knew there was more, skating just on the edges of my mind. I pushed it back. I wasn't strong enough to take it all at once. *Wasn't strong enough . . .* Lily leaned back and stood, pulling me with her. My thoughts vanished for the moment and blessed emptiness filled my head as I followed her toward the door, watching her hips sway as she walked.

She turned toward me, standing so close I had to tip my head down to look into her face. The night was gathering darkness, but the few lights that were on in the house cast a muted glow.

"Will you show me where you sleep, Boy Scout?" she asked softly. My heart picked up speed and my mouth went dry as I nodded.

"It's . . . just . . . right up the stairs," I said stupidly.

She nodded, opening the door and going inside. I followed her, trailing behind, a case of nerves suddenly assaulting me. God, I hoped she meant what I thought she meant. When we both reached the top of the stairs, she stopped and let me lead the way to the small bedroom I'd chosen at the end of the hall. I flicked on the light and for a moment Lily stood in the doorway, looking around. The room was simple, with only a queen-sized bed covered in a dark blue comforter, a wooden dresser, and a bedside table. I hadn't wanted to sleep in the master bedroom. Something about that had seemed disrespectful. That was Brandon's room. My duffle bag was on the floor by the closet.

I watched as Lily approached me, reaching for both my hands. "I want you," she said softly.

I swallowed heavily, blood rushing to my cock, causing it to swell and strain against my jeans. "Are you sure?" I asked, my voice shaky. "There's still so much—"

She put her fingers up to my lips. "Yes. In this room, tonight, where we can just be . . . *us.* Can we let all the rest of it go? Just for tonight? Here, just let it be you and me and nothing else. Nothing else at all." There was something so very knowing in her expression. "We deserve that, don't we?"

I was lost to her. Lost and found at the same time. *How was that?* "Do we?" I asked.

"Yes, I think we do."

"And you . . . you want *me?*" I asked, feeling awed, bewildered, grateful.

Her lips tipped up into a smile. "Is that so very hard to believe?"

"I . . . I don't know." I frowned.

She nodded. "Then let me believe for you." And she leaned up on her tiptoes and kissed me. I moaned at the taste of her. Sugary marshmallow and Lily. I cupped her delicate face in my hands and tilted my head so I could taste her more deeply, tease her tongue with mine. She clutched my shoulders and blood rushed in my ears as lust spiked through my veins. I wanted her. I wanted to learn every part of her. All the kissing we'd done over the past week had served to drive me wild with want. I'd come back to the lodge night after night aching for her, yearning to hold her through the night. I was desperate now. I wanted her in a way I'd never wanted a woman before. Right here, right now, I could believe she was the only woman I'd ever touched.

Lily turned on the small bedside lamp and then turned off the overhead light before returning to me. She rubbed her body against mine, causing my erection to throb and pulse. I let out another moan as I cupped her breast, using my thumb to rub her nipple through the thin material of her dress. Lily gasped out a tiny sound of pleasure.

Lost . . . lost. And found.

I pulled back and looked at Lily's face, her eyes lowered with passion and her lips swollen and red from my kisses. I brought my hand back to her face and used my thumb to trace the line of her cheekbone. "You're the most beautiful woman I've ever seen," I whispered.

Lily's eyes lowered, her lips curving up. She used her feet to kick off her loosely laced boots and met my eyes right before turning and moving her hair over her shoulder and tilting her head forward. I reached up and slowly began lowering the zipper of her dress, leaning in and kissing down her spine as more of her skin was revealed. She shivered, and I smiled against the warmth of her bare back, continuing to move my mouth along with the zipper, inhaling the clean smell of her skin, my tongue darting out to taste her. When I got to her bra strap, I leaned up and unhooked it.

Lily turned around and let both the dress and the bra fall to her feet, hooking her thumbs into her white underwear and letting them fall as well. She stood before me naked, her eyes lowered so her lashes brushed her cheeks. She moved from one foot to the other, looking unsure, moving her arms as if she wanted to cover her breasts, but was resisting.

I reached out and put my hands on her forearms. "Please," I said, my voice gravelly, "please let me look at you." She let her arms hang loosely at her sides, licked her lips, and raised her eyes to meet mine. I was as hard as stone, and all I wanted to do was lay her down and make her mine. I allowed my eyes to roam over her naked body, from her slender shoulders to her small, round breasts with their deep pink nipples—puckered under my stare—to her flat stomach, and down farther to the V of dark curls between her thighs.

"You're perfect," I told her. There wasn't another man on the planet who had gazed upon her like this. *Only me.* "My Lily, my ghost," I smiled, "my dream. Only mine." I leaned back in and kissed her again, deeply, moving down her neck as she arched her head back and panted sweet little sounds of pleasure. When my mouth found her nipple, she jerked and mewled, grinding her pelvis into mine. I licked and sucked, bringing one hand around her waist to hold her steady as I tasted her. My other hand skimmed down her ribs, my fingers moving over each tender bone, skating over her belly and finally down to the warm place between her thighs. Warm and so wet. So ready. "Lily," I choked, shivering slightly at the power of my desire for her.

She broke from my embrace, stepping backward and sitting down on the bed behind her. I pulled my shirt off and kicked off my shoes, bending to quickly remove my socks, and when I stood again to unbutton my jeans, Lily had pulled the sheets back and was lying naked on the bed. For a moment my hands stilled, and my mind went completely, utterly blank. I let my jeans fall and stepped out of them and then my boxers, kneeling on the bed between her thighs and kissing her lips. When I pulled away, I cupped her warmth with my hand. She moaned. "Lily, you have no idea how much I want you, how beautiful you look." She gazed at me with such tenderness, my heart squeezed. I came down on top of her and rubbed my nose on hers, smiling, filled with so much love for the incredible girl beneath me. She was so soft, like silk.

She brought a hand up to her cheek and closed her eyes, raising her eyebrows and laughing softly. "Am I supposed to be this nervous?"

I smiled. "I think it's normal. But I won't do anything you don't want me to do, okay?"

"Okay," she whispered, pulling me in for another kiss. Her hand moved tentatively between our bodies, and I pulled back to let her explore, releasing a breath, trembling in an effort to control my own breathing. Her fingers touched the head of my erection, and I gasped as she explored me, the look on her face intent and awed. "You feel like velvet," she said and I smiled before kissing her again.

"Wrap your fingers around me. Hold me in your hand," I begged her. She did as I instructed, and I moaned. It felt like heaven. She ran her fingers up and down my shaft until I thought I'd explode in her hand. My knee was between her legs, and as she touched me, she pressed against my thigh, moaning softly.

"Are you sure you want this, Lily?" I whispered.

"Yes, yes," she said, "please."

I was trembling, and not from the pills this time. I could almost feel myself pushing into her warm, welcoming heat and knew just how she'd feel all around me. I nodded, leaning up and checking the bedside table for the condom I hoped to God was there. It was. Good ol' Brandon. I ripped it open and Lily watched me with wide eyes as I rolled it on. I leaned in and kissed her again, lowering my hand between her legs and bringing her silken liquid up to the swollen bud that made her cry out when I circled it with my finger. "Oh God, oh God," she breathed, bucking upward.

Leaning back in, I took one nipple into my mouth while I used my finger to touch and play between her legs. After a minute, she began circling her hips and moaning, and then she came with a gasping cry and a long shudder. So responsive. *Breathtaking.* Her eyes flew open, and she blinked several times the way she had the first time I'd made her come, as if she wasn't sure exactly what had happened. I couldn't help grinning as I kissed her again.

Watching her writhe in pleasure had practically undone me. I put one hand behind her knee and pulled her leg up, opening her to me. "Guide me in," I said. "I won't go deeper unless you tell me to."

She lifted her head and wrapped her fingers around me and lined me up at her entrance. Then she lay back and looked up into my eyes as I pushed just the head of my penis inside, hissing out at the tight clamp of her body. "Jesus, Lily," I said. "You feel so good."

"More," she said, and a shiver ran down my spine as I pushed inside.

"That okay?" I choked out. I wanted to pound myself inside her so badly I was aching, desperate. She nodded her head, but her expression had become pained.

"More," she said, but there was an edge of hesitation in her voice. When I didn't move, she repeated the word with more force. "More."

I breathed deeply for a second, lowering my face to the crook of her neck and then with one swift motion, I pushed all the way inside her, growling with the intense, gripping pleasure, pinpoints of light bursting before my eyes.

Lily's body went rigid, and when I lifted my head she was biting her lip and there were tears in her eyes. "That's the worst of it," I said. "I promise. I'll make it better now, okay? Trust me?"

Her eyes met mine and there, joined with her, the moment felt profound. It felt more than physical. It felt like our hearts were joined, too. I'd never experienced this before. Never. "Yes," she whispered again, touching my face very gently. "Yes, Boy Scout, I trust you." My heart squeezed as I felt her body relax. I understood the gift she was giving me—not just her body, but her open trust, her willingness to be so vulnerable. Though instinct was instructing me to thrust and pound, I moved slowly, gently, letting her body grow accustomed to mine.

"Better?" I asked. "Okay?"

She nodded. "Yes, better. That feels nice." And I began to move, in and out, her body wrapped so tightly around me, I thought I'd die of pleasure. "I love you," I chanted. "I love you." I did, I loved her. I had never loved anyone like I loved Lily, and I knew I never would.

"I love you, too," she whispered into my ear. I felt the wetness of her tears on my cheek and wondered why she was crying, hoping it was because of the intensity of this experience. "I love you, Boy Scout."

Thrusting into her once more, my abdomen tightened, and I pressed deeply as my body shuddered in release, the pleasure spreading from my cock, down my thighs and all the way to my toes. "I love you," I said again, circling my hips to milk the pleasure and then stilling. "I love you."

I burrowed my face into the side of her neck, inhaling her sweet scent, as her hands moved caressingly over my back, her fingers stilling here and there as she traced a scar, circling her finger around a small one on my shoulder blade that I couldn't remember how I'd gotten. My brain felt cloudy with happiness and pleasure. Smiling and kissing up her still-wet jaw, I ended at her lips. She was smiling, too. She tasted both salty and sweet.

"Lily of the Night," I whispered. "*My* Lily of the Night. Are you okay?"

She smiled sweetly at me and nodded. I kissed her one last time before I pulled out of her and she yelped softly.

"I know. I don't like that part either," I said. I made a quick trip to the bathroom where I flushed the condom and returned to bed.

I lay back down and pulled Lily to me, hugging her against my body. She was soft, and sweet, and warm. "Will you come home with me?"

"We are at your home," she said distractedly, running a fingertip around my nipple, watching as it hardened beneath her touch. I shivered.

"No, my real home. I don't mean tomorrow. I mean in a couple weeks. Once I'm . . . feeling better. Will you come back to San Francisco with me?"

She was quiet for a moment, her finger stilling. "I can't. My mother . . ." A slight look of confusion crossed her beautiful features, but then it disappeared, making me wonder if I'd just imagined it.

"Your mother could come with us. Hell, I'll buy your mother her own house."

She smiled. "She'd never allow that. It's just not possible."

I tilted my head to look down at her. "Lily, she can't expect you to live on the edge of the woods for the rest of your life. What kind of life do you really have out here?"

"You don't know what my life is like," she said, her voice sounding harder. "Not really."

I sighed. The last thing I wanted to do was fight with her or push her after what we'd just done. "I know. I just mean . . . aren't you lonely?"

She hesitated before answering. "Yes. Sometimes. But not tonight." She snuggled closer, covering a small yawn. "Hold me." I pulled her tighter, kissing her head. We would talk about this in a couple days when I'd gone through the worst of the withdrawals. My body tensed at the thought alone. *Here we go again.* But I'd worry about that tomorrow. Tonight I had Lily. I fell asleep holding her in my arms, the smell of *us* bringing me happiness and comfort.

At some point in the middle of the night, I woke up to hear her whimpering softly and pulled her to me more tightly. "Shh," I crooned.

"You're just dreaming."

"Don't leave me," she murmured, a note of fearful distress in her sleepy tone.

"Lily," I said, shaking her a bit. "Wake up, you're dreaming."

I could barely see her eyes open in the dark and for a second she just stared at me as if she didn't know where she was or who she was with. "Boy Scout," she finally murmured as she relaxed against me, wrapping her arms around my waist and falling back to sleep. I waited a few minutes and then got up as slowly and quietly as possible. I went to the bathroom and relieved myself and then retrieved a couple pills from the bottle I'd left in the medicine cabinet. I raised them to my lips and then hesitated. I stared at myself in the bathroom mirror for a moment, thinking of Lily, thinking of all she'd given me, feeling my love for her flow through my body like a healing balm. *I love you, Boy Scout.* I wanted to be better for Lily. She deserved more than the man I was right now. I tossed the pills in the toilet and flushed. And then I took the two bottles Taylor had brought and emptied those into the toilet, too, and flushed again, exhaling a long gust of breath. I tossed both empty bottles in the trash. That was that. Jesus, that was that.

Nestled back in bed with Lily's warm body, I somehow fell immediately back to sleep.

I woke to the sunrise streaming through the window. The beast inside was clawing at my guts.

And I was alone.

CHAPTER TWELVE

Holden

It hurt. Oh God, it hurt so badly. My body was a flaming ball of fiery pain, each muscle screaming in agony. *You can do this. You can do this. Lily. Lily.* I was just so damned thirsty. Thirsty to the point of pain. But whenever I'd tried to drink anything, it came right back up. I wanted Lily. But I couldn't let her see me this way.

You can do this.

I wanted to be back in that bed with her. I just wanted to live there forever.

You can. Once you get through this. You can.

I needed air. I groaned, managing to drag myself from the couch out to the deck where I gulped in big breaths of fresh air. A muscle in my leg seized and I screamed, grabbing the back of my thigh. I hopped a couple steps, my leg coming out from under me. I hadn't realized I was right near the top of the stairs until I was plunging down them. I heard something crack and more pain exploded in my body. I couldn't even pinpoint where—it happened too fast. And then I slammed into the concrete below, stars bursting before my eyes, right before everything went black.

I was in the woods.

I hurt and yet I kept moving forward, moving toward Lily.

I just needed Lily.

I had to find her.

Everything ached and I didn't know how long I could keep walking.

Shaking so violently I could barely see.

Lily.

I moved forward anyway, tripping, falling here and there, losing time, coming to as I stumbled forward some more.

Lily.

And then I stepped into nothing. I yelled out loudly as the earth dropped out beneath me.

Lily.

Falling.

Falling.

Pain bursting.

Lily.

****

My head was throbbing, the light too bright behind my closed lids. I grimaced, turning my head and moaning, falling halfway back into the sleep I'd been pulled from in some way I couldn't remember. My hand felt heavy and numb.

I heard a voice. Lily, it was Lily's voice. The answer to a prayer. She was talking to someone in whispered tones. I tried to pull myself out of sleep, but was too tired. Too tired. Random words and phrases floated my way, but I didn't have the strength to try to grasp them.

"Quiet, he'll hear you," Lily said.

"So what? I only said he's handsome. I'm sure he's aware, right?"

"Yes and no," Lily whispered brokenly.

"What does that mean?" the other woman demanded.

"I'll tell you once he's taken care of," Lily said. Why did she sound so sad?

I drifted away again, only momentarily. "Dangerous?" I heard Lily ask.

"Yes, the handsome ones are *always* the most dangerous," the woman muttered.

"He's not dangerous," Lily said.

"That's what you think now."

I floated closer to the surface, trying once more to pull myself from the drugging grip of sleep. *Trying. Failing. Falling back down, down, down. Lily.* I heard Lily's voice again, scattered words, but couldn't string them together.

I came to and the light beyond my closed lids was different. How much time had passed? "Lily," I croaked, grasping on to the one word that made me want to fight to come awake, try to open my eyes. The light was too bright, though, and I clenched them shut. "I tried to get to you, I tried so hard . . ."

"Shush. Lily's not here, but she'll be back shortly. Just rest. You almost killed yourself, but Lily brought you here. You're safe now."

I fell back to sleep, my last thought being that I'd been abducted by a witch.

When I woke again, I was in a tub of water in front of a fire. "Are you cooking me?" I asked dazedly, not sure I cared.

"Your muscles were seizing," came the female voice. "Hot water will help. How long have you been addicted to pain medication?"

I laid my head back, her question causing me to try to use my brain. It felt all muddled. I brought my hands up and used the heels of my hands to massage my temples. "Not that long. A couple months."

The woman snorted. "That's plenty long enough."

"How did you know?"

The woman paused for a moment. "I just do."

"How'd I end up here?"

"You threw yourself right off a cliff I guess."

That didn't feel right. I searched my memory. "No, I didn't," I said. "I tripped."

"Okay. Well, your finger is broken and your ribs are bruised. You're lucky that's the extent of the damage. You were also dangerously dehydrated."

I opened my eyes as her footsteps came closer, and she stoked the fire. An old woman with short, salt-and-pepper hair and a face that was still lovely despite her advanced age. She vaguely resembled Lily.

"Who are you?" I asked. "Where's Lily's mother?"

"That's nothing for you to concern yourself with. You have enough problems of your own. Focus on getting better." I cringed from a muscle spasm in my calf.

I waited for more, but she didn't offer it. My brain was still foggy, and my body felt like a dead weight. I decided not to press the issue. "Lily?" I asked.

"I sent her away for a little while. Detoxing is messy and involves lots of personal bodily functions. I didn't believe you'd want her cleaning you up."

I grimaced. No, I didn't. "Thank you," I said. "Thank you for that." I felt grateful to this woman for giving me that small dignity.

She shrugged. "The worst of that is over, I think."

"How long have I been here?" I asked, sinking more deeply into the hot water. It felt so good. I opened my eyes long enough to glance around. The room looked like an old library, with an ornate, marble fireplace taking up a large portion of one wall, bookshelves filled with books all along the others, and a sitting area right behind the tub.

"Four days." *Four days.* Four days of no pills. A surge of pride ran down my spine. The worst was over. It must be.

"When will she be back?" I asked.

The woman paused, not looking at me, still stoking the fire. "Tonight. Are you hungry?" I considered her question, realizing I actually was.

"I think I could eat. Maybe I should. Maybe that'd be good."

She handed me a towel and looked away but didn't seem embarrassed by this situation. I thought maybe she was uncomfortable with me being there in general, though I wasn't sure why. My brain was still so foggy, and I was disoriented. I stood up slowly, using the towel to cover myself, and stepped gingerly out of the tub onto the faded Oriental rug on the floor. I wrapped the towel around my waist. "How'd you get me into this tub?"

"You walked. I just supported you. The fogginess should start diminishing now that you're moving around. And your clothes are in that bedroom." She pointed to an open door.

I nodded and walked toward it. My legs felt like they weighed ten tons each. It took all my energy to pull on my clothes. The woman brought me to the sitting area, and bending over a coffee table in front of the small couch, I ate some kind of vegetable stew filled with potatoes and a thick, rich broth. It was delicious and I'd have eaten more if I had the strength. I drank two glasses of water and could barely keep my eyes open.

The woman helped me back to the small bedroom where I'd changed my clothes and this time, I took a moment to look around. It had a twin bed in the corner and a dresser against the wall. There were personal knickknacks everywhere—a pink stone that was so smooth it looked like it'd been polished that way, a bird's nest, feathers of all colors and sizes, a basket full of pine cones, even a small, chipped arrowhead . . . things from the forest. "This is Lily's room, isn't it?"

As I walked past her, the woman nodded and inclined her head toward the bed, telling me to get in. I wasn't going to argue. I'd just sleep for a little while and be awake when Lily got back. "Thank you," I murmured, not turning around. "Thank you for helping me." The woman didn't reply. I only heard the click of the door being shut. I undressed quickly and climbed into bed. The pillow smelled like Lily. I fell asleep immediately, only coming to momentarily when I heard hushed arguing on the other side of the door. I could only make out Lily's words.

"You don't know that. You don't know unless . . ."

". . . there must be a way." Quiet weeping.

"I can be. I can be what he needs."

More weeping.

Lily.

I tried to pull myself fully out of sleep, pull myself toward her, but couldn't.

I dreamed of Ryan. He came to me through the fog, speaking to me, reminding me, telling me his story because I'd forgotten. *Oh God, I'd forgotten.* No, I hadn't forgotten. I hadn't wanted to hear. I'd shut it out, abandoned him. Abandoned *myself.* Yes, I'd abandoned myself. Because I'd thought I deserved it.

My best friend held out his hand to me and I gasped, the image becoming clearer and clearer as he moved closer. I wanted to look away in shame and an overwhelming sense of . . . fear. I was going to be lost, alone. But he was smiling, and he looked . . . happy. "Forgive me," I choked.

"There's nothing to forgive. It wasn't your fault. None of it was your fault," he said. "I did what I was meant to do in this life. It's time to let me go now." No, no, no, no.

I woke up with tears on my face and warm arms wrapped around me. "Shh," she crooned. "I'm here. I'm right here."

"Lily," I choked out, burrowing my head into her chest. "Oh God, Lily." She held me as I cried, held me as it all came back. She was my strength as the truth dragged me under. When the final sobs wracked my body, I tipped my head back and looked up into her sweet, gentle face. She brushed the hair back from my forehead and kissed my cheeks tenderly. There was so much understanding in her expression. "Do you know about me? Do you know?" I asked.

She nodded slowly and then kissed me again. "Yes, love."

I moved my eyes over her face, trying to read her expression, trying to understand what she felt for me now that she knew. I didn't know what *I* felt for me now that *I* knew.

"It shattered me, Lily. Losing him, it," I took a big shuddery breath, "it shattered me."

"I know, Boy Scout, I know."

And it sounded as if she *did.* "He was the other half of me."

She shook her head. "No, he was your best friend. You're a whole man. You're not half of anyone."

Her face was so beautiful, so sorrowful, so filled with compassion. It was all too much, too much. I grimaced from the pain in my head. "No,

I'm *not* a whole man. Maybe you don't even know me. Do you feel that way? You must."

"No," she said softly, and then with more force, "no. I know your superpower is flying." She smiled. "And I know you like football, and Star Wars, and jazz music, the old kind." Her fingers skated down my cheek, and I leaned in to them. "I know you like comic books, and museums, and fireworks, and travel. If I cooked for you, I'd make you pancakes even if it was midnight, and then I'd take you to a movie in an empty theater on a Tuesday, in a snowstorm. And then," her voice grew even quieter, "we'd come home, and you'd make love to me so sweetly I'd want to cry and sing at the same time. I know you're kind and good and that you love people with your entire heart and mind. I know that when you love someone, you'll love them forever. Are all those things true, Boy Scout?" Her fingers found the scars on my back and traced them lightly, lovingly, her fingertips finding the small, scattered divots.

"Yes," I breathed. "Yes, Lily," I murmured. It was the only thing in me right then. Only her. Only how much I loved her.

Under the blankets, Lily's hand roamed across my hip, her fingernails raking softly down my outer thigh. I shivered, hardening. Her smell, the soft feel of her was all around me, and I needed her so desperately. I needed her to remind me that I was real.

"Lily," I whispered again, my own hands roaming her body now. She was only wearing her bra and underwear and she quickly removed them, helping me take off my boxers. My body hurt, felt bruised all over, but I didn't care. Her lips found mine and I sighed, tasting her, basking in the comfort of her mouth on mine, her tongue tangled with my own. Moaning softly, she gripped me in her hand and stroked me several times until I was throbbing. She positioned her hips and guided me inside her under the blankets. I moaned at the soft, wet grip of her flesh around my own. "Oh," I moaned. "Oh God." Lily moaned, too, as our lips met. This was relief. This was heaven. Warm under the blankets, a safe haven, my body connected to Lily's as we moved together, seeking to find comfort in each other's bodies.

Minutes later, we came together, gripping one another and both crying out as softly as possible. We kept kissing for long minutes as we came back down to earth, Lily smiling softly against my mouth. I wanted to fall asleep again. Making love to Lily had zapped the very last of my energy. Despite her smile, a tear rolled down her cheek. "You know you don't need me anymore, right?" A numb sort of panic arced through me.

"No, no, I'll always need you. Always. I'll always love you." Why did it sound as if she was saying goodbye? I struggled to think. And I was still so tired . . . so very, very tired. I still felt like a ten-ton boulder was sitting on my head. It hurt to think.

Her expression was sad. "No, you need to go get your life back, Boy Scout. You're strong enough now." I tried to keep my eyes open—to keep them on her—but my lids were so heavy. I wondered blearily if the woman who'd cared for me had given me something to make me sleep.

"I'll always love you, Boy Scout. Always." It was the last thing I heard before sleep claimed me once again, stealing me from Lily's arms.

****

"**H**ey, buddy, you awake? Wake up, man." I blinked, grimacing against the bright light coming in through the window. Squinting, I opened my eyes, adjusting to the light.

"Brandon?" I asked, my voice scratchy.

"Yeah, it's me. How are you? Jesus, you look like you've been beaten up."

I sat up slowly, looking around. I was in bed at the lodge. I scratched my head, things slowly falling into place inside my head. How had I gotten here? I'd been in bed with Lily. How in the world had Lily and the other woman gotten me back to the lodge? I took a few more minutes, just staring into space as all the pieces came together . . . thinking about everything that had happened since I'd been here. I looked down at my naked chest, bandages wrapped around my torso. There were large black and blue bruises everywhere, a few just turning a sickly yellow. My ribs still ached. A good portion of me still ached. My finger was in a splint and wrapped with bandages as well. Inhaling a sharp breath, the weight of it all—everything I'd experienced, everything I'd realized—crushing my chest. I leaned back against the headboard, gripping my hair with my good hand. "Where's Lily?"

Brandon frowned, sitting down at the end of the bed. "Lily?"

"You haven't seen her?" I asked, pulling myself up just a little bit more. "I just can't figure out how they got me back here." I still felt groggy, but my body felt decent, and my mind was mostly clear, or clearing anyway. Clearer than it'd been in months. I thought about the rooms I'd been in. My God, I'd been at Whittington. The height of the ceilings, the way the paint had been peeling on the walls, the similarity to the pictures I'd looked at online. I didn't understand why Lily had brought me to an abandoned hospital, why she had a room set up there, but . . . "She must have gone back. I have to go find her." I sighed, closing my eyes again, gathering the strength to get out of bed.

"Okay, but wait, I . . ." He pursed his lips, his expression worried. "Things went well for you here? You're feeling better? Taylor finally 'fessed up that she came out here. Sorry about that, by the way. But she said you were still acting a little strange."

"Yeah, I was I guess. I didn't exactly expect to see her." I sighed. "But I'm feeling better now. I don't know. I just need to see Lily."

"But you're clear, right?" He eyed me. "You know your name, don't you? You know why you're here?"

My eyes met his. *I did. Oh God. Oh God, it hurt.* "Yes," I said, my voice wobbly. "Yes, my name is Ryan. Ryan Ellis."

He released a relieved breath. "And you know that Holden—"

"Holden is dead, I know," I said, an intense ache gripping my chest. My shoulders began to shake. "I know. Yes, I know it all now. I remember. I know."

CHAPTER THIRTEEN

"What are you doing out here all alone? The party's inside," Holden *slurred, weaving slightly before falling down in the chair next to mine and running his hand through his short, dark hair.*

I took a sip of my beer and glanced over at him. Despite being drunk, he looked miserable. He always looked miserable lately. "I needed some quiet," I said. "I guess I'm just not in the party mood."

"When are you ever in the party mood?"

I raised my beer to him in agreement. "Not often." But I'd come tonight to look out for Holden. He seemed to want to mess his life up these days. As if he was going out of his way to fuck up.

He made a sound of annoyance. "Taylor's looking for you. Pretty sure she wants you, man."

She did. She'd made that plenty clear. "Not interested. Taylor's a bitch only interested in her own status. I don't know why you went out with her at all."

"She's good in bed."

"I'm sure she is. She gets plenty of practice."

Holden gave a short laugh that died on his lips.

"What's the plan, Holden?" I asked, staring over at him. He knew what I was asking.

His head fell back on the chair. "My plan is to be amazing and awesome," he said dully, delivering the line he'd used so many times. Until recently, it had been said with humor and vibrancy. It used to make me smile.

127

"You used to be amazing and awesome all the time," I said, clearing my throat. My voice sounded scratchy. Now he was just . . . sad. Why? Why was he so fucking sad?

"How about we get out of here?" I asked. "Away from all these people. I'll treat you to some breakfast. Denny's? Moons Over my Hammy?"

"You're the one who likes breakfast for dinner. And you just like saying Moons Over my Hammy."

I gave him a wan smile. It was true, I did. Best breakfast name ever. "What's not to like about breakfast for dinner?"

He shrugged, looking genuinely confused. "I don't know. It's like I can't find it in me to like anything these days."

"That's the pills, Holden. You've gotta get off the pills. Your knee's been healed for months now."

"The pills might be the only things I actually do like."

I pressed my lips together, at a loss. As I stood, I said, "Well, if you're not going to help yourself, Holden, there's nothing I can do for you." Feeling useless, I walked to the sliding glass door leading inside.

"Jesus, have you seen this sunset?" he asked.

I paused and glanced back. Holden had walked to the rail of the balcony. He looked . . . lost, yet eerily calm.

"I never fucking look at sunsets anymore. You ever just . . . enjoy something for the sake of it anymore, Ry?"

I released the door handle. "Yeah," I said. "I mean, I try."

He nodded. "That's good," he said, and I heard the tears in his voice. I went still. Was Holden crying? He leaned over the wrought-iron rail of the balcony. "It's so high up," he said, leaning even farther.

"Holden, what the fuck?"

"It's good to feel something, though, isn't it?" His voice was muffled and upside down.

I took a step toward him and in that moment, he flipped over the railing. "Holy fuck!" I shouted, lunging toward him. He let out a yell, grabbing one of the rail spindles, hanging by one hand. I went down on my knees and wrapped my hands around his. "Help!" I yelled behind me,

"Help!" But the party inside was too loud. No one could hear me. "Don't let go, Holden." I was panting, my heart beating out of my chest in terror. "I'm going to stand up and lean over and I want you to grab my hand. Okay, Holden, grab my hand. I won't let you fall. I won't let you fall."

As I stood, my legs were shaking so badly, I could barely move. But I stood and I leaned over, holding my hand out to him. "Grab on," I choked out. "Grab my hand, Holden." His eyes were wild as he reached up and took my hand. I let out a whoosh of air, my heart hammering so hard. "Okay, okay, I've got you, okay? I'm going to pull you up now. Work with me, okay?" I started to pull him up, both my hands clasped around his, his other hand on the balcony. He suddenly let go of the ledge and only held on to me. I grunted with the sudden pull of holding over two hundred pounds of weight. My hands were shaking and my arms were throbbing. I couldn't even force out words.

"I'm sorry, Ry. I'm just too tired," he said, something coming into his eyes that caused a sharp spike of terror to stab through my gut. Something . . . something. I didn't know what. His hand loosened in mine, our sweaty palms slipping apart as I screamed. And as his body hit the ground below with a loud thud, I shattered.

He was gone.

He was gone.

Gone.

My hero was gone.

CHAPTER FOURTEEN

Ryan

I'd convinced Brandon to take me to Whittington. He'd humored me with a worried frown on his face. But I hadn't cared. I'd been desperate to find Lily. When we got to the gate, though, there was a rusty padlock on it that hadn't been there before. "It was open last time," I'd mumbled. After walking around the perimeter, we found a broken portion of the gate next to the garden and squeezed through.

The garden obviously hadn't been maintained in a very long time, but it was bursting with color, perhaps even more beautiful for its wildness, the way vines grew up the brick wall and everything blended together. Funny the things you notice even when your heart is breaking.

"This is the creepiest shit I've ever done," Brandon had muttered, as he'd followed me inside the building through the front door that was still unlocked from the last time I'd been here. "But kinda awesome, too," he'd admitted, a small chuckle following his words. For fifteen minutes, we'd wandered the mostly empty hallways, stepping around rusted wheelchairs, pushing aside heavy metal doors, looking inside small rooms that must have been cells once upon a time, me calling Lily's name again and again. That's when I'd found the rooms I'd recognized— the rooms I'd detoxed in. They were empty. There was no furniture, except a metal bedframe in the room where I'd made love to Lily.

I had, hadn't I?

I'd sagged against the doorframe, massaging my head, gasping for breath, whispering her name. *I knew this place.* I'd *been* here before.

No, no, no. "I don't understand," I'd gasped out.

Brandon's hand had gripped my shoulder. "Man, there's no Lily. Okay, whoever you thought you saw—"

"No!" I'd insisted, shrugging his hand off, despair racing through my veins. "No, I didn't fucking *imagine* her. No. Lily! Jesus, Lily, please, please," I'd choked, gripping my head in my hands. God, had I made her up? Jesus, Jesus, *Jesus.* No, no, she was real. I wouldn't believe otherwise.

"Did you bring drugs with you, Ryan?" Brandon had finally asked. "Did you sneak drugs into your bag?"

I'd let out a shuddery breath. "Yes, but they weren't *hallucinogens.* They were pain pills. And . . . Look," I'd said excitedly, going over to the fireplace mantle, "no dust. How *could* there be no dust in here unless someone *had* been using it?" I'd looked at him expectantly, perhaps a little desperately.

Brandon's hands had been in his pockets and he'd stared at me piteously and shrugged. "It's in the middle of the building? Sealed up tight. I don't know," he'd said. Clearly he hadn't been convinced pain pills couldn't make me high enough to see shit, *or* he'd thought I was completely off my rocker. God, I *was.* I was off my rocker.

Oh my God. I was insane.

My father had told me I was crazy, and he was right.

He was *right.*

I was crazy.

I was worthless.

"No," I'd said weakly.

I had let Brandon lead me out of there. No. *Lily, Lily, Lily . . .*

CHAPTER FIFTEEN

Ryan

I saw her everywhere. Walking down sidewalks, in crowded restaurants, once in the brief flash of dark hair and white lace right before an elevator door closed. Without thinking, my heart thundering in my chest, I'd run up four flights of stairs only to find that it was someone else. Someone holding a little boy's hand. She'd pulled him closer to her side as she'd exited the elevator, looking at me warily as if I might grab him and run.

Those were the times I still doubted my own sanity, still questioned whether she had ever existed at all. But then I'd remember the feel of her fingertips on my skin, the slippery silk of her hair, the sound of her laughter, and the way I loved her still, and I'd know, *I'd know*, deep down to my soul that she was real.

I dreamed of her, and in the darkness, she held me in her arms. In the darkness, she whispered that I was strong enough to hold on, that I was worthy of the love she'd given, and she reminded me who I was before I was anyone at all.

My Lily of the Night. Only of the moon.

Because now, just as then, when daylight came, she was no longer there.

CHAPTER SIXTEEN

Ryan

"**D**uring the time you were in Colorado, did you ever question whether you were really Holden?" Dr. Katz asked. She never wrote anything on the notepad on her lap, so I wondered why she had it sitting there. Maybe she vigorously scrawled out notes between appointments and wanted to make sure it was at the ready. Maybe she just held it to look professional. Did I want a doctor who needed props to convince her patient she was professional?

I'd seen a psychiatrist the first six months I was back in San Francisco, but he seemed less interested in hearing my story than in prescribing medication. The last thing I'd thought I needed was more damn pills. And so about a month ago, I'd made an appointment with a psychologist. Maybe I just needed to talk to someone. This was only my third appointment, and despite her notepad prop, I liked her.

I shook my head. "No. I mean, there were places I think I kept myself from going in my mind, things that felt wrong that I didn't choose to investigate, but . . . no. I never actually questioned it. I had all his *thoughts*, all his *feelings*, all his *memories*. For that time, I *was* him. Only . . . I *wasn't* either. It's so damned confusing. Even for me."

She nodded her head. "Ryan, had you ever 'gone away' in your head before this?"

I sighed, moving my thoughts back to her question. I'd thought about it a lot. "Yeah, when I was a kid. My dad, he, well, to put it bluntly, he beat the shit out of me on a pretty regular basis." I paused, swallowing. Goddamn, the very memory of that man was still so painful. He had put me in a cage sometimes to punish me like a worthless animal. *Bark like a dog! Bark like a dog, you dirty fucking animal. Bark like the dog you are and I'll let you out.* He'd died seven years ago, and I hadn't even flown back for his funeral. I'd never said goodbye. I'd thought of it as a small way to get him back, but in reality, maybe I'd been the only one damaged. I'd never gotten closure. As if that was even possible. "I tried to harden myself, but . . . I never could. I just never could." I sighed. "So instead, I got pretty adept at going somewhere else in my mind, you know? I'd just . . . leave. I got so good at it that after a while I didn't even feel the punches, the burns. Pissed him off, you know, me not reacting. But I couldn't blank out and still pretend it hurt, so I just got beat extra hard. Didn't matter though." I shook my head.

"Why didn't it matter, Ryan?"

"Because there was nothing I could do to stop it. I just had to figure out how to survive it."

"Did you ever become someone else during those times, Ryan?"

"No. Never."

She nodded, chewing on the end of her pen, regarding me pensively. *Did she not believe me?*

"I saw in your file you were hospitalized one time. What was the reason for that hospitalization?"

I took a deep breath. "I . . . I was in college. I was under stress, lonely—"

"Holden wasn't with you then."

"Right. I went to Arizona State. I wanted to get far away from Ohio, far away from my father. I just didn't realize how hard it'd be . . ." My words floated away.

"Go on."

"I just . . . I had a lot of anxiety. I just wasn't doing well."

"But your hospital stay, that helped you?"

"It did. I got back on track and was able to return to school, graduate, start my career."

Dr. Katz watched me again for a minute and I shifted in my seat under her penetrating gaze. "So, initially, with your father, you just removed yourself mentally from the situation. That's how you survived it. Until Holden?"

Pain squeezed my heart. Would I miss him forever? *Would I want it any other way?* I relaxed, breathing deeply. "Yes, until Holden. He befriended me." I laughed softly. "I mean, that sounds passive. And Holden was never passive—not like me. He'd practically demanded I be his friend. It's the only way it would have worked, you know? I was so mistrusting of everyone. But Holden, he was like this *force*, this force of just . . . energy and goodness."

"You worshipped him."

I paused, considering that. "I guess . . . yeah, I guess. But it wasn't because he was a great football player, or that he was a big shot or a celebrity. I loved Holden because he had this way about him . . . somehow he made every single person in the room feel like they were the most important one there. And how did he *do* that? It always amazed me. He . . . it's hard to explain. You had to know him." I paused again. "He was just so genuine. And his parents were such good people, too." Running my hand through my hair, I allowed the memories in. "I got to finally experience what a family was supposed to be." *If you're not going to help yourself, there's nothing I can do for you,* I'd told him. I'd said that to him after everything he'd done for me. After all the times he'd come to my rescue. After all of his persistence, I'd left him to fend for himself that night. If only I'd stayed to talk to him, to reassure him, to force him off that balcony before . . . I'd failed him. God, I'd *failed* him, and it still burned like a knife that would forever be planted in my gut. It sliced into me each time I moved. I felt my mind get foggy with grief and fought to pull myself to the surface.

Dr. Katz nodded again. "Did Holden's parents know what your dad did to you?"

I swallowed. "Yeah. I mean, they saw the bruises. They wanted to turn him in, but I refused. I didn't have anyone else, and I didn't want to go into foster care."

"Did it bother you that Holden's parents didn't offer to adopt you?"

"They practically *did* adopt me, even though they didn't have much money either. And once they understood what was happening at home, Mr. Scott went to see my dad. I don't know what was said, but my dad mostly laid off me after that. Mostly."

"So they did protect you?"

"Yeah," I choked out. "Yeah, they did."

"And they passed away the year before Holden?" she asked.

I nodded, a lump moving up my throat. "They were older. They'd had him later in life." It'd hit us both hard. Sometimes I almost felt like I took it harder than he did . . . But I also knew it was part of the reason Holden had gotten addicted to the pills, why they had been so appealing to him.

"I can understand why you were so attached to Holden, why you saw him as not only your friend, but your hero, your savior. I can see that, Ryan."

My chest felt tight. "Yeah," I sighed. "We did everything together. We went to different colleges, but then he got drafted to the 49ers and he helped me get the interview for the job as their athletic trainer." He'd been different after that, though. Somehow the fame had seemed to . . . *dim* him. It dimmed the light that had been Holden's spirit. And then he'd gotten injured and started taking pain pills . . . The same pain pills I'd eventually started taking to take up where he'd left off. Somehow it'd been less painful than accepting he was dead. It had been the only way I had to keep *him* alive and make myself disappear. "Do you think I'm crazy, Dr. Katz?" I tried to laugh, but it came out strange, choked.

"Crazy? I try not to use that word in my diagnoses, Ryan." She smiled. "We're all crazy in our own ways. Would I diagnose you with a mental illness? I would say that I somewhat agree with the psychiatrist you originally saw, Dr.—"

"Hammond," I offered.

"Yes, Dr. Hammond. He diagnosed you with a dissociative disorder brought on by trauma. I would tend to agree, based on our sessions so far, although the disorder generally pertains to the patient having two or more personalities. You present differently than some other patients in that you took over a real person's identity and gave up your own. Nevertheless, that would be my diagnosis if I had to check a box. Unfortunately, the mind doesn't always fit itself into neat little boxes, does it?" She gave me a faint smile before continuing. "In your case, though, it makes sense, does it not? You learned early on how to separate your mind from grief, from pain. And then when Holden died, you experienced trauma once again and fell back on your reinforced and conditioned response: mental removal. You blamed yourself for his death. You blamed *yourself* for not seeing the extent of his unhappiness, and for not being able to do anything to help him. I think that in an effort to understand it, you *became* him. You looked to save him as he saved you, and in so doing, escaped a bit of your own grief. And the pain pills made it easier, of course, to distract yourself from the true issue, although they did not cause this disorder."

I leaned my head back, looking up at the ceiling. "That sounds . . . crazy. How did I even manage to put one foot in front of the other while I was that out of my mind?"

When I looked back down, Dr. Katz gave me another small smile. "The mind can be very mysterious. There are things that can break us all. But people with mental disorders still often hold jobs requiring complex skills, and contribute to society in a number of valuable ways. But if we're using the word crazy to cover the broad spectrum of mental sufferings, including yours, then yes, you were crazy for a time. Do you still feel crazy?"

I released a breath of air, looking out the window, unseeing for a moment. Did I feel crazy? Mostly, no. I recalled that sense of being in a dream that I'd felt after Holden died and the entire time I was at Brandon's lodge. I had walked and talked, convinced myself I was Holden, lived his life, picked up right where he'd left off, but I'd had no real connection to anything. *Until Lily . . .* It's how she'd brought me back, made me *want* to face reality again. "No," I finally answered. "I still feel sad. Maybe I'll always feel sad." It wasn't the kind of sorrow that brought tears anymore, though. The sadness simply was part of me now. It had settled into my bones and I just kind of figured it'd always be there. "But I don't feel crazy."

I couldn't help but think of Whittington. If I'd lived a hundred years ago, I'd be one of those people drooling in a corner somewhere, perhaps lobotomized, my organs removed. At the very least, I'd be forgotten . . . invisible, worthless. A shameful stain on my family and society.

She nodded. "Ryan, do you think that, in part, you became Holden because you believed you should have been the one to die that night? Did you wish it had been you instead of him?"

I studied my hands. "Yes. Sometimes I *still* think that."

"You realize, of course, that's your father speaking, right? Neither of you deserved to die. Not Holden, and not you."

I sighed. "I know," I finally said. But especially not him. Not him. *He* was the superhero, the golden boy.

"Good." Dr. Katz paused. "Do you still think about the girl? Do you still question her existence?"

That was a more difficult question to answer. I'd been back to Whittington every month for the first nine months. I'd wander the halls, calling for Lily, looking for anything that might indicate she'd been back. I'd go into the woods and call for her, but she never appeared. She wasn't there. I looked for any evidence that she'd existed, but couldn't find a thing. It made me feel like she *had* been a part of what my mind had done while I was there—just a beautiful part of my crazy. But how could that be? She'd expressed thoughts that weren't mine. She'd said things I wouldn't have even known. *Hadn't she?* I'd made love to her, learned her body. I ran my fingers through my hair, the memory of Lily doing the same that first night on the rock coming back to me. "I don't know," I said. "I don't think so, but . . . I have no proof other than the fact that I still miss her so damn much. Do you think she was a figment of my imagination?"

"I can't say, Ryan." She chewed on the end of her pen for a moment. "The fact that she just disappeared right at the moment you admitted to yourself who you really are indicates there was some connection . . ."

Sadness filled my chest. "I know. It does seem like too much of a coincidence."

"But maybe it is just that—a coincidence. Perhaps the girl, Lily, had some other reason to leave."

"Maybe." I sighed. "The thing is, if I really did create her—created a whole *person*, created feelings around that person—then it just adds to my insanity. It could indicate I do require several diagnoses."

"No one *requires* a diagnosis. A diagnosis of something doesn't change the disorder, it just makes it easier to treat. But if Lily *was* a symptom of your grief, she's gone now."

"I know," I said dismally. "But, God, she *saved* me. In so many ways . . ."

"And perhaps that was her role. Perhaps you *created* her to save you. Perhaps if you search your memory, you'll find that you'd done the same thing before. Perhaps not. The point, though, is that she did her job and then it was time for her to go. It was time for your mind to let go of her."

You know you don't need me anymore, right? But I did. I did need her.

"Wow, that sounds *really* crazy," I murmured.

Dr. Katz laughed softly again. "They say crazy people rarely question their own sanity."

"Who's *they*?"

"The crazy people," Dr. Katz deadpanned.

I laughed and she grinned. "And the *other* piece of good news is that dissociative disorders respond very well to therapy, specifically individual psychotherapy. I'm glad you found me."

"Yeah, me too."

She smiled momentarily and then her expression became serious. "It has been almost a year since you've been back in San Francisco, though. Are you going out with friends? Are you dating again, Ryan?"

"No," I said. "I haven't been interested. And truthfully, I've felt like I needed to focus on getting myself better again."

"Good choice. But don't cut yourself off from other people. You deserve happiness, Ryan. You deserve love. It might be time to make a few social plans, get out, test the waters."

I smiled. "Okay, I'll think about it."

"Good. Very good. You've made wonderful progress today. Our hour's up, but I'll see you next week."

CHAPTER SEVENTEEN

Ryan

Returning to work had been one of the easier transitions. The guys had welcomed me back with open arms. Of course, they had never completely understood the extent of what had been going on inside my head. They'd seen me fall apart, start taking pain pills. They'd seen me participate in the same behavior as Holden before he'd died: partying, meaningless sex, reckless driving. They'd even seen me refer to myself as Holden, but apparently they'd just thought it was me acting out as part of the grieving process. Or perhaps as an effect of the drugs and alcohol. They hadn't understood how deeply disturbed I'd been. Otherwise, I'd probably have been committed instead of flown by private helicopter to a remote, luxury lodge. They hadn't known, and that was good because they'd probably never trust me again if they *had* known the whole truth. Only Dr. Katz knew . . . Dr. Katz and Lily.

Of course, maybe Lily knew it because *I* knew it. "Jesus." I sighed, despair making my head ache.

"Ryan my man," Jameson, a team member said, entering my office. "How's it hanging?"

"Hey, Jameson. Not bad. What's up? How's the shoulder?"

Jameson rotated it as if in habit. "Better. A lot better. Hey, a bunch of us are going out tonight. Join us."

"Oh, nah, I gotta work in the morning."

"I didn't say you had to get trashed. I know you're past that. I just meant you haven't hung out with any of us in almost a year. We miss you, man." He slapped me on the back and I smiled. "Come on, it will be like your coming-out party. Your quinceañera." He did a few salsa steps. I laughed. "What do you say? There's a whole world out there, sport."

"What the hell? Okay." I had been nervous about going out, about being around the team, around alcohol. But maybe the doc was right. I had to live in the world at some point.

"Good deal. Go home and get yourself dolled up in your party dress and meet us there at nine."

I chuckled. "See you then."

****

The team had decided to go a bar in the financial district of San Francisco, decorated to mimic a pirate ship with old wooden barrels on the walls and ceilings. Jameson had texted to let me know the guys had a table on the mezzanine level. I made my way through the crowded bar and the guys all stood and gave me a round of cheers as I took a seat. I motioned for them all to sit down, embarrassed. "Okay, okay," I said as they laughed. "Very funny." Mike, a team running back grabbed my shoulder and shook me.

"Welcome back to the land of the living," he said and I couldn't help laughing. It was either that or cry and I figured I'd cried enough for one lifetime. I tried my best to tamp down my anxiety, tune out the overly loud, drunken noise all around me, ignore the smell of alcohol, and just focus on my buddies.

We talked and laughed for a while, and I was genuinely having a decent time, but someone ordered a Jack and Coke.

That had been Holden's drink.

Melancholy assaulted me, and my mood shifted. Suddenly, I was hyper aware that Holden wasn't there, and he never would be. I kept a smile plastered on my face anyway. But I couldn't maintain it once

Taylor arrived, sitting down on Jameson's lap and whispering something in his ear. For the next ten minutes, she alternated between making out with him and shooting me glances that looked half suspicious and half mocking. I didn't need any of it—*this*. This had been Holden's downfall or at least part of it. I didn't think anyone noticed that I'd grown very quiet. "Hey, I'm gonna go use the bathroom. I'll be back," I said to no one in particular, standing up and walking toward the stairs.

I used the bathroom and then headed to the bar, not ready to return upstairs yet to the boisterous laughter of the team, to all the girls milling around the table, some taking pictures, some even filming, looks of desperation on their faces, hoping one of the team members would notice them, even if it was only for a night. When the busy bartender pointed to me, I ordered a water. He scowled and I gave him an apologetic look, sticking a ten in his tip jar even though I should have told him to fuck off. People get thirsty.

"You get stuck as designated driver, too?"

I looked to my right and there was a pretty girl with dark hair and red lipstick standing next to me, apparently waiting for her drink order. In the dim light of the bar, her hair looked almost black and it made me think of Lily. *Enough. Stop chasing ghosts, Ryan.* I nodded at the girl and looked back to the bartender who was serving some people at the other end of the bar.

"I'd forgotten how obnoxious drunk people are when you're not drinking," she said, rolling her eyes and giving me a small smile. When I didn't say anything, she looked embarrassed. "And if I have to hear one more bad pirate joke . . ."

I furrowed my brows. "Pirate joke?" I couldn't help asking.

She used her finger to wave it around the room. *Ah, the pirate theme.* "Fetch me a flagon of ale, wench!" She said this in a deep voice, apparently mimicking the person who had requested she make a bar run. "I mean, seriously, right?" She bit at her lip.

I laughed. She really was pretty.

The bartender set my water in front of me and before I could even thank him, he was back down the bar, pointing at another customer. I

143

turned toward the girl, raising my water glass. "Good luck." *Stupid thing to say.*

But she gave me a big smile anyway. "You too."

I walked back toward the stairs, but couldn't bring myself to climb them. Suddenly this was the very last place I wanted to be. But it would be rude to just leave without saying goodbye. I'd take a breather outside for a little bit, and then I'd go back in and say my farewells. Make it look like everything was fine and dandy. Setting my water glass down on a table, I exited the bar and stood to the side of the door in the dim light of the awning, my hands in my pockets, wondering why I hadn't guessed it would be this bad. This had never been my scene. Why would I be good at it now? I watched a group of girls giggling as they pushed an obviously drunk friend wearing a white dress and veil with plastic penises pinned all over it into a limo. The sign stuck on her ass read, "I like being spanked."

The doors to the bar opened and someone exited, coming to stand next to me. We both looked at each other at the same time, her eyes widening, her expression one of growing embarrassment. It was the girl I'd talked to for a minute at the bar. "I did not follow you out here, I swear."

I laughed. "Sure you didn't."

She rolled her eyes. "No, really, I didn't. But since you're here, do you have a cigarette?"

"I don't smoke."

"I don't usually either, but my ex-boyfriend just showed up with his fiancée and—"

"You're not drunk enough to deal with that kind of thing tonight."

She laughed. "Exactly. Not nearly."

The door opened again and for a second before it closed, raucous laughter flowed out, someone screaming as if in glee.

"Sounds like adult Disneyland in there," she murmured.

"No wonder I'm out here."

Her eyes widened. "You don't like Disneyland?" She looked around, as if making sure no one had heard me, like I'd just told her I was a terrorist.

I laughed and shook my head. "No. But in all fairness, I've never been there. I'm just assuming based on the fact that I don't like roller coasters. Or magic. Or wonder."

She leaned forward and laughed. "Right. Magic. Wonder. *So* boring. No wonder adult Disneyland isn't really your speed."

I shook my head and pointed across the street to a coffee shop. The sign was making a strange buzzing sound and one of the F's in coffee was missing. An old man was sitting at a booth at the window, his head down on the table, either sleeping, or possibly dead. "That place over there's more my speed."

She gazed over at it sadly. "Yeah, there's definitely no magic or wonder there. Probably very little hygiene either."

I nodded, looking over at her, and giving her a slow smile. "Ah, but there is one thing. Donuts."

Her eyes widened. "Let's go."

I laughed. "You can't just leave your friends."

"I'll text them to let them know where I am." She nodded to the door. "It's not like I won't see them if they come outside. We'll sit by the window. By the way, my name's Jenna."

"Ryan." I smiled. "Okay, why not? Let's go."

We waited for a few cars to pass and then jogged across the street, pulling the door open to the comforting scents of sugar, grease, and coffee. A waitress at the counter, who was reading a magazine, gestured her hand around the coffee shop, indicating we could choose our seat. I chose a table by the window, a couple down from the (probably) sleeping guy. Jenna slid into the chair across from me. Once the waitress had taken our order, two coffees and two maple-glazed donuts, Jenna asked, "So Ryan, what do you do?"

"I'm an athletic trainer."

She laughed softly. "Is that a job or an undergarment?"

"Ha ha." But I gave her a genuine chuckle.

"So seriously, what does an athletic trainer do?"

I shrugged. "I'm basically the team's favorite employee. I tape ankles, rub sore muscles, and rehab injuries. In a nutshell."

She raised an eyebrow. "So you work for, like, a sports team?"

I nodded. "I work for the 49ers."

Her eyes widened. "No shit? That's so cool." The waitress brought our coffee and Jenna dumped a couple packets of sugar into hers before saying, "I'm a fan. What happened with Holden Scott last year was so tragic. Did you know him well?"

"Yeah," I said, and cleared my throat when it came out croaky. "Yeah."

Apparently there was something in my face that gave Jenna pause because she took a sip of her coffee and then said, "I'm sorry."

"It's okay," I said. *It so wasn't okay. I missed him. But I hated making others uncomfortable.* "So what do you do, Jenna?"

She smiled, obviously relieved to change the subject. "I'm in marketing." She told me a little bit about her job and the company she worked for. I mostly listened, although my mind wandered just a little. There are all these little milestones after you lose someone. Mostly, they pass by in ways that others don't even recognize, but they still continued to jolt me. I wondered how long that would last? Those few moments after Holden's name was mentioned when I had to work to regain my equilibrium, those few moments when I had to focus on not sinking to my knees.

Be proud of those victories, Dr. Katz had said. For that's what they are, small personal triumphs of strength. And they matter.

I tuned back in to Jenna. "Anyway," she sighed, "I like it. I like the job, and the travel it involves."

"How often do you travel?"

"At least once a week. I'm actually leaving for Chicago tomorrow. Part of the reason I offered to be the DD." She smiled, tilting her head. She was flirting with me, and I wasn't sure how I felt about it. She was pretty, definitely pretty. But would I ever feel that intense rush of feeling for another woman that I'd felt for Lily? I guessed not, especially if that had been purely in my own mind. It would be impossible to recreate a fantasy, I supposed. Maybe a reality check was exactly what I needed.

Maybe spending time with someone like Jenna—someone inarguably real—was just what the doctor ordered, so to speak.

We drank our coffee and ate our donuts, not lacking for conversation, and it was pleasant. When Jenna's friends texted her, I walked her back across the street and waited for them to exit the bar. I decided no one would miss me if I didn't go back inside and say goodbye. They'd all be completely wasted by this point. They could call a limo. Jenna looked at me hopefully. "This turned into a far better night than I thought it would be," she said. Her expression moved from hopeful to expectant. The look that said *I like you. I want to know more.* Lily had looked at me like that. *Deep breath, Ryan. Lily is . . . gone.* And spending time with Jenna had felt . . . easy.

"For me, too." I smiled. "Can I call you, Jenna?"

She released a breath. "Absolutely. Here, let me give you my card." She pulled a white business card out of her small purse and handed it to me, biting her lower lip. "I really look forward to hearing from you, Ryan."

I smiled. "Good night." When I'd walked to the corner, I turned back once. Jenna was still standing on the sidewalk, watching me leave. I held up my hand and waved and she waved back.

CHAPTER EIGHTEEN

Lily

Are you a dream? Or maybe a . . . ghost?

Maybe. Yes, I think I might be.

I don't feel like my life is . . . real.

The words skittered through my mind as I stood staring at the small portion of the Golden Gate Bridge I could see from the window of the hospital. My eyes moved to a woman walking by pushing a baby in a stroller on one of the garden paths below. Somewhere nearby, a car horn blared. Did I feel like my life was real now? Maybe. At least more so than it had been. Here, I could people watch, interact with others, walk in the grass . . . even go out now that I'd been given more freedom.

"You've gone to see him again, haven't you?"

I turned my head from the window to glance at my grandmother as she entered the room. I crossed my arms over my chest.

"He didn't see me," I murmured.

My grandmother sighed. "Lily, darling. He's doing well now. It's time to let him go. In fact, we need to talk about returning to Colorado. My lease on the house in Marin is up next month."

I turned from the window and moved quickly to the small sofa where she'd just sat down. I took her hands in mine. Ignoring her comment about the lease, I said, "That's just it, Grandma; he's doing so well. He's back at work. He seems to be . . . himself again."

My grandmother gave a short laugh. "Himself? Lily, you don't even know who that is. You have no idea. And he has no idea who you are either."

I shook my head, denying her words. "That's not true. I know him. I know who he is in here." I pulled one hand away and used it to tap against my chest. *He's in my heart.* For some reason, the vision of those hands—fingertips just barely brushing—that had been carved into the rock in Colorado raced through my mind. Grasping for each other in the dark. *I'd felt him. I'd known him.*

My grandmother shook her head. "We've gone over this and over this. We agreed to move here temporarily while you were treated. We *agreed* to that. But you promised you'd let me be the one to check on him. And that we'd go home once your treatment was complete."

"I haven't broken that promise," I said, pulling my other hand free and leaning back on the sofa. *I'd go home with her. First to the rental house and then to Colorado. But would I stay there? Could I bear it?*

My grandma gave me a sympathetic look. "I understand, my love. I know exactly what you're feeling. I know how much it hurts. And that's the reason I won't let you involve yourself with Ryan Ellis again. I won't let you hurt him or hurt yourself. It isn't fair to him. If you love him, you'll let him go." She ran her hand over her short, coiffed hair. *I wanted to cry because I knew in my heart she was right.*

I bit at my lip. It was pointless arguing with her. And if I persisted, she'd just cry, and I didn't want to see her cry. I couldn't deal with her sadness—her disappointment—and my own pain. It'd been almost a year and I still felt *desperately* sad. She'd said it would end, and yet it hadn't. Not really. I worked so hard to stop the hurting. I pressed my lips together and stood. "I'm going out to get some coffee."

"You're going out?" she asked.

"Yes, to the coffee shop up the street." That was something I loved about being here in San Francisco. No matter what it was I wanted or needed, it was generally within fifteen minutes walking distance.

My grandmother jumped to her feet. "We could have coffee here. In the cafeteria."

"No, I need to get out." I was tired of being inside, tired of the smell of disinfectant. "And I'd really rather go alone."

She frowned. "Okay. Are you sure that's a good idea?"

Sighing, I turned to her. "It's just coffee, Grandma, I'll be fine. And I have to get used to living in the real world again."

"Okay, Lily," she said again. "You're right. Of course you are. I guess I'll get going then, too." I pretended I didn't notice she was clasping her hands as if she was wringing out a rag.

"Oh, Lily," she said, following me as I pulled on my sweater. I thought she was going to try to stop me. "I forgot to tell you. My friend, Cora, from the tennis club, is hosting a charity event in Marin for those Guatemalan kids she's always talking about and she wants you to attend. I told her it'd be a wonderful way for you to get out. I thought you'd probably love that. It's on your birthday—your twenty-first. We could celebrate there."

I hesitated. "A charity event for Guatemalan kids?" I *would* love that. And it was my grandmother's way of apologizing to me. I offered her a small smile. "That sounds wonderful."

"We can look at dresses online later. Or I could call the personal shopper from Bloomingdales. I'm sure they'd bring some samples here for you to try on."

I grimaced. How embarrassing for a stranger to bring dresses to me here. "Or I could go there," I said. My grandmother nodded, but her smile faltered as if me going to a small coffee shop was tolerable but a big department store crossed the line.

I kissed her cheek, put on my shoes, and left, walking quickly through the grounds and smiling at George as I exited the front gate. "Be careful, Lily," he called as he always did.

"I will, George."

It was a foggy, drizzly morning and I couldn't help but recall that day in the forest under the branches of a tree. My heart clenched. *Ryan.* Sometimes it was still difficult for me to refer to him by that name, even in my mind. I'd met him as Holden. I'd fallen in love with him as Holden. But Shakespeare had been right because what was there in a name?

Holden, Ryan . . . I loved the *man.*

I loved the man who was intense and quiet, gentle and shy, smart and funny. I loved the man who'd looked at me like he wasn't sure how I'd come to be his and was counting his lucky stars. I closed my eyes against the tears. I'd never be his again, and yet I felt like he'd always be mine. Did he wonder why I'd left? I knew he probably didn't understand, and that was my biggest regret. Maybe I should have left a note . . . something. But my grandmother had agreed to help him in exchange for us leaving that night. She'd agreed to help him as long as I promised I wouldn't have any more contact with him. And once I'd told her about why he was there . . .

And I'd known he needed to get better. I'd *known* that he needed to go back to his life and find a way to reclaim it. I just hadn't anticipated it hurting so much when he did and I wasn't a part of it, nor could I ever be.

The coffee shop was warm and bustling with activity. I ordered a latté and found a table in the corner. At least I had something to look forward to with the charity event. My grandmother would be comfortable with me attending because it was across the bridge in Marin, where she was staying at a rental home.

I pulled out my phone and quickly googled the 49ers, looking for any recent pictures of Ryan. I knew I should stop. It only brought me pain to see photographs of him. But it also brought me pride and happiness to see him doing well. There were some recent photos from a bar on one of the tabloid pages. I caught a glimpse of Ryan in the background of one of the shots, sitting at a table, looking off to the side. He was smiling. I used my index finger to trace the tiny outline of his face on the phone screen. I thought back to the moment I'd realized he was suffering from some sort of mental disorder.

The moment my heart had dropped into my feet and I'd felt like I might sink to the floor right in front of him. The picture of the man on the cover of the magazine, a stranger I didn't know, but labeled "Holden Scott." I hadn't understood exactly, but I'd known he wasn't lying to me by the look on his face. He believed himself to be Holden Scott. He didn't know who he was. And suddenly his confusion—his sadness—had made some sort of sense. And what was I to do? I had already fallen in love with him. I *still* loved him. "Boy Scout," I murmured, wondering if the smile on his face in the photograph was real, wondering if he was truly happy.

Wondering if he still thought about me.

CHAPTER NINETEEN

Ryan

I threw my jacket on the couch and kicked off my shoes. I'd taken Jenna out to dinner and had a good time. She'd told me all about her trip, making me laugh with funny stories about the co-worker she'd gotten stuck sharing a hotel room with after her room reservation had been mistakenly cancelled and they'd had no other rooms available.

I collapsed into a chair. I liked her and enjoyed spending time with her, but it also felt strange. And the intensity I'd felt when I'd first spent time with Lily wasn't there. But should it be? I'd been half out of my head when I'd fallen for Lily, when I'd kissed her, when I'd made love to her. That whole time seemed almost like a dream now—as if none of it had really happened at all. As if I'd never even flown to Brandon's lodge in Colorado. As if my life had stopped the moment Holden's hand slipped from mine and only just recently resumed. And yet, inside, I still felt half asleep—as if a part of me remained missing, incomplete.

I looked around my apartment. Everything was neat and tidy. Growing up, my house had always been trashed, had always smelled like garbage, rot, and dog shit. I hadn't thought about it too much until I'd started hanging out at Holden's house. I hadn't known that some homes smelled like baked goods and fresh laundry. I hadn't known that some parents lit seasonal candles that smelled like vanilla or spiced apple or lavender fields. It'd made me intensely aware of the stench of my own house. It'd made me wonder if *I* smelled as foul as my home to people at school. Even though I tried my best to keep my clothes clean, washing them in the bathtub with bar soap when my dad wasn't home if I had to, surely stink like that soaked into a person's skin after a while.

It was why I was so fastidious now. I vacuumed and dusted regularly, changed my sheets once a week, and made sure dirty dishes weren't left in the sink. I would never live like an animal again. I'd never *smell* like an animal again.

Walking back to my bedroom, I undressed and tossed my dirty clothes in the empty hamper in my closet. My gaze caught on the duffle bag I'd thrown in the corner and still hadn't unpacked. I wasn't sure why I grabbed it now. I set it on my bed and pulled on a T-shirt and boxers and then went and stood in front of it. A strange feeling of loss moved through me. No, that trip had been all too real.

The trip at least . . . Lily, I still . . . I raked my hands through my hair and then unzipped the bag. I rummaged through it, but there was nothing except clothes—dirty clothes that were long overdue for a wash. Gathering them up, I walked to my small laundry room and tossed them in the washing machine. A pair of jeans fell out of my hands onto the floor. Sighing, I picked them up and went to toss them in the machine, too, when I stopped, holding them up and then reaching inside one pocket. Why I did that, I wasn't sure. The pocket was empty. I switched hands and reached inside the other pocket, pausing when my fingers came upon something hard and smooth. I grasped it and pulled it out and stood for several long moments just staring down at it: the white arrowhead Lily had given me. *It looks so delicate, and yet it could take down a large animal or even a man.* Her words echoed through my head and I sucked in a breath. "Lily," I whispered. I held the arrowhead up to the overhead light and then grasped it in my hand. It was solid. It was real. I clenched my eyes shut. *Was she?*

Was it possible I'd been running through the forest alone, an entire make-believe scenario going on as I collected actual objects and drew stick figures on rocks to support the fiction of my own life? *Jesus, had I been that fucking nutty?* I cringed. Walking back into my bedroom, I set the arrowhead down on the top of my dresser and took a deep breath. *Crazy people rarely question their own sanity.*

I took a quick shower and then, still unable to get that arrowhead off my mind, went into the living room and opened my laptop. I googled Whittington and got the same results as the first time. I scrolled through the site I'd originally looked at. Sitting back, I chewed on my bottom lip, thinking about everything I hadn't considered yet. Lily had told me about two escapes. I searched for any information on either one of the two but didn't find anything. It could be that Lily had actually read the stories in old newspaper articles she'd found inside the hospital and the stories just weren't put online for some reason, *or* it could be that I made the whole thing up. Back to square one.

After a brief pause where I stared at the screen of my laptop, I did a search for the owners of Whittington. I thought I'd remembered reading that it had been a privately owned hospital. It took me about five minutes of clicking to find the information: Whittington and its surrounding property was owned by Augustine Corsella, a real estate mogul from Colorado who had made the purchase in 2008. He was deceased, but it appeared it was still owned by the Corsella family. I scrolled through, looking for more information on him, but there wasn't anything I was interested in. Yawning, I closed the laptop and put it aside, disappointed in my fruitless online search. But what had I really been looking for anyway? *Something. Anything.*

I had the arrowhead though. *It* was something, wasn't it? *Wasn't it?*

I thought for a moment, remembering the myriad of things Lily had said to me.

I logged on to my iTunes account and did a few searches. Love songs from the forties she'd said. "All of Me" started playing, filling the silence of my living room. I listened to it from beginning to end wondering if this was one of the ones Lily would have liked. As the collection of songs played, "I'll Be Seeing You" and "Tenderly" and "Some Enchanted Evening," I stared vacantly at the ceiling, my head resting on the back of the couch, my hand in my hair. And I wondered if these songs were *supposed* to be so very sad and create the intense ache in my chest.

And what of the lingering sadness that was ever-present in my heart? Could I miss someone who had never existed? Could I pine for a dream? I was back to *myself,* and yet without her, everything just felt . . . *off.* Exhausted by my own thoughts, I climbed into bed, Lily's face the last thing in my mind as I fell into a dreamless sleep.

****

"**H**ey there, handsome," Jenna said, standing up from the stair of my building where she had been sitting, waiting for me. She was wearing a slim black skirt and a white blouse, obviously having come straight from work, like I was.

"Hey," I said, smiling. "What are you doing here?"

"I found out earlier today I have to fly to St. Louis tonight—emergency packaging problem." She rolled her eyes and I chuckled.

"Sounds serious."

"It's solvable. Hopefully. Anyway, I can't go to dinner tomorrow night and I'm bummed. I thought maybe we could spend a little time together now before I have to go home and pack." She tilted her head, looking hopeful.

"Oh, uh, yeah, okay."

She grimaced. "You're busy. I should have called. This isn't a good surprise. And I looked up your address and just showed up, which is probably crossing the line. I'm being too forward. God." An embarrassed blush rose in her cheeks, and it was endearing.

I couldn't help but smile as I held up my hand. "No, no. I don't mind. It's a good surprise. I was just going to the gym. But I'd rather spend time with you." I nodded toward my building. "Let me just change and then we can go grab some food?"

Jenna let out a breath. "Yeah, cool." She still looked unsure and so I leaned in and kissed her cheek.

"Nice to see you, by the way."

She grinned. "Nice to see you, too." I took her hand and led her up to my apartment.

Half an hour later we were strolling along a street near the marina headed toward a casual Italian restaurant I hadn't been to for over a year. "Oh, I wanted to ask if you're available two weeks from now? Friday?" Jenna asked, turning to me slightly as she walked.

"I think so," I said, stopping in front of the restaurant and holding the door open as she passed through. "What's going on Friday two weeks from now?"

"One of my biggest clients is helping host a charity thing in Marin. I told her I'd be there."

"What's the charity?"

"Guatemalan whatnot. They're building a school or something like that."

I chuckled and raised one brow. "A cause close to your heart, then?"

She laughed. "Not really, but there'll be free champagne. What do you say? Do you have a tux?"

My mind was momentarily blank as I recalled a very different reaction to people in need. *There's always someone society chooses not to see. There's always someone who is invisible through no fault of their own.* And yet she hadn't existed? Confusion and despair tugged at my heart, but I did my best to push the feelings aside. Refocusing on the woman before me—the real woman—I quickly thought back to what she'd asked me. A tux . . .

"I could get one."

"Awesome."

The hostess led us to our table, and we ordered wine.

"So what are you doing this weekend then?"

I cleared my throat. "Actually, I have to clean out Holden's house. I was considering doing it this weekend. It's been a year and a half and I still haven't touched anything."

Jenna's mouth opened slightly. "Oh, geez. I didn't realize you were that close to Holden Scott."

I nodded. In truth, Holden had left everything to me—his money, his house, all his things. I'd thought about it and decided I was ready to go through some of it, at least get rid of his clothes, meaningless stuff like that. I'd do a little at a time, take it slow, see how I felt. At least that's what Dr. Katz had advised at my last session. "Yeah. Yeah, I was. We were best friends since childhood. We both grew up in Ohio."

Her eyes grew wide. "Oh God, Ryan. I'm sorry. What are you going to do with his stuff? I bet some of it would go for insane prices if you auctioned it."

"I wouldn't auction Holden's stuff," I said a little too defensively.

She put her hand on top of mine on the table. "I just meant that it could bring in some cash that you could use to help people. Was he a supporter of some charity or another?"

I sighed. "Yeah. I'll think on it." God, even talking about it like this was making me tired. Could I really even do it?

Jenna paused, giving me a small smile. "If you can wait a few days, I can come along and help."

I resisted grimacing. "No. No, thank you, Jenna. This is something I have to do on my own."

Her face fell as she pulled her hand away. "I understand."

"Thanks." Thankfully, the waitress interrupted the ensuing awkward pause with our wine. I fiddled with the silverware sitting on the table in front of me. "Listen, Jenna," I said. She stilled as if waiting for bad news. "I think I should tell you something about me. I mean before this goes any further. I don't want you to feel duped down the road and—"

"You're dating someone else," she said.

"What? No. No, nothing like that. No, it's about *me*."

She appeared to relax. "Okay, what is it?"

I paused, searching for the right words. "When Holden died, I . . . lost it for a while. I," Jesus, this was hard, "went a little crazy."

Jenna tilted her head, looking confused. "Okay. Well, I think that's only natural. I mean, it had to have been a huge blow. Now that I know you were best friends . . . it must have been devastating."

I nodded. "Yes, but . . . I don't think I'm communicating the severity of my breakdown. The truth is, I didn't just go a little crazy, I went a lot crazy." I let out a small laugh containing little humor. "I think you should know. And I won't blame you if you want to run in the opposite direction."

She watched me for a moment, and I shifted in discomfort, looking down. "Ryan, are you trying to tell me you're damaged goods?"

I met her eyes. "Uh, yeah, I guess that's what I'm trying to tell you. That's exactly what I'm trying to tell you."

She reached out her hand and put it over mine once again. "I'm sorry you went through such a hard time. And I'm sorry you lost someone you loved. But I think the fact that you took it so hard shows you're someone I want to know better, not someone I want to run away from."

I opened my mouth to say something and then closed it again. *That was really nice.* I wasn't sure I had properly conveyed the extent of my insanity, but I also wasn't sure I owed her all the details either. I felt better just having given her the bare bones.

Jenna raised her glass. "Okay, so, to new beginnings," she said. "To wonder and magic." The candle on the table flickered and for a moment, the light hit her eyes and they appeared almost violet. *Lily.* I blinked just as the light shifted, and they returned to their true hazel color.

I smiled and it felt a little bit wobbly. Holding my glass up and inclining my head, I said, "To Disneyland."

Later, I drove her back to her apartment and walked her to her door. And then, because she was pretty and nice, because she'd made me genuinely laugh for the first time in almost a year, and because she'd made me feel like I might *not* be damaged goods, I kissed her. Her lips were warm and soft and tasted of a new beginning.

CHAPTER TWENTY

Lily

"What do you think?" my grandmother asked.

I looked around at the plain room in the rental house, just a bed, a dresser, and a bedside table. The linens on the bed were white. Sterile. It didn't look much different than the room from which I'd just moved. At least it didn't smell like disinfectant. "It's nice," I said.

My grandmother smiled. "Well, it's just temporary anyway, but get yourself settled. I took the liberty of ordering a few dresses for you. They're in the closet. Try them on when you feel up to it, darling."

I stiffened, not turning as I nodded my head. "Thank you," I murmured.

When I heard the door click closed behind me, I walked over to the closet and opened the door. Hanging inside were two garment bags. I took them out and unzipped the bag on top. Inside was a long, black, sleeveless gown, simple yet elegant. I relaxed slightly. Okay, so I hadn't picked it out myself, but it was lovely, I'd give my grandmother that. And it was even my size. Putting it aside, I unzipped the second bag. My eyes widened as I pulled the stunning dress free from its plastic closure. It was a one-shouldered, floor-length ball gown in a shade of purple so deep it appeared almost black when turned away from the light. It was reminiscent of a gown from the forties, something Lana Turner or Rita Hayworth would have worn to a Hollywood movie premier. I loved everything about it. I quickly stripped out of my jeans and long-sleeved T-shirt and pulled it on. Even with the white straps of my bra showing, it was beautiful and fit as if it had been made just for me. I twirled, watching as the skirt swung out around me. Something about that brought a sense of happiness I hadn't felt in a long time. A surge of hope filled my chest. *Life can still hold miracles, even very small ones.* And maybe if there were enough small doses of joy, sprinkled just often enough, I'd survive. As if the path of my life was a dot-to-dot puzzle, the spaces between the dots of joy filled with uncertainty and perhaps even pain. But eventually I'd make it to the end and there would be some sort of picture. Some sort of *point.*

There was a knock at my door. "Come in," I called, expecting my grandmother. The door opened and my body froze. It was my grandmother's butler, Jeffrey. He smiled.

"Hello, Lily. My, how beautiful you look. What's the occasion?" He came up behind me and I met his eyes in the mirror—the color so dark brown they almost looked black.

"I . . . I was just trying on a dress for an event Grandma's taking me to." I cleared my throat. I didn't like this man. He made me nervous, but I would not stutter in front of him. I would not give him that.

He smiled again, his eyes moving down my body. I resisted the urge to cover myself with my arms, resisted the urge to pull away. "Lovely," he murmured. "So lovely. So grown up." After another tense moment, he pulled back, as if coming out of a trance. "Well, I just came to say hello and let you know I was here if you need anything." I nodded, not breaking eye contact.

"Good," he murmured, walking to the door. He looked back at me. "I'm glad to see you well, Lily. Very, very glad."

As soon as he left, I walked quickly to the door and locked it, standing against it for a moment and breathing deeply. Then I undressed, returned the dresses to their garment bags, and hung them back up carefully, resenting Jeffrey for sullying what had been a happy moment. What was the point of looking beautiful in a new dress anyway when the one man I wanted to see me in it, never would? I quickly re-dressed in my jeans and T-shirt.

As I tiptoed quietly down the stairs, I heard my grandmother talking to Jeffrey. I caught my name, but didn't care to hear exactly what they were discussing. I slipped on my coat and opened the door slowly. Just before closing it, I called behind me, "I'm going out. I'll be back soon." I needed to get out and clear my head.

I heard a few sudden footsteps coming my way, and so I closed the door behind me and fast-walked down the block, letting out an exhale when I'd turned the corner. I didn't want my grandmother to worry, but I also didn't feel like dealing with her fretting over me going out for a simple walk around the neighborhood. I loathed being treated like a child despite being almost twenty-one. It was tedious and exasperating. Half my life had been spent feeling like a princess locked in a tower. *A damaged princess.* One who shouldn't expect to be rescued. And now I knew creepy Jeffrey was here and it made everything worse. So much worse. Why my grandmother trusted him, I had no idea.

There was a park a couple blocks from my grandmother's rental, a walking path weaving around the perimeter. I turned at the entrance, moving to the side in case a jogger or bike rider came up behind me. It was an unseasonably chilly day for California bringing to mind being in the woods in Colorado on cool fall evenings. I stuffed my hands in my coat pockets to warm them.

Children made loud sounds of delight—reminiscent of forest birds twittering—as they played on the playground. I closed my eyes momentarily, attempting to relax, smelling pine and dead leaves floating on the crisp evening air. As I walked, the sun began to set and the daylight dimmed. I walked into a section of path that was shaded by massive eucalyptus trees and for some reason, looking around, the entire landscape suddenly looked like it'd been drawn in black ink, the color leeching from the scene. I blinked, trying desperately to hang on to it.

No. Not now. The bench. Get to the bench. Quick, shallow breaths. *In and out, Lily. In and out.* My lungs felt as though they were stinging from the sharp cold of the air. My heart slammed against my ribs. *Oh God.* A panic attack. *Get control. Get control.*

Focused on the ground at my feet, my breathing finally slowed and my heartbeat became regular again. My vision slowly cleared and I was able to sit up straight. The scene resumed. Sound and color burst forth and I let out a relieved sigh. *Why does this keep happening?*

Move forward.

Move away from the pain.

When I felt calm enough to continue on, I stood on shaky legs and completed the lap, ending up back at the park entrance again where I hurried back to my grandmother's home. I would never tell her about my anxiety. She'd only worry and use it to contain me. And I wanted freedom. All I wanted was freedom.

Where would you fly, Lily?

Anywhere I wanted.

Anywhere at all.

CHAPTER TWENTY-ONE

Lily

"**A**re you sure this isn't too much makeup? I feel sort of like a Vegas showgirl."

My grandmother laughed. "Silly girl. Of course not. Would your grandmother let you wear too much makeup? You look stunning. As you should. It's your birthday."

I smiled. "Yes . . ." I turned to the mirror, taking one last look at myself. I was wearing the deep purple gown and a pair of strappy heels. My hair had been tamed into a swept-up style, and my grandmother had ordered a deep purple lily—almost the exact hue of my dress—from a florist and stuck it in the back of my hair. I smiled as I looked at it in a small mirror held up to see the larger mirror behind me. My makeup was dramatic with dark eyes and nude lips. I didn't quite feel like myself, and yet I couldn't deny that I felt pretty, perhaps even beautiful. Perhaps even like a girl who had a life ahead of her. And if not, maybe, just for tonight, I could pretend it was more than just a misplaced dream.

The limo was already waiting for us in front of my grandmother's home, and we rode to the hotel where the event was being held in one of the ballrooms. Stepping out of the limo, I closed my eyes and took in a deep, calming breath. I couldn't help smiling.

Do you feel real, Lily? Yes. Yes, tonight maybe I do.

My grandmother and I checked our coats and made our way to the ballroom, our heels clicking on the marble of the hotel entryway. Lights sparkled and I could hear the low strains of music drifting to us from inside the event. "Now, Lily," my grandmother, said, leaning close to my ear, "if you get overwhelmed, just squeeze my hand and we'll leave immediately. You don't have to say a word."

"Grandma, I'm fine. I promise. Please don't follow me around. I love you, I do, but I'll be okay."

"All right," she said, offering me a small, nervous smile. "Yes, okay, darling. Have fun. Mingle. The night is yours. Of course it is."

We entered the ballroom, and I looked around as my grandmother led us to our table. Men looked handsome in their stylish tuxedos, and the women glittered and shone, dressed in every beautiful shade of ball gown that existed. They seemed to know the art of easy mingling, some sitting at large tables and others standing to the side. *Watching them socialize effortlessly made me feel like an imposter.* The tables themselves were decked in orange tablecloths with bright red, purple, and dark orange runners that looked as if they were handmade, Guatemalan I assumed. And in the centers were large bowls of bright, tropical-looking flowers. The sweet, heady fragrance wafted in the air as I sat down in front of the place card that spelled out my name in elegant hand-written calligraphy.

"The raffle items are over there, if you'd like to come with me to look at them," my grandmother said, pointing to the other side of the room where I could see large baskets and other items on high-top tables. Guests walked the rows of items, many sipping colorful cocktails and glasses of champagne.

"Yes, I would," I said, standing.

"Good. And bid on a few things," my grandmother said. "It's for a wonderful cause."

I smiled at her just as an older woman wearing a long white gown approached our table, greeting my grandmother. My grandmother introduced me to her, and we said our hellos. "I'll meet you over there," I said to my grandmother, indicating the bidding area and nodding again to the woman.

"Yes, I'll be over in a few minutes," my grandmother said, turning back to the woman in white.

I wandered through the crowd, taking a tall glass filled with pink liquid off one of the trays and taking one long drink of the sweet, but tart, cocktail. I licked my lips. "Oh, excuse me," I said to the woman who was carrying the tray. "What is this?"

"A pomegranate martini."

It was delicious. I might just have two. I'd finish them quickly before my grandmother found me.

No, no I wouldn't. It was my birthday, after all, and I was twenty-one. I was allowed.

I walked up one aisle, looking over the baskets first then moving on to the vacations, and the tickets, and the other items that were described in detail on small placards. I wrote my name down on a basket full of spa items. Why not?

What about you? What do you like, Lily?

I don't know.

So maybe it was time to find out. I signed my name below tickets for two to a Broadway show performing at a theater in San Francisco, and then to a hockey game, and a day trip to Napa Valley, including a hot air balloon ride. I had money. Maybe it was time to figure out what to spend it on. Although, should I win, I might not be in San Francisco long enough to use any of it. I took another sip of the pomegranate martini. Looking over my shoulder across the room, my grandmother was still in deep conversation with the woman in white. And now another woman had joined them. She was gesturing wildly with her hands, and my grandmother and the other woman had astonished looks on their faces. I rolled my eyes. They were probably discussing the latest gossip at the tennis club my grandmother had joined.

"Oh look, a trip to Paris," a man said. I stilled, ice moving up my spine.

"Have you ever been?" a woman asked. With auburn hair swept into a chignon and wearing a black gown that dipped down her back, she was the picture of elegance.

"No. But I'd love to go someday," the man next to her said, a smile in his voice. My body froze completely. I *knew* that voice. Would know it anywhere. Oh *God*. Shock hit me like a physical blow and I backed up several steps, bumping into someone behind me.

My pulse jumped crazily, and I tried to apologize to the man I'd bumped into, but no words came out. He gave me a strange look but then smiled politely, moving aside. I looked back to the couple still in front of me. My blood was buzzing in my veins and I felt like I might throw up. This could not be happening. Life could *not* be this cruel. *Oh yes, Lily, it can. Life is pissing itself right now at the opportunity to be this cruel. Life is rubbing its hands in excited glee at this very moment.*

They were both still looking in the other direction. He was laughing now, saying something in her ear, his hand on the small of her back.

He . . . Ryan.

Oh no, no, no.

It was definitely him. I would know him anywhere by the way he held his shoulders, the tilt of his head, the deep golden hue of his hair, the cadence of his laughter. The woman he was with tipped her head back and laughed along with him. Then she turned, and taking his face in her hands, she kissed him. *Oh God.* He appeared briefly surprised but then he was kissing her back. They were kissing, and I was standing there behind them, shaking, a martini tipping out of my hand. I sucked in a breath, my knees almost buckling, reaching my arm out, placing my glass on a table to my right. Or maybe I'd missed completely. I had no idea. Static filled my head and bile rose in my throat. My guts churned painfully. *Run, Lily.* All you have to do is turn and run. *Do it now.* Only I couldn't. I was rooted to the spot, unable to move, watching them kiss, his eyes closed, the lips that had once moved over my skin so lovingly now locked with *hers.*

"Lily, darling. There you are," my grandmother sing-songed loudly, coming up behind me, breaking through the painful spell I was under and causing me to gasp out loud. As if in a dream—*a nightmare*—I watched Ryan's muscles tense, and the girl pulled away from him, looking at him quizzically. The look on his face must have given her pause because she tilted her head, her lips moving. She must be asking him what was wrong. His head turned toward me, and I tripped backward again. He was turning. *Oh, God.*

"Lily, what *is* the matter? You look positively pale, darling. I'm trying to introduce you to Mr. Bradley. He's the—"

"I have to . . . I can't . . ." I choked out breathlessly.

Where do you fly, Lily?

Away. I fly away.

His eyes were on me now, wide, unblinking.

Ryan, it was Ryan.

Just as I'd already known. His face, his beautiful face. He looked shocked, pale. The woman next to him was saying something. And oh, I couldn't do this. I was going to fall down. I was going to fly away. And suddenly in what seemed to be an instant, he was right in front of me.

"*Lily,*" he choked, grabbing on to my bare upper arms. I squeaked. I couldn't make my mouth move. "Lily!" he almost shouted. He shook me and I let out another small squeak. My heart lodged in my throat. He was *here,* in front of me. With another woman. *Oh God, why?*

"What in the world?" someone demanded. "What are you doing? Miss Corsella, do you require assistance?" My eyes darted briefly to him and then back to Ryan. I could barely breathe let alone answer him.

"Let go of her," my grandmother said shrilly to Ryan, ignoring the man next to her.

Ryan turned to the man. "Do you see her?" he demanded. The man's face became a study in confusion.

"I beg your pardon? Do I see Lily? She's standing right in front of me. Are you all right, young man?" He turned to my grandmother. "Bianca?"

Ryan ignored the man and turned back to me. "Lily? How? How?" he asked, his voice cracking, panic in his tone. Or was it joy? Oh no, that was worse. That was far worse. *Wasn't it?* His eyes moved quickly down my body and then back up to my eyes in one quick blink of movement. "Jesus, *Lily,*" he breathed. "*Lily.*"

"I . . ." The single syllable died on my lips. I tried to pull away from him, but he latched on harder. *Oh Ryan, Ryan, Ryan.* And I wanted to scream, because mixed in with the shock and intense jealousy of seeing him with someone else, I felt joy of my own. A dazzling spear of elation that spiked straight through my heart. *Ryan, my Ryan,* my mind insisted.

Only he wasn't mine at all.

"No," he said, "no."

"Ryan, what's happening?" the woman he was with asked softly, standing just to his side and a step behind, looking around, probably embarrassed and confused. I only saw her in my peripheral vision, unable to take my eyes off Ryan. He ignored her, his eyes still trained on me as well.

"Let go of her," my grandmother repeated, more loudly. She didn't want to attract any more attention than we already had.

"Please," I finally managed, "please let me go, Ryan." Time seemed to stop as his real name fell from my lips, the room seeming to grow brighter around me. Ryan's eyes widened even more.

"You know my name," he said. "You do know who I really am. I wasn't sure . . ."

The woman he was with took a tiny step back, looking between the two of us.

"Let her go, Ryan," my grandmother repeated for me. "You're making a scene."

"Grandma, it's okay . . . " I glanced at my grandmother, and Ryan, following my gaze, finally looked from me to her.

"You," he said. "You were *there.*"

"Yes, now let go of her and we can step outside and talk. Let go of her." She looked around, offering a small smile to the crowd in general, some milling nearby, some looking at us and whispering. *Nothing to see here, folks, nothing at all.*

Ryan looked back to me, his eyes wild, his expression still arrested. He dropped his hands from my arms, and I stumbled back slightly. He stepped forward to steady me, but my grandmother was closer and wrapped one arm around my waist, holding me up. "Let's just step outside," she repeated. She smiled at the man she'd been talking to, the man who I briefly noted was watching the scene with a worried frown on his face.

"Yes, please, I'd just like to go," I said, turning, my grandmother moving with me. My legs felt like they were weighted as she led me out of the ballroom. I had to focus to make them move. Behind me, I heard Ryan speaking to the woman he was with momentarily, and then I heard his steps on the marble floor behind us. I was woozy as if the half of a martini I'd consumed had gone straight to my head. As if I were drunk.

I felt his heat behind me before I turned, his hand again on my arm. "Lily, please," he said. We were just outside the ballroom now, the music filtering out into the vestibule where we stood. "You're real," Ryan whispered, his hand took mine and his thumb made a circle over my pulse as if he was checking to make sure I was really alive. I blinked. "You're *real*," he repeated as though he needed to say it twice to convince himself.

I felt my face move into a frown. "Did you think . . . that I wasn't real?" I finally asked, confused.

He let out a gust of breath. "I, Christ, Lily, I wasn't sure. I questioned it. I've *been* questioning it."

Something about that *hurt*. "I . . . see," I said. If he hadn't known if I was real or not, he couldn't have missed me, pined for me as I'd pined for him. He couldn't have. He mustn't have. That's why he was with that woman, giving *her* his body and his heart. He'd forgotten about me, moved on. He'd dismissed me as nothing more than a dream.

"You left. *Why?*" he asked. "Why didn't you tell me you were here? In San Francisco? How long—"

"Let's move aside," my grandmother said, walking several steps so we were farther from the open doorway. I followed her and so did Ryan. Ryan was staring at my grandmother.

"You *were* there," he said, repeating what he'd said inside. He turned to me. "She's your grandmother."

"Yes," I whispered. "My grandmother," I hesitated and then added,

"Bianca Corsella." I had considered not offering her name, but there were a hundred people inside the ballroom who could tell him *both* our names. It hardly seemed worth withholding now. Ryan's eyes were moving over my face, his expression still shocked, confused.

"Where was your mother, Lily? I don't understand any of it. Please tell me."

My grandmother took my hand. "My daughter, Lily's mother, has been dead for a long time," my grandmother said calmly. "My granddaughter is ill, Ryan, just as you are. Everything you know of her is a lie. It was Lily living a lie." She looked around to make sure no one had heard her. I squeezed my eyes shut and then opened them. "Please, you have to understand that she can't see you again." Heat was rising up my chest to my neck, filling my head, making me feel like I might pass out. I didn't want him to know. It was irrational because I'd understood him, I'd understood that he was ill, but I just . . . didn't want him to know. *Not about me.* I felt humiliated and small and filled with despair.

Because now he'd realize what I had already come to understand: We could never be together. There could never be an *us*. It wasn't possible. I wasn't good for him, and truthfully, he probably wasn't good for me either. The woman inside the ballroom, the woman waiting for him, the beautiful woman in the black dress who he was going to take home tonight and make love to, *she* was better for him than I was. I knew nothing about her, but I knew that. And it filled me with pain and a sick, fierce jealousy. I pictured his naked body moving above hers and sucked in a miserable breath.

Ryan was staring at me, clearly trying to understand. "Lily?" he asked.

I closed my eyes momentarily. "It's true," I said, meeting his gaze. "My mother is dead. I've been in a hospital this year. I'm sick, Ryan. I've been . . . getting better. It's happened before, I . . ." My voice grew smaller. I didn't know what else to say.

"Okay," he said, "we can work through this, Lily—"

"There's nothing to work through," my grandmother said, latching her arm through mine.

Ryan glared at her, the first sign of anger coming into his expression. "Can Lily and I have a moment alone, please?" he asked, his jaw tight.

"Absolutely not. Lily, darling, we need to go. You look positively shaken anyway." She looked at Ryan. "Can you *see* how delicate she is? Can you *see* what this has done to her?"

"It's for the best," I said weakly. "What my grandmother said is true. Everything you know of me is all a lie. It was me living a lie. It's for the best that I walk away, Ryan."

"For the *best?*" he asked incredulously. "For the best?"

He looked back and forth between my grandmother and me, his eyes slightly wild again. "You can't just walk out of here!"

"We certainly can," my grandmother said, leading me away. "Lily's right. It's for the best. You'll come to realize that. Go back to your date, Ryan. It's good to see you doing well." Ryan stood there, shaking his head in disbelief as I allowed my grandmother to lead me away. I felt like my knees would buckle at any moment. Everything in me was screaming to run back to Ryan and beg him to take me out of there, take me with him, but I couldn't. More misery engulfed me.

Ryan, take me back to our woods where we can be together, where we can just be us, where you were free to love me and I was free to love you back. Take me there. Oh please, please take me there.

But, no. My grandmother was right to separate us, and the woman inside was waiting for him.

"Lily," Ryan repeated bleakly, but he didn't attempt to stop us again. He let us walk away. *He let me go. Just as I must let him go.* I dared to look out the window of the limo as it pulled away from the curb. Through the glass doors, I could see Ryan still standing in the lobby, watching as our car drove away. He grew smaller and smaller as the distance between us grew, all my hopes shrinking the farther we drove, until he finally disappeared completely. *Again.* Finally, unable to hold the anguish off for one minute longer, I put my face in my hands and sobbed.

CHAPTER TWENTY-TWO

Ryan

The glass struck the wall and shattered, the sound breaking the silence of my apartment, jolting me free of the shock still holding me tightly in its grasp.

Lily.

Here in San Francisco.

She was real—she'd been right in front of me.

And she knew who I was, too. I'd been certain she'd figured out I wasn't Holden.

Do you know about me? Do you know?

Yes, love.

But I hadn't known if she knew who I *really* was. Hadn't known if she'd made the connection. Of course, I hadn't even known if she was *real* so I hadn't allowed myself to think too much about that aspect. Each time I did, it made me wonder if I was going crazy again—even considered whether it would *cause* me to go crazy again—and so I would shut it down. *Christ.* I didn't have to wonder anymore if she was real, and so I let myself think about it now. About how she'd stopped using my name, only calling me Boy Scout after she'd looked at the picture of Holden on the magazine cover. Yes, she'd definitely known. *My God.*

Maybe you don't even know me? Do you feel that way? You must.

No, no.

Lily. I'd *found* her, and I'd watched her walk away. What else could I have done? Tackle her? She'd *wanted* to leave. She'd looked as if she was going to collapse. But truthfully, I'd only allowed her to leave because I knew her name. Lily Corsella. Her name was Lily Corsella and her grandmother was Bianca Corsella. Her family owned Whittington. Holy *fuck.*

And *she* was mentally ill? She'd been hospitalized? For a *year?* I didn't know *what* to do with that, didn't understand. My mind was still reeling. I loved her. God, I did. I still loved her. If I'd had any doubt before tonight, seeing her in front of me, feeling a wild surge of joy as if she'd suddenly come back from the dead—which in essence, for me, she had—took away any and all question about the depth of my feelings. Her mental illness—that was why she thought we couldn't be together. She'd spent the last year in a hospital and she thought . . . what? That I'd have looked down upon her for it? Why would she think that after what she knew of *me,* of the battle I'd been fighting the entire time I'd been in Colorado? Of the battle I *might* fight for the rest of my life.

She'd looked so hurt when I had told her I'd wondered if she were real. Sitting here now, alone in my apartment, I wondered how in the hell I ever could have questioned it. *Her eyes.* Those violet eyes. Even I couldn't have dreamed up eyes like that. I ran my hand through my hair, letting out a grunt of frustration. What did I do now? A million questions swirled through my mind.

The ding of my phone interrupted my chaotic thoughts. Jenna. I felt terrible about Jenna, but Jesus, how was I supposed to handle that situation? Seeing Lily had hit me with the force of a hurricane. I'd driven Jenna home right after that, not offering her much of an explanation other than I'd met Lily when I was in Colorado, and she'd disappeared. I hadn't known what happened to her and seeing her there was a shock. I'd told Jenna the whole situation had given me a headache, and I just needed to be alone. Which wasn't a lie. My head was throbbing in a way it hadn't in a year. Still, the crushed look on Jenna's face had left me feeling like a complete and utter asshole. I threw my phone aside. I'd answer Jenna in the morning when I could come up with a better explanation—when I knew *what* to say to her.

Pulling out my computer, I again looked up Augustine Corsella, specifically looking for information about his family. Now that I knew what I was looking for, I was able to narrow down the search and came upon a few scraps I was able to piece together: he was survived by his wife Bianca. Augustine and Bianca had a daughter named Rachel. There was one other name attached to those names on the people search sites I looked at—Lily Corsella. Rachel must be her mother. I couldn't find any information about her father. And she went by her mother's last name . . . I had to assume her father wasn't in the picture for some reason or another.

Unfortunately, the only address I found for any of them was an address near Telluride. *Shit.* They were here in San Francisco. Her grandmother had said she was taking her home. How was I going to get her address? Okay, I'd worry about that tomorrow. I had several ideas. Hell, I'd call a private detective if I had to. Lily was not going to disappear again.

I went back to trying to find information on Lily's mother. That seemed to be at the heart of the mystery. *Why the hell am I not getting answers directly from you, Lily?* After clicking around for another fifteen minutes, I was able to confirm that Rachel Corsella was deceased. There wasn't very much information about her. I couldn't find anything about *how* she'd died. But she was definitely dead. So Lily had been . . . what? Keeping her alive in her mind? She had been living at Whittington, in that dusty, deserted house of horrors, imagining her mother was there with her, walking alone through the woods day after day, finally finding me. *God, Lily.* I shut down the computer, finding it too difficult to continue trying to fill in the many blanks without Lily's explanation. I owed it to her to hear the story from her lips. And she owed an explanation to me, dammit.

Everything you know of her is a lie. It was Lily living a lie.

I clenched my eyes shut. No. I refused to believe our feelings for each other were a lie. I had been sick, too. Possibly even sicker than Lily. And yet, I loved her. That had been real. *It was still real.* No one would convince me otherwise. Not even myself, not again.

I set my computer aside and then stood up, rubbing my palms on my jeans. I was antsy and still had a headache, but all I wanted to do was run across town to Lily. But I really had no idea where she was. Helplessness coursed through me, causing my gut to twist painfully. What if she *did* try to disappear? What if her grandmother took her somewhere I couldn't find her? No, no, her grandmother was obviously trying to protect her—misguided intentions or not—she wasn't going to hide her away somewhere. I had let them leave tonight, just walk right out. I'd *let* them leave, and I had to believe that my actions had soothed her grandmother's mind. Plus, they were here in San Francisco. If her grandmother imagined I was that much of a threat, surely she wouldn't have agreed to put Lily in a nearby hospital. God, she'd probably been less than thirty minutes from me this whole time. All those nights I'd sat alone in my apartment or walked the streets aimlessly, ending up in odd places, *consumed* by misery, hearing her voice in my head as if it were drifting to me on the wind . . . and she'd been a few miles away. I'd dreamed of her, over and over, visions that twisted and turned and caused me to wake up in a cold sweat, swearing her scent hung in the air all around me like a benediction. And all that time, *she'd been right within my reach.*

I grabbed my jacket. I couldn't stay in this apartment. I left and walked a couple blocks to a bar I'd never been in before. I hadn't had a drop of alcohol in the year since I'd left Colorado, but if anything called for a sudden fall off the wagon, this was damn sure it. *Lily.*

CHAPTER TWENTY-THREE

Lily

The aquarium was somewhat crowded on a Sunday at eleven in the morning. Dim and cool, marine life occupying tanks on both walls and even overhead, it was like walking underwater, like being in a different world. Lost in thought, I wandered past the floor-to-ceiling tanks, trailing my finger along the glass when a fish swam right up to it, following its movement with my hand. I'd been holed up the entire day before and I'd needed to get out or I'd go crazy. That particular argument had made my grandmother pale and had her suggesting I go into San Francisco to the aquarium where she'd bought a pass several months before. She had an appointment—thank God—and so I'd been able to get out alone. I wasn't particularly interested in the aquarium, but that wasn't really the point. The point was a small dose of freedom, something to occupy my mind. And so here I was. Of course, I was certain the woman with an aquarium badge hanging around her neck who seemed to be trailing me wherever I went was not a coincidence. My grandmother had called someone to make sure I didn't run away again. I supposed I didn't exactly blame her. I'd obviously taken years off her life already. And now after what had happened at the charity event, I was sure she thought I might break at any moment. And, God, maybe I would. Still, feeling like a mental patient, even in the outside world, was intolerable. I couldn't live like that. It was no life at all.

I felt his body heat behind me—an awareness that made the small hairs on the back of my neck stand up—before I heard him speak. My body stiffened.

"You still smell the same. Even here." His voice was low and slightly hoarse right behind my ear. "It's like I can smell the forest all around us, even now. Pine, and," he paused and I somehow knew he was closing his eyes, "those wildflowers that grow at the side of the stream—the white ones." His breath fanned the side of my neck and I shivered, closing my eyes briefly, swearing the rush of the water in the tanks was the stream flowing past us. *If only.*

"You shouldn't be here," I said, but it came out breathy and unsure. More a question than the statement I'd intended. My heart was beating out of my chest.

"No?" He moved my hair over my shoulder and leaned in. "Then where should I be, Lily?"

"This isn't the forest, Ryan. It's the real world and—"

My words died as Ryan's hand moved slowly down my arm, his fingers weaving through mine. I clenched my eyes shut. "And what?"

"How did you find me?"

"I called the car company you used, told them I'd forgotten something in their vehicle, had them confirm the address. I followed you here."

"Inventive," I said, pulling my hand from his. I was trembling, and I suddenly hated him just a little for doing this to me. Hated him for making this *hurt* more than it already had.

"I went back, you know, every month for nine months straight. I went back to Whittington and I searched for you. *You haunted me. I walked through the forest. I called your name.* And all this time, all this time, Lily, you were a few miles away from me. You just disappeared. Were you really going to leave me without so much as an explanation again?" The hurt in his voice made my chest ache. "Didn't you think of me, too?"

Oh, God. Oh, Ryan. Please don't do this to me. He'd gone back. He'd searched for me. He pulled my arm and I stumbled around a corner with him into a small alcove on the other side of a tank of jellyfish. Moving light danced all around us in the dim space and I was face to face with him now. He was right in front of me—too close—his blue, blue eyes, his high cheekbones, his straight nose, and those lips . . . the lips I would never kiss again. The lips I had watched kiss someone else. "Wasn't what my grandmother told you enough?" I averted my eyes. "Everything that happened between us, none of it was *real*. None of it. You were a fantasy, nothing more. Don't you see, now that you know about me? We were just two sick people running through the forest like children playing make-believe."

He leaned back suddenly as if I'd hit him. "You're wrong. You don't believe that. You can't even look at me when you say it. *This* isn't real. *This* is fake, Lily. A *lie*. You acting as if what we had meant nothing is *false*. What we had in the forest was real and it was right. What I felt for you, what I *feel* for you is real."

"You didn't know who I was," I whispered. "You didn't even know who *you* were."

He watched me for several moments. "Is that part of this then? You not being able to get past *me* being sick? Damaged goods?"

"I . . . yes," I lied, steeling my spine. "That, and the fact that I'm sick, too. I'm sick. That girl you were kissing at the charity event, you should be with her. Someone normal, someone . . ." I trailed off, not knowing exactly how to end that statement. *Someone better, healthier . . . someone not me.* Oh God, just the thought *hurt* with an intensity that stole my breath. I felt like I was dying inside.

He regarded me for several tense moments, his eyes moving over my features. "Is that what you want? You want me to be with her?"

"Yes," I said, feeling as if I might be sick. "Yes, that's for the best." My body was cold and shaky. Ryan took a step backward. I opened my mouth to beg him not to go, but snapped it shut. This was for him. And really, this was for me, too. This was for the best. *Wasn't it?*

"Why'd you come to San Francisco?" he demanded.

"Why?"

"Yes. If what you felt for me wasn't real, then why are you here?"

"The hospital . . . it's one of the best and—"

"That's a lie. There are plenty of good hospitals all over the United States. Why here?"

I released a breath. "I just . . . I wanted to make sure you were doing okay. I wanted to be able to check on you, to see you. I was worried, I—"

"You did care."

"Yes, of course I cared. I know what it's like to be sick and alone. But that's all. I checked on you, but I never meant to see you again."

"You *were* following me. I *saw* you. God, Lily, I thought I was going crazy again." He put his hand on his forehead and leaned his head back, gazing at the ceiling for a moment before looking back down, directly into my eyes. No. *No*, he was never meant to notice me.

I blinked. "I didn't know you saw me. I'm sorry."

"You're sorry? Jesus." He ran his fingers through his hair, already tousled as if he'd been running his hand through it before he even got here. I remembered the feel of that hair, remembered the texture as if it were a memory branded into my skin. "You're sorry," he repeated as I chewed at my lip.

"You thought I was nothing more than a vision," I said, the hurt of that, the ridiculous, irrational hurt finding me again. But maybe it would make it easier for him to walk away now. And that was a good thing. It *had* to be.

"And yet I still longed for you. I should have known." He looked off behind me for a moment. "It's just that everything was . . . and I had a hard time trusting myself—"

"I know. I understand."

Something came into his expression. Something I couldn't read, something intense. "You don't think it's fate? That we met each other? And then that we were at the same damn party? How is that not fate? We found each other once, through that huge expanse of forest—two people reaching for each other in the dark. Take my hand, Lily. Grasp on to me now. *Please.*" He reached his hand out toward me, begging me with his eyes. I sucked in a gasp of air, raising my hand. Just as I knew the soft texture of his hair—longed to run my fingers through it again—his strong, graceful hands had touched me intimately. They'd touched my body and my soul. I *ached* for his touch again. *Just one touch, Lily. Feel his love one more time.* Our fingertips brushed.

Behind Ryan, I saw the woman with the aquarium badge walk past, glance at us and hurry away. There was my answer. There was my fate. Not Ryan. Never him . . . "I have to go," I breathed. I dropped my hand. "No, Ryan, I have to *go*. We can never be together. Never. Don't contact me again. I have to go." Ryan stared at me for a second and then dropped his own hand, stepping aside.

"Go then."

I moved around him and hurried toward the entrance, resisting the urge to break into sobs.

****

"Hey, girl," Nyala said, swinging the door open and turning away immediately. "Close it behind you. I'm writing." I shut the door and headed toward her office, the despair of my run-in with Ryan making me feel slow, sluggish, heartsick.

I had left the aquarium needing a friend, needing Nyala. I'd called her, but she hadn't answered. I knew that didn't mean she wasn't home and available, though—she rarely answered her phone—so I'd hoped for the best and taken the bus to her duplex in The Mission.

"Sorry, Nyala. I don't want to interrupt you." Ny had only been home for a couple months, and I'd only visited her here once in that time. She would check herself into the hospital when she felt as if she were unraveling. She'd been there a handful of times over the year I'd been treated, and we'd become fast friends despite not having a whole lot in common—on the surface at least. She was in her fifties, wore her hair in long dreadlocks that fell down her back, and usually dressed in bright African-print dresses. She was warm and wonderful, and I thought of her as a mother figure, albeit one who was unpredictable and given to flights of fancy. At least, that's how I put it. The doctors would describe it differently I was certain.

"No, no, I can put the writing aside for now. I can just as easily talk while I sculpt. Let me just close this file, and I'll get my hands busy doing that." Nyala was in one of her manic-creative moods. It was either create or die, or at least that's the way she described it. Sometimes she'd stay up three or four days straight, moving between writing, sculpting, and painting. Then she'd sleep for a week. She never minded me visiting when she was in one of these moods, though. In fact, the more things she was doing at once, the better, or so it seemed, even when she was in the hospital and art supplies were limited. She hit some keys on her computer and then stood up, gesturing for me to follow her. She opened the door to the room at the back of her apartment, the one that overlooked the garden and had windows on three walls letting in lots of natural light. She had several easels set up and a table where it looked like she was creating the bust of a woman. She sat down in front of the clay and started working it with her hands.

"Sit down," she gestured to a berry-pink, overstuffed antique settee on the wall opposite her. I took a seat, leaning against the back and sighing loudly.

"Uh oh. What's that?" Nyala asked.

"Ryan. I ran into Ryan at a party and then he . . . found me." Nyala's hands paused only momentarily before she started working again, but her eyes remained on me.

"He did, did he?"

"You don't sound surprised."

"I'm not."

I tilted my head. "Why aren't you surprised?"

"Fate."

I groaned. "That's the second time today I've heard that word."

Nyala glanced up at me. "Fate is the language God uses to speak to us, baby. It's up to us to listen, though. What happened?"

I tilted my head, taking in her words. I was surprised Nyala believed in God, that anyone with an illness of any kind could believe in a loving God. Why couldn't he heal us then? Were we not worthy? But that was for another day, I supposed. I moved that aside and told her about running into Ryan at the charity event and then about him showing up at the aquarium that morning. "Damn," she said, the word filled with surprise. It was difficult to surprise Nyala when she was in one of her creative moods.

"Yeah," I said. "I know."

Nyala was quiet for a moment, focusing on what her hands were doing to the clay in front of her. "You never let go of him," she said.

I let out a long breath. "No. I still love him. And it still doesn't matter." And to grieve for him the way I had for months and months . . . I couldn't do it. Not again.

"Oh, it matters. I'd say it matters a great deal."

I shook my head. "I won't do that to him, Ny."

"What? Strap him with the burden of you?"

I let out a small laugh lacking in humor. "Basically, yes." I paused. "He looks so good, Nyala." I couldn't help the small smile that tugged at my lips. "He looks healthy and . . . happy."

"And you're not? Healthy, I mean?"

I shook my head. "No. And I probably never will be, not entirely. You know my past, Ny. What do I have to offer him other than the promise of a chaotic life? Of always wondering if I was just going to . . . go into one of my episodes at a moment's notice?"

She raised a brow, but her eyes remained on her work. "Episodes? Is that what the specialists are calling them these days?" *No, that's what my grandmother called them, and I'd taken up the term.*

"You get my point, though, Ny. After everything Ryan's fought through, does he deserve dealing with that? Dealing with *me?* Does he deserve *that* fate?" I bit at my lip, pondering the question as misery settled over me.

Nyala shrugged. "*Deserve* it? Do any of us *deserve* what we get in this life? Is that how it works?" She shrugged, answering her own question. "Sometimes I suppose. Mostly, no."

I sighed. "I just . . . why do I have to be this way? I just want to be free of it all. God, I just want to cast it all off."

Nyala was looking at me with sympathy. "You can't. Some things must be carried, and that's just the way it goes. It's not for us to know the why. Listen, baby, life is a series of things we choose and things we carry." She stood up, grabbing a rag on the table in front of her and wiping her hands clean before coming to sit next to me on the settee. "The things we choose, well, those are ours. But we don't get a vote on the things we carry. Some are heavier than others, some we can put down eventually, and some are ours to keep. We don't have a choice in the burdens we're given to bear, but we do have a choice in how we hold them. We can strap them to our backs and walk through the world hunched over under the weight like someone who should spend his or her days in a bell tower. Or we can stand tall and straight like one of those African queens carrying a woven basket on her head." She straightened her spine and held her head high, demonstrating her words, and then she smiled gently. "No, baby, we don't get to choose what we carry, but we do get to choose the grace with which we carry it."

I let out a small sniffle, a tear streaking down my cheek. I smiled and swiped at it.

"Now, are you Quasimodo or are you a queen?" she asked.

I laughed softly, wiping at another tear. "I want to be a queen."

Nyala gave me a dazzling smile. "*Good.* Then stand tall. Stake your claim, my love. Ryan—or any man for that matter—would be *lucky* to have you, brave, beautiful girl." She stood up and returned to her sculpture.

"Even if I'm a queen, I'm still difficult to love," I insisted.

"I don't find you difficult to love. I find it quite easy actually."

I smiled. "That's because you just . . . accept me."

"Maybe he wants to accept you, too."

"I shouldn't let him." *I want to let him. I want to let him so much.*

"It might not be your choice. And, baby girl, the ones who see what we carry and want us anyway, those are the ones to hold on to."

"How could it ever end well, Ny?" I asked.

"Oh, Lily. Happily ever after doesn't mean a lifetime of perfection.

I don't think *anyone* believes that happily ever after means there are no unhappy days, even unhappy years. It means loving *forever*, despite all the many reasons it's easier not to."

I sighed loudly again thinking that Ryan didn't know the extent of what he might be dealing with, what *forever* might mean between the two of us. "Oh, the angst," Nyala said and laughed. "I should write this into one of my novels."

I gave her a mock stern look and then smiled. "I should write a novel of my own. I obviously have the imagination for it."

Nyala nodded. "You have the heart of an artist. It's why so many of us lose our minds."

I laughed. "What?"

"No, it's true. Go into any institution in the world and take a poll. I don't have any scientific data to support it, but from my personal observation, the majority of crazy people are artists. They're more sensitive souls—they have to be to create art others respond to. But it means they're more easily broken."

I shook my head, smiling. "*I'm* not an artist."

"Maybe you just haven't found your art yet." She pulled her head back and gave her clay an assessing look and then went back to work. "Think about what it means to be a writer, for example—you have to create an entire world in your head and then fashion characters so believable you know their every thought, their every dream, every intention, every potential, every motivation. You have to *live* in their head enough to understand them, to tell their story. You have to make them so believable that sane humans actually fall in *love* with that character. Or mourn their losses, or feel anger on their behalf, feel *authentic* emotion for them. I think a writer needs to be at least partially crazy to manage something like that."

Yes. Yes, that's exactly how it could be for me in my own mind. I should never, *ever* try my hand at writing because I had *no* problem going there. My problem was that I would *stay* there. And I wouldn't know whether the world I'd suddenly found myself in was real or not real. That's what it was like to go crazy—like jumping straight into a novel. In any case . . . "I think most authors would say they have a vivid *imagination*," I corrected.

She snapped her fingers, a small bit of clay flying away from her hand. "Yes! And you and I have the most vivid imaginations of all. Next time one of us sees a person who isn't there, or knows all the thoughts and feelings of a vision, we'll say about the other, 'Isn't her imagination *particularly* vivid?' What a wonder! What a marvel! It's not just vivid, it's strikingly vivid. *Astonishingly* vivid. The most vivid of all."

I laughed, my soul feeling lighter. Nyala somehow managed that. Always. I guess some people might call her crazy—and there were times when she sunk into a dark abyss where only she went—but I called her my miracle. She was somehow able to magically change my outlook on an entire situation, to provide that tiny shift in perception that gave me hope to rise above the problem. And it always felt right because she was able to put voice to that which was already in my heart. How she did that, I wasn't sure, but if that didn't speak of miracles, I didn't know what did.

"Those quacks and pill pushers might try to diagnose us with something else, but Lily, girl, our *real* diagnosis is a particularly vivid imagination. And we both know it." She gave me a big grin.

Oh, if only that were true. Still, sometimes you had to laugh. And that's just what I did, collapsing back on the couch.

****

I felt a little bit better when I left Nyala deep in her clay, although seeing Ryan at the aquarium still weighed heavily on my heart. As I walked, I pulled out my phone to call my grandmother. She answered on the second ring. "Hello, darling."

"Hi, Grandma. I just wanted to let you know I'm headed home."

"Okay. I need to run out to the store in a little bit so if I'm not home when you get here, I'll be right back. I have a pot of gravy on the stove. Did you have a good time at the aquarium?"

I hesitated. "Yes. Grandma, did you call someone to follow me around there?"

There was a pause. "No. Why would I do that?"

"Because you don't trust me." *And could I really blame her?*

She sighed. "I do trust you, Lily. And I want you to get out. It's good for you. I just don't want—"

"I know. You don't want me to see Ryan. We talked about that. I agreed."

"Right. Speaking of which, I scheduled the movers. We fly back to Colorado two weeks from tomorrow."

I swallowed. "All right."

"All right. I'll see you soon?"

"Yes, see you soon."

It took me a little over forty-five minutes for public transportation to get me from downtown San Francisco to Marin. From there, I walked to my grandmother's rental house and let myself in the door. "Hello?"

There was no answer. I followed the scent of Grandma's "gravy"—rich tomatoes, basil, and garlic—and saw it simmering on the stove. Grabbing the wooden spoon she had set on a spoon rest to the side of the stove, I lifted the lid of the pot, leaning in and inhaling the comforting smell. I stirred the sauce and replaced the lid, moving over to the sink to wash my hands. I'd make a salad to go with dinner.

"Lily," came the deep voice behind me.

Startling and turning abruptly, I found Jeffrey standing in the doorway. My heart began hammering in my chest. "H-Hello," I said. "I was just going to make a salad. Will you be joining us for dinner?"

He shook his head. "No. I have an appointment tonight."

"Okay," I said, glancing at the nametag pinned to the lapel of his suit. Why would he be wearing a nametag? I frowned, blinking at it, unable to read it from across the kitchen. He suddenly began advancing on me, and I sucked in a breath, my eyes shooting to his face. I pressed my butt against the sink, unable to back up any more than I already had. Jeffrey came to within a step of me. He brought his hand up and ran his knuckle down my cheek. I flinched. "You seem so jumpy around me.

Why? I'm here to help you. I only want—"

"Lily," my grandmother called from the foyer. Jeffrey stepped back.

"In here," I called loudly. Jeffrey gave me one last assessing look and then turned and left the kitchen. I heard him chat briefly with my grandma and then the front door closed. A few seconds later, my grandma came into the kitchen carrying a bag of groceries. I took the bag from her and she leaned toward me as I kissed her on her cheek.

"Are you okay? You look peaked."

"I'm okay," I said softly. "I was going to make a salad." I turned toward the refrigerator.

"That would be great. All the ingredients are in the crisper."

"Grandma, about Jeffrey—" The chiming of the doorbell cut me off. "I'll get that," I murmured.

I walked through the living room and into the large foyer, peeking through the curtain next to the door. It was a woman, turned halfway away, but I recognized her immediately. She was the woman from the charity benefit. The woman who had been with Ryan. "Good grief," I whispered. *What more?* She turned and saw me peeking at her. Taking a fortifying breath, I opened the door. "Hello?" I asked, pretending I didn't know who she was.

"Don't pretend you don't recognize me," she said. "I can tell by your expression that you do. My name is Jenna. May I come in?"

I stared at her. She was somehow even more beautiful when dressed casually in jeans and a sweater. Her auburn hair was down and curled around her beautiful face, and her deep brown eyes were a stunning contrast to her creamy complexion. "How did you know where I live?"

"I'm good friends with a client who helped organize the charity event," she said, not elaborating. I supposed she had access to the guest list and all the information pertaining to that. I sighed and stood back, holding the door open to her. What a wonderful way to wrap up a *wonderful* day.

"Who's there, Lily?" my grandmother called.

"Someone for me," I called back, gesturing for Jenna to follow me to the formal living room to the right of the foyer. Doubtless my grandmother would listen in at the door, but I couldn't bring myself to care. Not today. I took a seat on the couch and Jenna sat down on the loveseat, facing me.

"I guess I'll just get right to it," she said. "I know who you are. I know about you, and I've come to tell you to stay away from Ryan."

What the hell?

I let out a small laugh. "You *know* about me? You know what exactly?"

"I was listening when you talked to him in the lobby. I heard what your grandmother said about you being ill. About you being in a hospital—a mental hospital, I assume. A whole *year*? You must have been very, very disturbed. Are you still? Disturbed that is?" She cocked her head to the side and narrowed her eyes as if she could tell more about my mental state if she looked hard enough.

I felt myself pale and clasped my hands in my lap. I wasn't sure I had ever felt such deep loathing for someone before. *Snake.* "I'm not sure how my situation is any of your business, Jenny, was it?"

She gave me a smile, but it dissolved into something verging on a sneer. "Jenna," she corrected, her voice dripping phony sweetness. "Listen, Lily, Ryan told me in detail about his own struggles, poured his heart out actually. He's finally healing from his loss. Do you really think he needs to bring more unpredictability into his life? More chaos and uncertainty? If you care about him at all, which I suspect you do by the way you looked at him at the event, surely you see that I'm right."

I paused, regarding her, trying my very best not to let her see how much her words affected me. It was the crux of my pain regarding Ryan, in fact. How did this horrible woman know that? It was as if she could look right inside my heart, and that was not tolerable. And the fact that he'd shared his deepest secrets with her just . . . *hurt. This* was the woman Ryan had feelings for now? I supposed I should be personally offended by his poor taste in women. He'd been *kissing* her. *His* mouth had been on the mouth of the woman in front of me now, capable of spewing such ugly, hateful things. And I had told him he should be with *her*? I had practically demanded he choose her. Because I'd thought it was right, *better.* I didn't answer her question.

"He and I are just beginning something very special. I suppose he feels some attachment to you being that you were there during a very rough time in his life, and I suppose he feels as if he can't turn you away now. He must feel very sorry for you." She shook her head as if the thought was one that made her sad. "So, do the right thing—do him the favor of not having him make a choice that will cause him guilt. He doesn't need one more thing weighing on his mind."

"I'd like you to leave my home now."

"Happily. I'm done here." She stood. "Think on what I've said. I'm sure you'll realize I'm right."

"Goodbye, Gemma."

She narrowed her eyes at me again. "Goodbye, Lily. Be well." But the look on her face belied her words. If a person could be assassinated with a final glance, I'd be lying on the floor in a pool of blood.

I didn't stand up. My hands were shaking with anger but also with humiliation. It was almost as if Jenna was the very embodiment of all my deepest insecurities. She walked out of the room, and a moment later I heard the front door close quietly behind her. I heard the soft sound of my grandmother's shoes moving back toward the kitchen and let out a long exhale. A moment later I heard a clatter from the kitchen and my grandmother say, "Oh dear, what a *mess.*"

CHAPTER TWENTY-FOUR

Ryan

My legs didn't want to cross the threshold, but I knew in my heart it was time. Holden's house. Taking a breath, I stepped inside. *I'm here, buddy. I'm finally ready.* Everything looked exactly the same, and yet a still emptiness filled the space, a sense of loneliness that had never been here before. *God, I've missed you.* Holden's housekeeping staff had been kept on, so everything was neat and clean—no dust, and fresh vacuum lines were visible on the living room carpet. I wanted to flee this place, flee the feelings it was bringing alive inside me, flee the despair bubbling up my throat, but I didn't. With a heavy heart, I climbed the grand double staircase in the foyer to what had been Holden's bedroom. I'd do a little bit today, and then I'd save the rest for another day, as it didn't need to happen all at once. This house was paid for, and even if it wasn't, I had plenty of money to keep making whatever payments needed to ensure its upkeep. I went directly to Holden's massive, walk-in closet and took a couple suitcases off the shelves. Jenna had been right—people would probably fall all over themselves to bid on Holden's underwear, but that didn't feel right. I'd quietly drop this stuff off at a homeless shelter—or one of those charities that helped provide interview attire for indigent people—luggage included, and I wouldn't say a word about who had owned it. That's what Holden would have wanted, and no one knew that better than I did. He'd been generous to a fault but not showy. Never showy. And everything he had done for charity, he'd done anonymously.

Shoes were dumped unceremoniously in the suitcases, then jeans and T-shirts. I'd bring a garbage bag up here next time and throw away his personal clothing items. I was still so fucking pissed off, so maybe I really would auction them off on eBay. I just wasn't sure whom exactly I was so angry with—him, myself, maybe both. I sighed. "Sorry, man, but I am. I'm so damn mad. I fucking am. You should be here." I sat down on the small bench in the middle of the room and just stared around, letting a few tears fall. This was okay; this was normal. This was the way *normal* people grieved. And why had I come here today when I had planned to come weeks ago and decided I wasn't ready? And I was here *now*—the day after Lily had rejected me? Why? To prove I was strong enough to handle this? To prove I wasn't the damaged goods I'd been made to feel like? To *prove* I could grieve normally? "Christ," I muttered.

I carried the suitcases into the hall and took one last look around his room. Eventually, I'd have to do something with the furniture. Either that, or I could sell the house furnished. I walked downstairs, lugging the overstuffed suitcases and set them down at the front door. I looked back up the vast staircase. *The office.* It was the only other place I could think of that I'd need to clear personally, the only other place he might have personal items, personal correspondence, etcetera.

Inside the room, there were a couple bookshelves, but the only books in it were ones I could tell had been placed there for show by a decorator. Holden had never read or been interested in reading War and Peace in his life. I had to chuckle at that. Holden had been many things, but a bookworm had not been one of them.

We so rarely hung out in his office, I didn't recognize most of the items, but a box on the bottom shelf looked vaguely familiar. Picking it up, I placed it on the desk. What I saw when I opened it caused my breath to catch. *Oh shit.* Photos of us as kids. As I flipped through them, memories skated through my mind: how we would use BB guns to shoot at cans in Holden's backyard for hours after school when we were supposed to be doing homework. How Holden would get model car kits for his birthday and Christmas, and his dad would build them with us. How Holden would grow impatient and I'd end up finishing them while he chattered relentlessly about anything and everything, just there, keeping me company. The time a kid at school tripped me in the hallway and laughed as I wiped out, and later Holden spent his allowance money on shaving foam and squirted about fifteen cans of it through the vents in his locker. Watching R-rated horror movies when I spent the night at his house, even though we weren't allowed, and then being too scared to go to sleep. Tears were streaking down my cheeks, even after I closed the box. In some strange way, now that Holden was gone, I felt like I'd done all those things alone. It felt like I kept losing Holden in little pieces: first in his physical presence, then in the things I could no longer remember— the sound of his voice, the unique phrases he liked to use. Once his house was cleaned out, I would lose proof of him in the items he owned. And then I'd be truly alone. No family. No best friend. No one.

You never really lost him. He'll always be a part of you. Always, Lily had said.

Lily. And suddenly peace broke through one of the cracks in my broken heart, just like those small flowers that somehow—impossibly— grew out of fissures in the rocks at the edge of the forest stream. Holden had changed me; he had saved me, in so many life-altering ways, whether he was here now or not, whether I got to keep him forever, or whether I didn't. I clenched my eyes shut, holding back another flood of tears. Despite the peace that flowed through my heart, an aching sadness settled inside, too. I recognized this moment for what it was: I was saying goodbye. I was finally strong enough to let him go. I tilted my head back and held my fingers up in the shape of a V. "Thank you," I choked out. "Thank you so much, buddy."

On my way out of his house, I stopped in the downstairs bathroom. After I'd washed my hands, I opened the medicine cabinet. Inside were two prescription bottles—pain pills prescribed to Holden. I hesitated only briefly before I shut the cabinet and left the bathroom. I didn't even bother flushing them down the toilet—I felt no desire whatsoever to take them. As I closed the door behind me, despite the lingering sadness, my heart felt full of all the things Holden had given me in this life: peace, love, and strength. And I'd carry those healing gifts with me forever.

****

The doorbell rang just as I had sat down to a solitary dinner of grilled cheese and tomato soup. Wiping my hands, I got up to answer it to find Jenna standing there, biting nervously at her lip. My shoulders drooped. "Hey Jenna," I said, feeling the guilt of seeing her hurt face right in front of me. I held the door open so she could enter and led her over to my couch. "How are you? Do you want something to drink?"

She gave me a hesitant smile. "I'd love some wine if you have it."

"I'm sorry, I don't keep any alcohol in my apartment. I have soda . . ."

"Soda's good. Thanks."

I went to the kitchen and filled a glass and brought it back to her. She took a sip. I sat down next to her.

She put the glass on the coffee table and turned to me. "I'm sorry to drop by without calling—"

"It's okay." I shook my head. "I haven't called you back, and you deserve an explanation." I ran my hand through my hair. "I'm sorry, Jenna. I'm so sorry for what happened at the charity event. I can only imagine how you felt. If I had had any idea . . ."

She reached out and put a hand on my leg, squeezing it gently. "It's okay, it was a surprise. To run into someone from your past, it's such a confusing feeling."

I remembered the first night I'd met her at the bar—she'd said her ex-boyfriend had shown up with his fiancée. Still, she hadn't thought her ex was a ghost . . .

"Yeah, it was a shock."

She looked down. "Have you spoken to her? Lily, right?"

I paused. "I have. She doesn't want anything to do with me."

It looked as if Jenna's shoulders relaxed slightly. "And you?"

I sighed. "That's more difficult to answer, Jenna. And I'm sorry about that. I really am." She shifted, crossing her legs and removing her hand from my thigh.

"You're still in love with her?"

I bent my head forward, massaging the back of my neck, stalling because I felt terrible about this whole situation. After a moment, I looked back up at Jenna. "Yes, I'm still in love with her."

Her face crumpled a little. "And yet, she doesn't want you."

"No, she doesn't want me."

Jenna took a deep breath, sitting taller. "Listen, Ryan, we just started dating. I understand you have lingering feelings for someone else. And that sucks for me. But, why not see where this can go between us? I'm willing to stay and see what happens. I really feel like, given the time, we can have something special together."

I blinked at her. "Jenna . . ." I let out a breath, shaking my head from side to side slowly. "Lily doesn't want to be with me, but it doesn't change how I feel about her. It *won't* change how I feel about her—at least, not for a while. And Jenna, it wouldn't be fair for me not to end things with you when my heart is still wrapped up in someone else. That would be wrong."

"But you like me," she said, hurt evident in her voice.

I closed my eyes for a moment. "I do like you. I like you a lot. That's why this is so hard."

"But you're dumping me for a girl who doesn't want you? You won't even give us a chance?" Her face was a mixture of disappointment and confusion.

"I . . . no. I'm sorry." I shook my head. "I thought I'd moved on enough, but I haven't." God, this fucking sucked. But I owed it to both of us to be honest. There was no way I could continue dating Jenna, no way I could dredge up any interest in kissing her, touching her, when I knew Lily was on the other side of town. Just . . . no way. And I knew it made me a fool. I *knew* it made me pitiful and probably stupid. No, no probably about it—it definitely made me stupid. But I wasn't going to drag Jenna into my idiocy. Then I'd be stupid and immoral.

Jenna let out a long breath. "Well, then I guess that's that," she said sadly.

I almost apologized again, but there were only so many times I could say sorry before it would start getting plain annoying and possibly conceited. Jenna was a nice, beautiful, intelligent girl. She wouldn't have any trouble finding someone else, someone with far more to offer. I pressed my lips together and gave her a look I hoped conveyed the extent of my regret over this whole situation. She stood and I did, too. Her eyes looked misty. I stepped in to hug her, but she held up her hand and shook her head and so I stepped back. I almost said something else, something about hoping she found someone who wasn't an idiot hung up on someone else, how she deserved more, how awful I felt right then, but none of it seemed right. Everything that flitted through my mind sounded like a line or a platitude. In the end, I decided it was best not to say anything.

"Goodbye, Ryan. I wish you the best. I really do." Her expression was sad, but her voice was clipped. She wasn't going to drag this out. I felt guilty, but relieved.

I nodded. "Thank you, Jenna. I feel the same way."

She turned and left, closing the door quietly behind her. I sunk back down on the couch, resting my head against the back and groaning in frustration. *God, Lily, what are you doing to me?*

CHAPTER TWENTY-FIVE

Lily

$\mathbf{I}$ took a deep breath and knocked on the door in front of me. Ryan's door. He wouldn't be home, of course. It was a weekday, and he'd be at work, but I figured I'd try anyway, before putting the note with my phone number asking him to call me in his mailbox. So when the door swung open, I sucked in a startled breath and stepped back. Ryan stood there, wearing jeans and a black T-shirt, his expression one of immediate surprise. "Lily," he said, staring at me.

I opened my mouth to speak and then shut it, unprepared, not knowing exactly what to say. "I didn't expect you to be home," I finally managed.

He leaned his hip against the doorway and crossed his arms over his chest, his expression slightly wary, as if he was waiting for me to hurt him. *Again.* The way I'd done at the charity event and then at the aquarium. "So why'd you come here if you didn't think I'd be home?"

I bit at my lip for a moment. "I was going to leave you a note, with my number on it. I was hoping you might call me."

He paused, his eyes running over me quickly. After another moment he said, "Two days ago you told me never to contact you again."

"I know. I know I did."

He simply watched me for a moment, making me feel even more uncomfortable than I already was. All right, so he wasn't going to make this easy for me now. Maybe I didn't blame him—he was in self-preservation mode. "Well, now you can say what you were going to say on the phone, in person," he said, but not unkindly. He was perfectly still as if every muscle was tensed.

"I wasn't sure what I was going to say, honestly. I thought I'd have a little bit of time to think on it."

"Ah."

"So, um, why *are* you home?"

"I called in sick."

"Oh. Are you? Sick, I mean?"

"No."

I paused, waiting for him to continue, but he just stared at me. He still had that slightly startled look in his eyes that he'd had at the charity event, as if he still couldn't quite believe I was real. I *felt* real now though. I felt very real. My heart—filled with pain and uncertainty—was reminding me with every heavy beat. "Oh, okay, well that's good." I took the note I'd written out of my pocket and handed it to him. He took it and put it in his pocket and then sucked his bottom lip into his mouth for a moment.

"Will you come in?"

"I . . . yes. I mean, if that's okay." *Gather your courage, Lily. You didn't expect him to be home, but he is. Roll with it.* He stepped back and to the side as I walked into his apartment, my eyes moving over the furniture, taking in the classic, simple design, noting that he was obviously a very tidy housekeeper. Although it looked like he'd been parked on his couch. His laptop was open and there was a bottle of water and what looked like the remainder of a sandwich sitting on a plate, a few books with papers sitting on top so I couldn't see the titles.

He waved his hand at a chair next to the couch and I sat down. He took a seat on the couch. "So what was the gist of what you were going to say when I called you? Which I would have. I would have called you right away." There was something moving behind his eyes—nervousness perhaps—but his expression remained neutral.

My fingers twisted in my lap, and I stared down at them before finally raising my eyes back up to his. "I owe you an explanation."

He was quiet for a moment. "Is that the only reason you're here? To explain things to me?" *And then leave again* was implied.

I blinked at him. "Well that, and to let you know that your girlfriend came to see me."

"My girlfriend?" He frowned. "You mean Jenna? Why?"

I nodded. "Oh, she didn't mention it? She was very clear that I should stay far away. That I was bad for you."

His lips thinned and he looked briefly surprised, but then his expression went blank. "So you two agree then."

"Yes. No!" Anger and indignation spiked through me. "God, Ryan. I understand why you want to make this hard on me. I understand why you're angry. But no, I don't agree with her. The way she put it . . . hearing it from someone else, made me realize . . ." I threw my hands up in the air. "I don't even know what it made me realize, but when she said it, it just sounded—"

"Wrong," he supplied.

I let out a frustrated breath. "Yes. Wrong. It sounded wrong."

His shoulders relaxed slightly, and he leaned his elbows on his knees, bringing himself just a little bit closer to me. "It is wrong. And Jenna isn't my girlfriend. Truthfully, we only went on a couple dates. I broke it off completely yesterday."

That surprised me after seeing the depth of her possessiveness. "Oh . . . I . . . I mean, why?"

"Because it's not fair to date one person when you're in love with another, that's why." His voice was suddenly filled with intensity as if he had been barely holding it back and with those words, could no longer contain it.

I let out a breath. *He still loves me.* "Ryan . . ."

"Come sit next to me, Lily. Explain what happened. Tell me about your life. I want to know about you. I want to know every little thing. Please don't be scared. Please know that there's nothing you can tell me that will cause me to feel any differently about you." When I stood up and sat back down next to him, he turned toward me and took my hands in his. I gave him a smile and felt my lips waver slightly. *This. This is where I've longed to be.* It felt so good to be touched by him. He smiled back, so gently, and then he pulled me toward him, wrapping his arms around me. I relaxed into his embrace. It felt so good to be held. I hadn't been held by anyone in the year we'd been separated. I'd missed him so much. I burrowed into his warm, solid chest as tears slid down my cheeks. When I leaned away from him, he used his thumbs to wipe them away. "Lily, Lily of the Night," he murmured. "You've been all alone, too. You've been lonely just like me."

I nodded. "Yes," I whispered. "But not just lonely, Ryan. Lonely for you. Only for you."

He planted his lips on my forehead for several moments before he said, "I missed you, too, Lily. I can't even express how much I've missed you. I've ached for you. I still do. I still do." His voice sounded hoarse and filled with pain. I wanted to raise my mouth to his. I was trembling from holding back, but we had so much to discuss. So many things that might cause him to run . . .

"Ryan," I murmured. He seemed to read my thoughts because he pulled back and took my hands in his again.

"Can I get you a glass of water? Some coffee?"

I nodded, the tension releasing from my body. It was as if he'd read my mind and knew I needed a moment. He seemed to know my needs so well, though we'd spent so little time together. "Sure, water would be great."

Ryan stood up and headed to the kitchen and I stood, too, walking to the window and taking a deep breath, readying myself. I'd never talked about my illness with anyone other than Nyala and my doctors. I'd never been afraid like this.

I stared out of Ryan's window, overlooking the vastness of Golden Gate Park. From here, I could almost imagine it was our forest. It made me feel . . . *homesick.* Although I supposed that was the wrong word since it hadn't actually been my home. Still, the feeling lingered. I'd been *happy* there, though at the time, I'd been the mere ghost of myself.

I turned when I heard Ryan enter the room and walked back over to the couch. He set a bottle of water on the coffee table and I took a long drink once I'd sat back down.

"Do you need a minute?" he asked.

I set the water back down and shook my head. "No, I just need to start. I need to tell you."

"Then tell me," he said gently.

I took a deep breath and dove right in. "The winter I was ten, my mother took me to see The Nutcracker in downtown Telluride. It was an icy night and we almost stayed home, but in the end, my mother decided to brave the weather. It wasn't far and the roads had been salted." I paused, remembering how beautiful it had been that night, the way the tree branches had been encased in ice, making them sparkle in the moonlight. It had looked like a land from a fairy tale. The whole night had felt magical. I had been enchanted by the ballet, swept away by the music the orchestra played. The hot chocolate my mother bought me during intermission had been thick and sweet, topped by swirls of whipped cream with a candy cane stirrer. My mother had been particularly beautiful in her white winter coat and red scarf, her blonde hair long and lustrous, her green eyes shining with happiness. When we left, I told her it was the most wonderful night of my life.

"We had parked in a lot several blocks from the theater, and because we were talking and reminiscing about the performance, we got turned around and ended up on a side street that only had one dim street light. That's when the man stepped out from the doorway of a building." Ryan took my hand in his, squeezing it to let me know he was there. "At first I was just confused, but I could tell my mother was scared, and so I became scared, too. We tried to turn around and walk the other way, but he immediately caught up to us. He put a knife to my mother's throat and demanded money."

"God, Lily," Ryan said. I paused as I picked up the water and took a long drink, needing the moment.

"My mother handed him her purse and he poured everything out and took what he wanted. But he wasn't done with us. He dragged my mom into a doorway and started ripping at her clothes—" I drew in a large, shuddery breath, even now reliving the confused dread that had gripped me back then. "I was crying, of course, and he kept telling me to shut up or he'd kill my mother. I . . ." I'd begun shaking and Ryan pulled me in to his chest, making soft sounds of comfort.

"You don't have to do this, Lily, not if you don't want to."

"I do," I insisted. "I do want to." And truthfully, I didn't know if I could stop now that I'd started. Telling this story was like a runaway train. I had to see it to its completion—it felt like I didn't have a choice in the matter. Still, it felt good to soak in the warmth of Ryan's body as I told it.

Without leaning back up, I said, "He raped her. He raped her in front of me and I couldn't do a thing. I didn't even fully understand what was happening, just that he was hurting her so brutally." I felt Ryan's body tense, but he kept stroking my hair. He never stopped. "He pushed her aside and he . . . he grabbed for me. His eyes were glazed like he was on something. He started ripping at my clothes, just as he'd done to her." Ryan's arms hugged me tightly again and I could feel him trembling now, too. *Ryan, my sweet love.* "My mother hadn't fought, not until then. It was like the minute he reached for me, she came back to life. She started screaming and clawing at him. I was screaming, too. It was . . ." My words faded as I wiped at the tears that had begun to fall. "It was as if we'd walked right into hell from that warm, wonderful theater." I paused again, breathing deeply, attempting to gather myself. "The man brought his knife to my mother's face and he started slashing her, again and again and—"

"Lily, Lily," Ryan crooned. "Sweet Lily, I'm so sorry." I buried my face in his chest, my heart rate increasing, my breath coming out in short bursts as the scene played out behind my eyes.

"There was so much blood," I gasped against his T-shirt. "I'd never seen so much blood. That was the first time I just . . . went away. I just—" I sucked in a deep pull of air.

"I know," Ryan said. "I know." Yes, he did know. Yes, he did. I burrowed deeper into his chest, focusing on the steady rhythm of his heart, the comforting, masculine scent of him. He rubbed my back, murmuring calming words in my ear, soothing me as if he knew just what to do, as if he'd done it a hundred times before. My heart rate lowered, becoming steady and even again. I finally leaned back up and gazed into his face. His expression was filled with so much gentleness and understanding and a raw pain I'd never seen there before, not even when he'd told me about Holden.

"I didn't know my father. Truly, my mother hadn't known him either. She met him one weekend when she was on a girls' trip in New York City. She'd spent the night with him and then the next morning she found the wedding ring he'd hidden in the nightstand drawer. She found out a month later she was pregnant with me. The doctors say that sometimes these things run in families, but I'll never know as far as that side goes."

Ryan smoothed a piece of hair back that had fallen across my cheek. "Would knowing help, though? I think about that sometimes, too. My mother died when I was just a baby, and I don't know a lot about her side of the family either. Truthfully, I don't know a lot about my father's side of the family, other than most of them are drunks or wastrels." He sighed. "I just don't know what difference it would make."

I gave him a slight smile. "It might feel better to be able to blame someone."

Ryan let out a small laugh on a breath. "Let's blame them, then. They can't do anything about it."

I laughed a small laugh. "Okay."

Ryan's gaze moved over my face. "She didn't die that day, though. She survived."

"My mother? Yes, she survived. Sometimes I wondered if she wished she hadn't. But, . . . yes. She'd been beautiful before and then suddenly, one side of her face was so terribly scarred, ravaged really. Before . . . she'd loved to go out—she was always planning things for us, vacations, day trips, plays, shopping. After that, she never went out anymore. We went to live with my grandparents on their estate, and she became a shut-in. And she didn't want me to go out either. She became afraid of the world, afraid something awful would happen to me. I was put into the hospital for a while." I shook my head. "I wouldn't accept that we'd been attacked, was living in one of my dream worlds." I bit at my lip for a moment. "After that, I was more than happy to stay inside with her where it was safe. I was afraid of the world, too. She took me out of school, hired private tutors. For years, we just . . . clung to each other."

"But you grew brave, didn't you? You wanted more than the small world your mother had created for you."

I nodded, feeling the familiar guilt claw at my throat. "Yes," I whispered raggedly. "I wanted more. We fought. We fought a lot back then."

"That's normal, Lily. What you were feeling was normal."

"I know . . . logically, I do know."

"It doesn't make it easier, though."

"No, it doesn't."

"Did your mother end up giving you more freedom?"

I shook my head. "I got sick again. That time it wasn't even for any particular reason." I frowned. "In any case, by that time my grandfather, who was big in the real estate industry, had purchased Whittington."

"You were sent to Whittington?" Ryan breathed.

I nodded. "At that time, only one wing was open. It looked different than it does now. The garden was still beautiful. The open wing was clean, and there were only a very few patients being cared for. My grandparents believed I'd get more personal care there than I would anywhere else."

Ryan sat back on the couch, looking surprised. "Wow, Lily."

I nodded. "I know. I can't remember much of what happened while I was there. They kept me highly medicated. It's all so bleary." I furrowed my brow. "But I wasn't there very long. I did get better, and I went home. And soon after, my mother died. An aneurism. Such a freak thing."

"Oh no, God, Lily. Baby, I'm so sorry."

"It sent me somewhere else again." I took a long, shuddery breath.

"And back to Whittington I went."

"Oh, Jesus."

I nodded, recalling how cold it'd been there, how the lights were always too bright, the noises too loud. "Again, I wasn't there for very long . . . I went home. But I couldn't cope. Couldn't cope with the loss of my mother, with living in the world without her. Maybe I wasn't ready. I don't know."

"Lily, you'd never been given a chance to grieve. Did your grandparents help you with that? Did *anyone* help you with that?"

No, no one had. "No, they wouldn't talk about her. I think they thought mentioning her name would drive me into a psychotic break. And maybe they were even right, but," I sucked in a breath, "not to talk about her, to just pretend she'd never existed, when she had been my whole world. My everything. It was . . . unbearable. God, Ryan, it hurt so much." I squeezed my eyes shut for a moment. *It still did.* She was the only person who knew the horrific images I'd seen. She was the only person who knew the crushing helplessness I'd felt that night. I missed her so desperately.

"I know, baby." He brought my hand to his mouth and kissed my palm.

"Last year, it happened again, and that's why I ran away." I lowered my eyes. *I could describe it from my doctors' perspectives, but I wanted him to understand it from mine.* "It's so difficult to explain and have it sound rational because it's not rational. It's not and I know it." I paused. "The world shifts, and something in me shifts, too, because I just accept it. I accept a new story, a new life, new characters. Sometimes it's only a slight variation of my real life, and sometimes it's entirely different." As if I were looking at the real world through a kaleidoscope, *there*, but changing, shifting with a thousand different colors, and patterns, and light. I watched my own hands fidget in my lap, feeling embarrassed and insecure.

"I know," he said softly, because he *did* know. I looked up at him and saw the understanding, the acceptance in his eyes and felt both love and sadness blossom in my chest. My lips tipped up into what felt like a sad smile, and I nodded, taking a deep breath before continuing. "Last spring, I began imagining my mother was still alive. My grandfather—who had been ill—had passed away a few months before, and my grandmother was planning to sell Whittington. And in my imaginings, my mother wanted to spend the summer there. Just a couple months of the two of us, of mountain air, and sunshine, and a reprieve from my grandmother who did nothing but stare at my mom and me with worry and walk around wringing her hands. I can't even tell you exactly why it made sense in my mind that we go there. I could tell you the conversations I had with my mom, I could explain it all, but it would make me sound like the crazy person I am."

"Lily, stop, don't say it like that." His voice was raspy.

"It's true, though, isn't it?"

Ryan sighed, pressing his lips together for a moment. "I guess we're both crazy people, then. And Lily, I think that sometimes, well sometimes, the only way to survive is to go crazy."

I thought about that for a moment, how similar grief and madness seemed, two sides of the same coin perhaps. I thought about how the grief stricken tore at their hair, their clothes, seeming to want to escape their skin. And I thought about how the mentally ill sometimes did the very same thing. I'd seen it often enough at the institutions I'd been at, felt like doing it myself. Perhaps that's what a mental illness really was—an extreme, long-lasting cousin to grief. *How* did you carry such a thing with grace?

And he had to understand . . . "It happens to me again and again, Ryan. It happens over and over—even when things are seemingly fine."

"You've been well for a year now."

"Yes, and I've been well for a year before. Is this really something you want to deal with? When you already have struggles of your own? When you're just getting well? Just feeling strong? You are, aren't you?" I felt tears stinging my eyes again, one spilling over.

"Lily," he said, the tone of his voice tortured. "I want you just as you are. I just . . . I want you, and—"

"Please," I interrupted. "Please don't say that now." I brought two fingers up to his lips. "Please think about what I've told you. Consider what you're agreeing to. Consider what a life with me would be like. What a life between the two of us would mean. Please, Ryan. Please do that for me. And if you think about it and decide it's not best for you, for either of us, then you'll be honest with me, right? You'll be honest with me because you're good and kind and because you love me." I brought my fingers from his lips and used my hand to cup his cheek. Slight prickles of a new beard lightly scratched my palm. He closed his eyes and leaned in to my hand for several moments.

When he finally opened his eyes, he nodded, his expression so very solemn. "Okay. Yes, I'll always be honest with you. Always."

I let out a breath and nodded. "I know," I said. "I trust you, Boy Scout." I gave him a tremulous smile. "I've trusted you from the moment I met you."

Ryan leaned in and placed his forehead against mine and we both breathed together for several moments. "Will you tell me what happened at Whittington? How you found me and how your grandmother came to be there?"

I nodded. "Yes."

Ryan sat back and I cleared my throat. "I found you in the woods, right near Whittington. You'd fallen into a very shallow ravine. You looked to be mostly bruised and scratched, more so from your walk through the woods than from your fall."

"I was trying to get to you."

I nodded, bringing my hand up to his cheek again. "I know." I brought my hand away and continued, "I used a thick quilt and moved you onto it and dragged you to Whittington. And then I used your phone to call my grandmother. She was a nurse before she met my grandfather . . . Anyway, I knew she'd be able to help you." I shook my head. "I probably should have called an ambulance, but I didn't think you'd broken anything vital, and there was no blood—"

"You did just fine. I was fine."

I nodded, still feeling guilty. "Anyway, my grandmother assessed you and agreed to help as long as I promised to check myself into a hospital. Finding me there, muddy and frantic, learning that I'd been living at Whittington with my . . . mother," I bit my lip and closed my eyes briefly, "she was worried and heartbroken to say the least." I sighed, recalling that confrontation, the arguments, the tears. "I said I would check myself into a hospital as long as it was one near you. When we returned you to the lodge, I found your bag with a luggage tag on it with your name, faded and hard to read, but there. It just confirmed what I already suspected—that your name is Ryan. Ryan Ellis. My grandmother looked up the rest of your information." I paused. That whole time was so murky. I'd been filled with grief, with fear. I'd let my grandmother handle the details while I walked through the days as if I was half asleep. Grief does that to you. "Later, my grandmother rented a house in Marin, and we were going to return to Colorado after my treatment was complete."

"So you and your grandmother drove me to Brandon's lodge and carried me upstairs?"

"Between the two of us, yes," I said. "You helped a bit, but my grandma had given you a mild sleep medication."

"I thought so," he muttered. "Thank you for taking care of me." He looked down for a moment. "God, Lily, what you did for me." He raised his eyes to mine and they were filled with an emotion I couldn't define. "You agreed to go to a hospital for an undetermined amount of time. Because of me. It's like going to prison. I *know*. I," his voice cracked, "I don't even know what to say about that, how to express to you how grateful I am."

I shook my head, looking down at my lap. "I would have done anything for you, Ryan, made any sacrifice. And deep inside, I knew I was sick, too. I knew. Despite my worry for you, I knew I needed treatment myself."

Ryan was silent for a moment, his eyes roaming my face. "You must have been so," he paused as if searching for the right word, "surprised to discover who I really was, what I was going through."

"Yes," I said. The word broke and I cleared my throat. "I knew we couldn't be together, knew I wasn't good for you, but I loved you. I still do. I still love you."

"Lily," he said, pulling me to him again, "I love you, too. We will never be perfect or without flaws, the lives we've been given are not like that. But, Lily, in my heart, you are perfect for me. Perfectly mine. And I'm yours."

The heat suddenly flowing through my veins surprised me. After everything we'd just talked about, after baring all my secrets, revealing every last skeleton, I could hardly believe I was capable of feeling desire. And yet I did. Ryan leaned away slightly so he could look in my eyes. "Can I kiss you?" he asked.

"Yes," I murmured softly, leaning in and brushing my lips over his.

He hesitated for the space of two heartbeats before he said, "Don't kiss me as if it's goodbye, Lily. Don't do that to me again. Just promise me that."

I squeezed my eyes shut and I shook my head. "I'm not saying goodbye." *I just want you to be able to, if you decide you cannot live the kind of life I'd give you.*

His hands came up to my face, and he pressed his lips to mine. He slid his tongue into my mouth and I sighed, the sound of pleasure mingled with sweet relief, with *hope.* It seemed that, in so many ways, I knew him better with my eyes closed—I remembered the taste of his mouth, his skin. I remembered the sounds he made when he was causing me to lose control, and the sounds he made when he was losing it himself. I remembered the feel of his body pressing into mine, and the way he trembled against me. We kissed and kissed, sitting on his couch, becoming familiar with each other once again, and it felt like coming home.

When I finally pulled away, I said, "I have to get back. My grandmother's expecting me." But I didn't move, instead kept nuzzling his jaw, his ear.

"You don't have to go. You could just stay here and we could . . . talk some more," he said, not moving either, moving his lips back to mine and kissing me again. I smiled against his lips.

"No, I really have to go. I don't want to, but I have to," I murmured, finally pulling back and meeting his eyes. "And, Ryan, if you think about *us* and decide it isn't right, if you decide we shouldn't be together, I won't blame you." I kissed him once quickly on his lips and then on his forehead, both eyes. "I'll understand, and I'll love you anyway. I'll love you, but I'll let you go . . . again."

"God, Lily," he said, rubbing his own lips on my forehead, "I already—"

"No. Please, take some time. I only ask that. I need to know you've taken some time. Please."

He nodded, more sure, and pulled away to give me room. "Yes, okay. Okay. I will. I promise."

I gave him a small smile and squeezed his hand, bringing it up to my heart and holding it there for a moment before letting it go. With shaky legs, I moved toward the door. My body wanted to stay. My heart wanted to stay. But I knew at that moment, I needed to go, and as Ryan slowly led me to the door—holding my hand within his—I knew he understood. When he opened the door, I walked through. I couldn't bring myself to look back. If he chose to let me go, it meant that I'd just left my heart behind.

CHAPTER TWENTY-SIX

Ryan

The contemporary one-level home was visible from the top of a set of darkly stained wooden steps that leveled out to a deck wrapping around the front of the house. I began descending, taking in the incredible view. From where I was standing, I could see the Golden Gate and the Bay Bridges, San Francisco, and Sausalito. The sun was just beginning to set, the sky burning with red and orange fire. The view alone had to be worth a cool million. Quite the rental home.

When I got to the front door, I knocked twice. After a moment, I heard footsteps and a few seconds after that, the door opened to reveal Lily's grandmother. "Hello, Mrs. Corsella," I said. She only looked mildly surprised.

"Ryan."

I waited for a beat. "Is Lily home?"

"No, she's not."

Disappointment hit me. "Oh." I frowned. I hadn't anticipated her not being here. I had tried to call her on the way over and she hadn't answered, but it was dinnertime and I figured she might be busy with that. Or maybe she really was here and her grandmother was lying to me. "Do you know where I can find her?"

"Ryan, please come in." I hesitated. I hardly wanted a lecture right now on why Lily and I shouldn't be together. I'd taken a second day off work and spent it doing just as Lily had asked me to do: thinking about us. I sighed and stepped over the threshold of the door she was now holding open. I followed her to a formal living room to the left, directly off the small front entryway.

She took a seat in an off-white wingback chair, and I sat down on the couch. I waited for her to speak first. "Lily told me this morning that she confided in you about her . . . past. Her situation."

Her situation. "Yes, Lily told me about her life, her illness," I said. "I accept everything about her."

Her grandmother stared at me for several moments, her look assessing, but not cold. "You accept her." She was silent again for a moment. "Do you really even know what that means? Do you understand what it's like to love someone like Lily?"

Someone like Lily. Someone like *me.* "Yes, it's the best thing that's ever happened to me," I said, putting the conviction into my words that I felt in my heart.

"You think that now, Ryan. You think that now because Lily's doing well, she's here with you in every sense. You haven't felt the heartbreak of watching her just . . . disappear right before your eyes, of seeing her talking to people who aren't there because she's living in a world of her own."

"No, you're right, I haven't. But I'm willing to accept that possibility, even the probability. I'm willing to accept it because to let her go entirely is so unthinkable, that for me, there's no other choice. I choose her willingly, every part of her, even the darkness." *Just as she accepted me, even the darkness.*

Her grandmother's face seemed to gentle. "You're in love with her."

"Yes. *Yes.*"

She sighed. "Well, that's a start I suppose."

"I like to think it's a really good start."

"And you'll care for her?"

"With my whole heart and soul."

The glimmer of a smile appeared on her grandmother's lips. "She's in love with you, too. She made that quite clear to me this morning. She made it quite clear a year ago, too, though to my mind, there were more dire priorities." She looked down at her hands for a moment. "We talked . . ." Her words faded away, but I didn't speak. It looked as if she was still pondering something. When her eyes met mine, they were filled with sadness. "Lily is the only family I have left, Ryan. And she has no one except me."

It was obvious that she loved her granddaughter very much. I didn't want her to think that with me in Lily's life she would be relegated to the sidelines. She didn't deserve that. *She* didn't deserve to be alone either.

"Had," I said. "She has me now, too. You both do."

She nodded slowly, her eyes soft. "She has money, you know, from her mother's estate. And I've left Whittington to her. I suppose she can do with it as she sees fit. That seemed right." *Whittington belonged to Lily.* She paused. "Still, I worry, you know, what happens to Lily when I'm gone." She put her hand over her heart. "My heart is weak, and I worry—"

"You don't have to worry anymore. I want to be here for her."

"And what happens if *you* become ill again? What then?"

I let out a breath. "I don't know. I don't have all the answers in this situation. But I think—no, I know—that Lily and I belong together, and I have to believe we will find a way to make things work, whatever that might look like, whatever that might mean."

Her grandmother nodded sadly. "So much uncertainty. It's what I've tried to avoid for Lily."

"You can't. I don't know if anyone can, but especially for Lily and me, there will always be uncertainty. It's love that will make it bearable. No matter what, it will always be our one sure thing, our one constant. It will *always* be the light to lead us from the darkness."

Lily's grandmother's eyes shimmered with tears as she nodded. "Okay, Ryan." She let out a deep sigh, perhaps resigned, perhaps relieved, perhaps some of both. "I'm sorry I tried to keep you apart. I'm sorry for that. You have my blessing."

My shoulders relaxed, and I gave her a small smile. "Where is she?"

"She went to the planetarium. She should be home any minute if you—" We were interrupted by the sound of my phone ringing.

"Excuse me," I murmured, taking my phone from my pocket. It was Lily. "Lily," I answered. I heard static on the line. "Hello?" I turned slightly away from Lily's grandmother.

"Ryan," Lily said. "Sorry, it's windy. Can you hear me?"

"Yes, where are you?"

"I'm on the Golden Gate Bridge. I'm walking—"

I frowned. "The Golden Gate? What are you doing there?"

She answered, but it was lost in a burst of static. "Lily, I'm coming to get you, okay? Stay there, I'll find you. Hello?" I heard her garbled voice and repeated what I'd said right before the line went dead.

I looked at her grandmother. "Go," she said, giving me a small, concerned smile. "Go get her."

****

The wind hit my face as I moved quickly through people walking along the bridge. The sky was dark now and the bridge was lit, but the lighting was soft and subdued. To me, the Golden Gate at night never looked as if it was illuminated by electricity, but rather as if it was bathed in starlight. I walked through the strolling crowd, moving swiftly, swiveling my head when I spotted dark hair, disappointment hitting me each time I realized it wasn't Lily. My heart had begun to beat faster. *Where was she?* I picked up my pace even more, practically jogging now, my breath coming out in short bursts of air. I finally spotted a lone figure with long, dark hair standing near one of the towers, her arms resting on the ledge, staring out over the bay. My heart leapt with joy. It was her. Lily of the Night. *My* Lily of the Night. I slowed down as I neared. Her head turned right before I got to her as if she had sensed me approaching and the smile that lit her face made my heart jump in my chest. "Hi," I breathed.

"Hi," she said, turning her body to face me.

"What are you doing here?"

"I've never walked across the bridge," she said. "The sunset was so beautiful tonight and it just called to me, I guess. And now, the moon." She glanced up and I did, too. "Do you see that?" And then I did. I couldn't believe I hadn't noticed it before, so intent on finding her. The moon above was full and bright, so brilliant it outshone the stars.

"I do now," I whispered. We looked back at each other and Lily tilted her head, her smile fading, and a slightly nervous look replacing it.

"What are you doing here?"

I took her hands in mine. "You told me I had to understand what I was agreeing to. What being with you means. That sometime in the future you *will* just . . . go away. And it won't necessarily be because something terrible happens and it won't be because you want to. And it won't be because I could have done anything to prevent it from happening. Or sometimes it *will* be because something happened that you couldn't handle. It's unpredictable and—"

"Yes," she choked out, sorrow moving across her face, averting her eyes away from me and then back again. "Yes, Ryan."

"Then I'll come find you."

She laughed on a sniffle. "What?"

I squeezed her hands more tightly. "If you go away, then I'll come find you, even if it means I have to get lost for a while, too."

She shook her head, her smile sweetly puzzled. "How will you be able to do that?"

"Because," I said, moving even closer so our bodies touched and she had to tip her head to look up at me, "I'm not afraid of the darkness. I've been there before. I'll step into it willingly, unhesitatingly, and I'll come find you. No one else could make that promise and mean it, Lily. No one. No one except me."

A tear spilled from her eye and streaked down her cheek, but I continued to hold her hands, neither of us wiping it away. "I don't want to bring you into the darkness," she said.

"*I* might be the one to go there first. I can't guarantee that I won't.

Would you come for me, Lily? Would you?"

"Yes," she said, a sudden intensity in her voice. "A thousand times, yes. But this is why people would say we're all wrong for each other. People would say we're encouraging each other to be sick."

"That's ridiculous. I'm not saying I *want* you to be sick. I'm not saying *I* want to be sick. What I'm saying is that if you get lost, I will find you. And I will bring you back. Wherever you are, *whoever* you are, I will come there, and I will find you. And I hope you'll do the same for me."

"I don't know if that's possible, Ryan," she said tenderly, moving a piece of hair off my forehead, "and even if it is . . . the world certainly isn't set up for that kind of thing. Unless you're Willy Wonka and you own your own chocolate factory."

I gave her a slight smile. "Then we'll make our own world. No one can know what's possible until they've been inside minds like ours. And I believe we'll figure it out. *Somehow* . . . Do you believe, too?"

She finally smiled again, her lips trembling. "You *make* me believe."

"Good, because it's true."

She breathed out a small laugh and looked down, tilting her eyes up, looking so beautiful it made my heart ache. And deep inside, I felt something stir to life, as if my soul itself was just beginning to wake. *Finally.* "I love you, Boy Scout," she whispered.

"I love you, Lily of the Night. I love you so much." I let go of her hands and reached up to hold her face, her beautiful face. I brought my lips to hers and kissed her. "I'm going to love you forever," I murmured between kisses. "Forever. In the darkness, or in the light." She smiled against my lips as the world moved on around us. And for just that moment, we *had* found our very own world, and we lived in it joyfully.

CHAPTER TWENTY-SEVEN

Lily

Ryan unlocked the door to his apartment and pushed it open. I laughed out a startled sound of happy surprise when he lifted me in his arms and carried me over the threshold. "I think this is reserved for brides," I said, laughing.

He grinned. "It sort of feels like today is our unofficial wedding day," he said. "I'll do it again when it's official." He headed down a hall where he entered his bedroom and kissed me as my feet touched the floor. At the mere thought of someday being his wife, happiness filled my heart. I smiled against his mouth and pulled free, looking around his room. It was as tidy as the rest of the apartment, with simple, masculine furniture and a red and blue quilt on the bed. He had neat piles of books everywhere. *A bookworm.* And he still read paperbacks. My eyes lit on a shelf filled with models of all types—old-fashioned cars, ships, trains, airplanes, helicopters. I leaned in more closely, looking at the details of them. Everything was so tiny, so precise, so perfectly placed. I took a moment studying them. "You have the heart of an artist," I murmured.

Ryan came to stand next to me. "Nah, they're just models. They come with instructions. You can't really mess them up." I tilted my head, looking at the details of a helicopter, the way he'd drawn a bird on the side of one, its wings spread in flight, the wind streaming through its feathers. Another one had the 49ers logo on it. Most of them had tiny people drawn at the windows, drivers, passengers, all so beautifully done, their expressions different, some happy, some pensive, some bored. Everything was so tiny. How had he done that? I blinked, a sense of déjà vu overcoming me as if I'd seen something similar before . . . on a windowsill once upon a time, the light streaming in as I'd passed by an open door. As quickly as it came, the feeling passed. I stood up straight and turned to him.

"No, they might be just models for others, but you've made them into art. They're amazing." He gave me a crooked half smile, looking like a little boy who'd just been given a compliment and wasn't sure how to respond. "My friend says that those with the hearts of artists are more sensitive than others. They can be more easily broken."

Ryan brought my hair behind my shoulder and leaned in and kissed my neck, smiling against my skin. "I feel anything but broken right now," he whispered. I laughed softly, tilting my head to give him better access. Right now I didn't feel broken either. Right now I felt alive and filled with a joy so startling, I almost felt giddy. My eyes fell on something small and shiny on the top of his dresser and I reached over and picked it up, smiling as Ryan continued to nuzzle my neck. Holding it up, I sucked in a small breath. "You found it," I said, gazing at the arrowhead. Ryan lifted his head.

"Yes, I found it in my pocket." He closed my fingers around it. "You keep it. We'll take it back to the forest. Maybe we'll go skiing in Colorado this winter." I grinned, thinking about the future that lay ahead of us, suddenly filled not just with uncertainty but also with possibility. It was a heady thought, unfamiliar. The tunic top I was wearing had a small pocket over my breast and I dropped the arrowhead in it, focusing again on the wonderful feel of Ryan's mouth as it slid down my throat and came to rest over the dip right at the base. He rubbed his lips there, causing me to shiver and my core to clench. I bit my lip as he stepped back and pulled his shirt off. My eyes slid down his body. *He* was a work of art. So beautifully male, so perfectly proportioned. I felt my face flush with longing. Hot sparks ignited between my legs.

I ran a finger down the muscles of his stomach and he tensed, a whoosh of air escaping his lips. He reached forward and pulled the bottom of my shirt up and I raised my arms so he could pull it over my head. He laid it on top of his dresser as I kicked off my shoes and stepped out of my jeans. Ryan's eyes ran down my body—my bra was simple white cotton as was my underwear. I hadn't exactly expected to be standing in front of him like this when I'd left the house earlier. But he didn't seem to mind. His eyes burned my skin from my breasts to my feet and back up again, pausing for several moments on my breasts, causing my nipples to harden. Ryan stepped forward and pressed his hard body against mine, gripping my butt so he could pull me even closer. And there was nothing more delicious than feeling his hot skin against my own. He held me as his mouth stroked mine. I gripped his shoulders, my hands sliding down the muscles of his upper arms. And somehow—from somewhere—came the sharp scent of pine as if we were back in the forest, in our own world, just the two of us. I smiled against his mouth, feeling as if I was falling though I remained on my feet.

I used my thumbs to bring my underwear down and then shimmied out of it. Before I even realized what was happening, Ryan walked me toward his bed and when I felt it against the backs of my knees, I sat down and scooted back until I could lie down. Ryan crawled over me, the expression on his face intense and filled with want, with love. My breath faltered. *I loved him.* I loved him with every part of me.

He touched my cheek gently, so lovingly, and a tear broke and ran down my cheek. Ryan wiped it away with his thumb.

"Why does this make you cry, sweet Lily of the Night?"

"Because I never imagined someone would consider my love anything but a curse."

"Your love is a gift, never a curse." He traced my cheekbone with one finger, down to my lips, where he traced those as well.

I stared into his eyes for several heartbeats, finally leaning up and kissing him. There didn't seem to be a better response than that. He groaned softly. He loved me back. Unconditionally. I'd never dared to consider such a thing. Something seemed to break wide open inside me, some kind of wonder. He knew everything about me—all the ways in which I was damaged—and *still* thought my love was a gift. The world seemed to brighten all around me.

He unhooked the front clasp of my bra and worked it down my arms until it fell away. His hand brushed up my ribs to my breast, his thumb circling my hardened nipple. I gasped, lightning arcing from my breast to between my thighs. His mouth came down and sucked gently at the budded peaks until I was writhing beneath him, waves pulsating between my nipples and my core. My hands came to his hair, and I wove my fingers into it.

When I felt his hand come up the side of my leg to grasp the back of my knee, my core clenched in a way that made me gasp. He lifted my leg so I was open to him, and I noticed that his hand was trembling just a bit. When he pressed himself inside me, our eyes met, the moment seeming to pause and then resume in a bright flash of pleasure. "Ryan," I groaned, "Ryan, Ryan."

He spoke words into the side of my neck as he began to rock slowly, words I couldn't make out, but knew all the same. Words of love, of happiness, of pleasure. I grasped on to his buttocks, loving the way they flexed each time he thrust into me. When my climax seized me, I gasped, my back bowing slightly, my head pressed back into the mattress. My orgasm seemed to bring on Ryan's because just as I was drifting back to earth, he shuddered and groaned, circling his hips as he breathed harshly against my skin.

We lay together quietly for several moments as I stroked his back and his breathing slowed. "She walks in beauty, like the night," he whispered. My fingers slowed and I smiled. "Of cloudless climes and starry skies; and all that's best of dark and bright." We were still for another moment, the beauty of the words uttered in his love-filled voice repeating in my head. He pulled out of me but continued to lie there. Under my fingers I felt the familiar divots and leaned up slightly to look more closely. His back was a roadmap of scars, some small, round, and purplish, the divots I could feel with my fingertips—cigarette burns perhaps—and others thin and white. *Oh God.* "Who did this to you?" I asked, my voice hoarse with sympathy.

Ryan moved a piece of hair away from my face. "My father," he said.

"Your father," I repeated in disbelief. Sickened. He rolled to the side and gathered me close, pulling the quilt over us. I had told him my story in all its pure truth. And now, wrapped in each other's arms, he told me his. As he spoke of the beatings, the scars, the burns, and the cages, I learned that he, too, had suffered terribly, yet had somehow survived and even thrived, and I fell even more deeply in love. He was damaged, but not broken. He was beautiful and brave, and despite the pain he'd endured, he had managed to retain a heart filled with love and kindness. *We will never be perfect or without flaws, the lives we've been given are not like that. But, Lily, in my heart, you are perfect for me. Perfectly mine.*

And I was his *forever*, in this life or any other.

****

I came slowly awake, attempting to open my eyes but squeezing them shut when the sudden light caused my head to throb with pain. I tried to bring my hand to my forehead, but it pulled against a restraint. My eyes popped open and I groaned at the sharp burst of pain, blinking against the light. I was in my bed at my grandmother's rental home, and my hands were tied to the bedpost with rope. I was still dressed in the clothes I'd worn the night before. My blood pressure spiked, causing my heart to hammer in my chest. My eyes adjusted to the light as I worked to control my breathing. *What was happening?* I grasped at my memory. I felt so woozy, as if I'd been drugged. Thinking *hurt*. Oh God. I'd come home from Ryan's the night before . . . we'd made love. *Ryan.* I'd been so *happy*. Ryan had wanted me to stay the night with him, but I wanted to be respectful to my grandmother, and so he'd driven me here. He'd kissed me good night . . .

The door opened and I went completely still, tense. Jeffrey walked in, wearing a white suit with a nametag. My vision blurred as he came closer and I let out a strangled sound of fear. His nametag had the Whittington logo. *Oh God, oh no. What was happening?* "What do you want?" I asked. "Why am I restrained?" I pulled against the rope. My voice sounded thick, garbled, as if I was listening to it from underwater.

He sat down on the edge of the bed and brought a finger to my cheek, stroking it. "You're so beautiful, Lily," he said. "So beautiful, but so damaged. So sick."

"I'm not damaged," I tried to say but wasn't sure if I'd managed to or not. He continued to stare at me with a look of such raw *hunger*, or was it anger? I couldn't tell. It was just like that other man—the one who'd hurt my mother. The world pulsed around me, the details of the room morphing into the black outlines of a scrawled drawing. I groaned.

"There, there," he said. "I don't mind that you're damaged. I like it, Lily. I like it a lot." He leaned in and kissed me, probing my lips with his tongue. He tasted of cigarettes and stale breath. I felt bile rise in my throat.

I turned my head, forcing the word, "No," out as harshly as I could, but it came out more a whisper than a yell. Anger flashed in his expression, and he raised his hand to slap me. I braced for it, but suddenly, a door closed somewhere else in the house and he looked over his shoulder.

"I'll be back," he said, standing quickly and exiting the room. I tried to yell, but my voice didn't seem to be working. And what if the noise hadn't been my grandmother? What if it was just a car door slamming or something? Was she even here? Would yelling make him return? I needed to get free. I pulled at the restraints, but the knots were tight. He'd left some give in them, but not much. I needed a tool . . . something . . . I looked around wildly. There was nothing on the bedside table except a lamp, nothing I could reach. I felt tears burning at the backs of my eyes. *Oh God, oh no.* Taking a shuddery breath, I lay still. My eyes suddenly popped open. *The arrowhead.* It was in the pocket of my shirt. *Please, please don't let it have fallen out.* With some effort, I brought myself up to a sitting position, the world dimming with my exertions. I breathed deeply, some clarity returning. *Okay, okay.*

Bending my wrist until it felt like it might snap and stretching my hand, I grasped on to the edge of the small pocket. I let out a whoosh of air and strained some more, sweat breaking out on my forehead at the exertion and the pain of my bent hand. When my fingers brushed the edge of the arrowhead, a surge of hope exploded inside me, and I pushed myself up farther . . . farther, my index finger and my thumb grasping the paper-thin edge in a pincher grasp. *It was still there; it was still there.* I took a moment to try to relax, my heart rate slowing slightly and my trembling decreasing. I moved my hand slowly upward, the barest edge of the arrowhead gripped in my two shaking fingers. When I brought it completely out of my pocket, I turned my hand slowly and let it fall into my palm, clenching it tightly and letting out a harsh breath of victory. A bead of sweat dripped down the side of my face. I thought I could hear footsteps upstairs, the clang of something metal against metal. Getting a good hold on the arrowhead, I held it in a tight grasp, turning my hand toward the rope on the frame so I could begin sawing at it. The arrowhead looked so delicate, as if the slightest pressure might break it, but it *didn't* break. It began sawing through the fiber of the rope and I almost started crying with relief. Now I just needed time. I upped my efforts, sawing at the rope with speedy strokes.

After five minutes or so, my wrist broke free, to the sound of the tiniest of dings as the arrowhead hit the metal of the bedpost. I sagged back against it, tears running down my face and sweat making my clothes stick to my body. I fought to stay alert. I was so woozy, so woozy.

I untied my other hand and stumbled off the bed, grabbing the bedpost so I wouldn't fall as blood rushed to my head. The world swam in front of me for several moments until it finally cleared enough for me to move forward, pushing my feet into the slippers on the floor. I headed toward the door, but heavy footsteps coming toward my room caused me to turn, stumbling toward the window. I pushed it upward, the scrape of the wood making my blood run cold. A blast of frigid air hit me in the face. I was crying outright now, almost sobbing as I climbed over the sill and fell clumsily to the ground, picking myself up and beginning to run as I heard him yell something behind me, his voice laced with rage, caught by the howling wind and tossed away somewhere behind me. It was snowing. Oh God, it was snowing, the ground already dusted with the barest cover of gleaming white. Everything shimmered and glistened around me. *So cold, so very, very cold.* I ran on, stumbling once and crying out, picking myself back up. I didn't know which direction to go, was turned around, blinded by the snow. Something flew by my head and I yelped, stumbling again, but when I opened my eyes, I saw the glow of owl eyes looking back at me and heard its quiet hoot as if it was telling me to follow. And so I did, following the shifting air in front of me, the movement left behind by the bird's wings. It felt as if the tears were freezing on my face and despite the fact that I was running, I was shivering with cold and with fear. And I was so dizzy, so turned around, so alone, so scared. I ran and ran, until I came to a big, heavy, iron gate. Mercifully, the padlock was hanging from the chain, unlocked. I gasped out a relieved breath and squeezed through the opening, running once again, slipping, moving toward the dark wooded area in front of me, the hoot of the owl finding me again in the dark. I ran toward the sound, letting it lead me, wondering if the man was closing in. *Hide, hide, hide* my terrified mind chanted.

The branch of a tree hit me in the face and I let out a small scream, pushing it away. I looked behind me and gasped to see not my grandmother's rental, but Whittington standing in the distance, massive and gothic, looming against the dark sky, the moon covered by clouds, the flurries of snow almost obscuring it now. *This had happened before.* A wave of dizziness hit me, causing my thoughts to scatter like feathers in the wind. And yes, now I could hear someone pursuing me and so I pushed forward, running between trees, over stones and small twigs that caught at my feet and caused me to stumble again and again, hearing one last, distant hoot that faded away into the black night.

And then I saw someone in front of me. He appeared out of the darkness, a beacon of light walking toward me through the white, swirling air. It was a man, a man in a heavy coat and boots. It looked like he had several blankets around his shoulders as he trudged through the blizzard, straight toward me as if I alone was his destination. My heart almost leapt from my chest, but I didn't move. Time stilled, holding me in some kind of wonder I didn't understand. I glanced once behind me and then turned toward the man again. The man who'd been out here in the snow. *Why?* I strained my eyes as he drew closer and when I saw it was Ryan, I cried out, a wild sound of joy and relief that broke the silence of this hushed, winter night. I ran toward him, and he caught me in his arms as I sobbed out his name, both of us sinking to the ground where he held me in his lap. "Shh," he said against my hair. "Shh, Lily."

"He's coming after me," I cried.

"I know," he said, but there was no distress in his voice. "He'll be gone in a minute."

I looked behind me, as understanding began to dawn. "He doesn't exist," I breathed.

"He did, once upon a time, at Whittington. But he's gone now. We escaped a long time ago. Whittington's closed."

I glanced back at Whittington and realized he was right. It was dark, abandoned. I raised my face to his, calming, trusting him with my whole heart. *He loved me.* He always had. *Perfectly mine.* "It's snowing," I whispered.

He smiled so gently. "I know, baby." He kissed my cheek, caught a tear on his lips. "I know."

He held me in his arms for several moments, his warm lips pressed to my forehead. "Last night, we were together on the bridge," I murmured.

He raised his face from mine, smoothing my hair back. "We were together," he said. "There was no bridge."

Where do you land?

In your arms. I land in your arms, and you land in mine.

My heart rate slowed as the dark world cleared, the snow fading into late morning sunshine. "We're back," I said. "Oh Ryan, we're back."

"Yes," he answered, kissing my cheeks, my forehead, my chin and my nose. He smiled. "We are. We're back." The air grew warmer, the sharp scent of pine and damp leaves registering, his arms tightening around me, pulling me closer.

"Yes, we are," I repeated through my tears, my lips turning up into a trembling smile. *My savior. My love.* He must have come back right before me. "Are you okay?" I asked softly.

"Yes, I am now." He smiled.

After several moments, he helped me to my feet, taking a blanket from around his shoulders and wrapping it around me. I leaned on him as we walked, feeling stronger, my mind clearing. I inhaled a deep breath of air, looking at the man walking beside me, the man who I loved to the depth of my soul.

"Thank you for coming for me," I said.

"Always," he answered.

EPILOGUE

Lily

"**W**ake up, my love," I whispered, kissing one of the purplish, circular scars on Ryan's back. He rolled over, smiling a sleepy smile. I put my hand on his shoulder and propped my chin on it, gazing into his blue eyes. As blue as the limitless sky. I took in the lines of his handsome face, my heart aching with tenderness. He was mine. Mine to fall in love with a hundred times over.

"We should go," I said, stifling a yawn. "Winter will be here soon. There's snow on the ground this morning. Just a light dusting, but whoever owns this lodge will be vacationing here. We've used it long enough."

"Hmm, okay," Ryan hummed. "But not before," he flipped me over and rose above me as I let out a surprised burst of laughter, "I ravish you a time or twelve in this huge bed."

I smiled softly at him, trailing a finger over his cheekbone, down his jaw, my thumb rubbing his full bottom lip. He kissed it and then nipped it lightly, his eyes darkening with promise.

"There's time for that." I smiled. "Take me home."

We made the five-mile walk through the cold, fresh air of the woods, hand in hand, talking about everything and nothing. A brisk wind rustled the mostly sparse trees and the very last of the late autumn leaves fluttered down around us.

Later, as the sun set over the forest beyond, the sky unabashedly gorgeous, flaunting herself in shades of mauve and lavender, I stood in front of the window on the very top floor of Whittington. There was a fire blazing in the fireplace, warming the room and making it dance with shadows and light. Miles Davis played softly on an old Victrola I'd found in the basement. "I wonder who we'll be next time," I mused. Ryan came to stand right behind me, wrapping his arms around my waist and resting his chin on my shoulder.

"I don't know," he finally said. "Maybe a doctor from Ohio." I considered that. *Always someone who could go back and help him* then. *Oh, Ryan, my sweet, tormented love.* No matter how many lives we led, some things remained constant. Always so much truth amidst the make-believe, but always having to come back to our true selves, our true stories, before we could walk out of the darkness. Always, always . . .

I smiled, turning in his arms. "Perhaps I'll be a nurse." I tilted my head up, thinking. "A blind nurse! You'll have to lead me around, of course."

"How can you be a blind nurse?" He smiled against my skin as he nuzzled my ear.

I shrugged. "As easily as I can be a ghost. We'll figure it out as we go along. As usual."

Ryan chuckled. "If only it worked that way. If only we could choose."

"If we *could* choose, I'd stop making your girlfriends so pretty."

He grinned, kissing my neck quickly. "They all end up looking like you anyway. I can't help it."

I smiled, but my heart squeezed slightly with sudden sadness. I thought of Nyala, and how though she wasn't real, I'd grieve for the loss of her all the same. And I knew Ryan would do the same for his version of Holden Scott, the football player. The price we paid for being sensitive souls. Perhaps made too sensitive for this world, our emotional volume set too high, drowning out the real world far too often. But in recent years, less often than before.

Perhaps we'd just be ourselves for a while.

"Do you get tired of it, Ryan? Saving me?" I glanced up at him and then away, but he put a finger under my chin and tilted my face, forcing me to look into his eyes.

He shook his head. "No. I made you a promise, and I meant it." He smiled a heartbreakingly sweet smile. "Most people only get to fall in love with their beloved once. I get to fall in love with you over and over in a hundred different lives. How *lucky* am I?" he finished on a hoarse whisper.

I leaned my forehead against his, holding back my tears.

"Do you get tired of saving *me*?" he asked.

"No," I said, shaking my head. "No. I'll venture into any darkness if I know you're there." Something about it even felt . . . healing. And I wondered about grief and madness again, how just as grief was both a malady and its own medicine, perhaps, too, madness was the same. Maybe if you walked toward it, rather than away, maybe if you dove right in and let it take you where it wanted, someday you'd walk out whole and healed. Or maybe that was only my fanciful mind speaking.

"I'll always come for you, Lily. Every time. I would travel through hell itself for you. Do you trust me?"

"With my soul," I whispered, smoothing a dark golden lock of hair off his forehead, my gaze washing over his face, his beautiful, beloved features. I kissed him softly, thinking back to the digital date display on the cable guide on the TV at the vacation lodge. "We weren't away for long—less than three months," I said.

"Is that good?"

I shrugged. "Hmm. I don't know. It doesn't have to be good or bad, I guess. It's just the way it is, for now anyway. And either way, I'll love you forever, no matter what. I'll love every version of you. Your soul doesn't ever change. I see it each and every time. I see it when I close my eyes. It calls to me in the darkness. I'll see it even when I'm blind." I smiled. "It's that bright."

"I see yours, too, my beautiful Lily."

"I know," I said, kissing him again. "I knew it when you picked me up out of the snow and carried me to that small cave carved into the rock and kept me warm. As if it had been made only for us by someone long ago who knew we'd need it someday. That we'd be out here all alone, reaching for each other in the dark."

"You weren't only lost in the snow—"

"No, in my mind, I was the daughter of a family visiting Whittington that day and you were the son of a rich executive from Connecticut. You'd climbed into our trunk. The cave was my family's stable."

"You found me. And then I found you. It's where we first fell in love."

"Yes," I murmured, remembering that day, remembering how cold I'd been, how scared, how lost. Remembering the world I'd created and how he'd found me there that very first time. "The doctors who used to work at Whittington would say we're still crazy."

He gave me the barest glimmer of a smile. "Yes, I suppose they'd see it that way."

"But now Whittington is our home, it belongs only to us."

"Hmm," he hummed.

"Anyway, I think maybe *they're* the crazy ones. Because they can't make that forest out there San Francisco, or Boston, or . . . Hawaii," I said, smiling at the last one, thinking of the island warmth in the middle of winter.

Ryan laughed. "*Wherever* it is we go, that's where we'll fly. We'll just fly away."

I put my hand on his cheek. He was my fate, and I was his. "And then we'll come back. To each other. Always. Again and again and again."

The poem referred to in this story (in its completeness) is:

She Walks in Beauty

By Lord Byron (George Gordon Byron)

She walks in beauty, like the night
Of cloudless climes and starry skies;
And all that's best of dark and bright
    Meet in her aspect and her eyes;
Thus mellowed to that tender light
Which heaven to gaudy day denies.

One shade the more, one ray the less,
Had half impaired the nameless grace
    Which waves in every raven tress,
    Or softly lightens o'er her face;
Where thoughts serenely sweet express,
How pure, how dear their dwelling-place.

And on that cheek, and o'er that brow,
    So soft, so calm, yet eloquent,
The smiles that win, the tints that glow,
    But tell of days in goodness spent,
    A mind at peace with all below,
    A heart whose love is innocent.

Acknowledgements

And now to the part I love the most . . . giving thanks to those who helped me tell this story.

Huge shout-out to my storyline editor, Angela Smith, for helping me fill the holes in this complicated story, for reading it once for one aspect, and then again for the second, and then a third just because you love me. And then for untwisting your brain so you'll be available to help me on the next one. I love you dearly. (Insert many crazy face emoticons). And I miss you sitting at my counter with a glass of wine in your hand more than words can express.

Eternal gratitude to my developmental and line editor, Marion Archer. You stretch me in ways I am so very grateful for, all the while making me laugh and swoon at the comments you send back in my manuscript. Someday I'm going to read through our three-page emails back and forth discussing the plot points of this story, and I'm going to wonder how we aren't both committed. (Or are we? Wait—where am I?) I think those emails in and of themselves could be used for a case study . . . ;) Thank you for continuing to teach and inspire with each new book.

To my wonderful beta readers who read Midnight Lily first and came back with comments ranging from, "WTF," at ten p.m., to "You're lucky I don't live in your neighborhood or I'd be at your door right now to discuss this," at five a.m. And then they went on to provide such incredibly insightful comments and suggestions; Heather Anderson, Cat Bracht, Elena Eckmeyer (who read Lily three times to provide invaluable psychology advice and may now need a short "rest" at Whittington ;)), Michelle Finkle, Natasha Gentile, and my author beta Gretchen De La O who takes the word cheerleader to a whole new level. Thank you for your friendship, your time, and your support.

My final eyes editor, Karen Lawson, who gives me such immense confidence in the quality of my final product, *thank you.* You take such good care of me, even when you're jet-lagged and still smelling of coconut oil!

Thank you to Amy Kehl and Sharon Broom for giving Lily one last read-through and saving me from having to do it, and in the end saving my sanity.

Huge love to A.L. Jackson and Katy Regnery who provided hours and hours of laughs, support, advice, craziness, and friendship, not to mention were really awesome promotion partners. This business can be solitary—to have "co-workers" like you two makes my whole world a brighter place. I have such immense admiration for you both as writers and as people. #SideEyesForever #TheGreatKind

Tina Kleuker, you kind, generous soul—thank you for all the hard work you put into this release, my website, and a million other things you do for me both personally and professionally. Not one of them goes unnoticed or unappreciated.

Thank you to my badass agent, Kimberly Brower, whose care and kindness, and passion for all things book-world has made her not only a friend, but my most trusted advisor.

To you, the reader, thank you for inviting my characters into your book clubs, your homes, your hearts. I know that there is a never-ending supply of new books to read. I am forever grateful that you chose to spend your precious time on mine.

Thank you to Mia's Mafia for providing me a happy place online where I can go to hide out once in a while. You all are so positive, so supportive, and so much fun. I value each one of you!

To all the book bloggers for whom reading is not only a passion, but a job. Thank you for doing what you do. Each review and recommendation is appreciated beyond measure.

To my husband: You believed in this story from the very start, even when it took a few turns neither of us expected. Without you, I wouldn't have had the courage to tell it. Thank you for listening to all my ceaseless babbling as if every word of it mattered to you. One night as I sat on our bed crying about all the reasons I was scared to put this one out into the world, you looked at me and said simply, "Honey, take a chance." You said the same words to me almost four years ago, and I have not regretted it. So no matter what, this one is for you. You make me brave, not only with your belief in me, but because I know that however it turns out, you will be there with open arms. For someone with the heart of an artist, there *is* no greater gift, and no softer place to land. Thank you for so very, very much, but especially, thank you for that.

About the Author

Mia Sheridan is a *New York Times*, *USA Today*, and *Wall Street Journal* Bestselling author. Her passion is weaving true love stories about people destined to be together. Mia lives in Cincinnati, Ohio with her husband. They have four children here on earth and one in heaven. In addition to Midnight Lily, Leo, Leo's Chance, Stinger, Archer's Voice, Becoming Calder, Finding Eden, Kyland, and Grayson's Vow are also part of the Sign of Love collection.

Mia can be found online at www.MiaSheridan.com or www.facebook.com/miasheridanauthor.

Book Club Questions

1. What were your feelings about Holden Scott when you first met him? Did he seem to fall into the category of a stereotypical athlete, or were there things that surprised you about his character, both physically and mentally? Did you look at these things as clues to something else going on?

2. What were your initial thoughts about Lily? Who (or what) did you think she was? Did those ideas change as the story progressed?

3. The forest unites Holden and Lily and they spend a good portion of time there in the beginning of the book. Why is this remote setting important? In what ways is the forest a character all its own?

4. Midnight Lily is built around several mysteries. Did you find portions of the story more mysterious than others? Were you forming hypotheses as you read? Did any of them end up being accurate?

5. What is the significance of the stone "cave" Lily shows Holden in the woods? In this scene, Holden tells Lily that when it comes to other lives, you should "dream big or go home." And Lily expresses more of an interest in living a simple life. When the true nature of the situation they've just experienced reveals itself at the end, does this exchange become more meaningful?

6. What were your feelings about Whittington? Did those feelings change at the end of the book?

7. What were your initial thoughts about the two people Lily describes as escaping from Whittington? Did you think there was a connection between them and Lily and Holden?

8. What are the overarching themes of *Midnight Lily*? Could you relate to any of them?

9. After learning the truth about the hero and heroine's situation, what are your feelings about the supporting characters? Specifically Nyala and Dr. Katz. Who were these women to the hero and heroine? What roles did they play?

10. Did you consider the conclusion of the story a happy ending? Why or why not?

11. What questions were you left with after the epilogue? What clues can you pinpoint that answered some of those questions (either in the story, or in the conclusion)?

12. What do you imagine happens after the end of *Midnight Lily?* Where do you see these characters in five years? Ten?

Made in the USA
Middletown, DE
29 May 2016